UNBROKEN
VOWS

PROJECT DEMON HUNTERS:
BOOK SIX

CHRISTINE POPE

This is a work of fiction. Names, characters, places, and incidents are either the product of the author's imagination or are used fictitiously. Any resemblance to actual events, places, organizations, or persons, whether living or dead, is entirely coincidental.

UNBROKEN VOWS

Copyright © 2020 by Christine Pope

ISBN: 978-1-946435-32-3

Published by Dark Valentine Press

Cover art by Christian Bentulan

Book formatting by Indie Author Services

All rights reserved. No part of this book may be reproduced in any form or by any electronic or mechanical means, including information storage and retrieval systems—except in the case of brief quotations embodied in critical articles or reviews—without permission in writing from its publisher, Dark Valentine Press.

Chapter 1

As soon as she saw Caleb Lockwood standing on the porch, Rosemary's first instinct was to slam the door shut. He'd obviously anticipated that maneuver, though, since he grabbed hold of the door and pushed it inward, forcing her to take a step backward. Even though her mind reeled at his completely unexpected appearance here at Will Gordon's home in Pasadena, she wasn't knocked so completely off-balance that she forgot to summon the angelic powers within her to come to her aid. The magic—or whatever you wanted to call it—surged around her, reaching out with bright flickering tendrils to dispel the intruder.

Except he only laughed and raised a hand, and the bright glow that had surrounded Rosemary disappeared at once. She let out a sound of dismay and backed away, and he took the opportunity to step toward her again, then slam the door shut.

Still smiling, he said, "You don't look very happy to see me."

"I'm not," she snapped, even as she did her best to resist the cold fear that threatened to overwhelm her. Her thoughts darted this way and that, but she told herself that she couldn't lose it right now. She just *couldn't*.

And she didn't even want to think about the hard drive that contained the *Project Demon Hunters* footage, hidden only a few yards away in the office closet. True, Will had locked up the hard drive in the little fireproof safe that also held the title to the house and other important paperwork, but Rosemary had no idea whether the combination lock that guarded the contents of the safe could stand up to an assault by Caleb Lockwood.

After all, he'd apparently come back to life, so who the hell knew what other powers he might command?

He pressed a hand against his heart. "I'm wounded, Rosemary. I thought you'd be happy to learn that reports of my demise were greatly exaggerated."

Even though her heart was pounding painfully beneath her breastbone, she somehow found the courage to say, "Not really. I was kind of hoping you'd stay dead."

"I suppose that would have been more convenient for you," he responded, not looking offended at all. He glanced around. "All alone?"

"You know I am, or I doubt you would be here right now," she shot back.

He pursed his lips, then shoved his hands in his pockets. "Oh, I don't know. I think you're giving Will Gordon more credit than he deserves. You must know that you're the real threat here, Rosemary, not your preacher would-be boyfriend."

How in the world could she respond to that remark? Deep down, Rosemary knew Caleb was right. Will might have assisted his friend Michael Covenant with several cases of possession and demonic infestation, had probably been a calm and steadying presence at an exorcism or the blessing of a house, but he certainly didn't possess any supernatural powers like she did.

Possibly sensing her mixed emotions, Caleb went on, "Anyway, I didn't come here to talk about Will Gordon."

"No, I assume you're here for the hard drive," she shot back, figuring she might as well address that subject directly.

"Partly," he admitted, although he looked remarkably unconcerned. "But I also wanted to talk to you, Rosemary. There are a few outstanding matters that require some…clarification."

She crossed her arms, somewhat relieved that he'd stopped moving forward and seemed content to remain a few feet away from her…for the moment, anyway. Eyes narrowed, she asked, "Clarification about what? How you came back from the dead?"

That question earned her another chuckle. "Oh, I was never actually dead."

Rosemary blinked. "What? But the police—"

"The police saw what I wanted them to see," Caleb broke in, still wearing a small smile, the sort of smirk that made her wish she was powerful enough to wipe it permanently off his face.

"Well, I saw it, too," she said. "The body, I mean. It was definitely you."

His mouth quirked. "You still don't get it, do you? We can be whatever we want, whoever we want." For just the briefest second, his features wavered, and she could have sworn that was Will standing there, although she knew the man she loved would never have smiled at her in such a smug, hateful way. But then it was Caleb once more, his face his own again as he said, "And we can use that power of illusion on others. You didn't see my body, Rosemary—you saw the body of a dead drug addict. It was easier to maintain the illusion on him because he was around my height and build, but he was no one you knew."

"But the dental records—" she protested, her mind stubbornly wanting to hold on to something real, to something solid, to facts and figures that couldn't be altered by magic or illusion.

"Yes, they eventually would have given my trick away," he said. "Which was why the body was accidentally cremated before they could get a match. A paperwork mix-up of some sort. I guess that kind of thing happens from time to time."

Of course, it hadn't been an accident, but rather meddling demons making sure their subterfuge wouldn't be discovered. Rosemary didn't bother to ask how they'd made it happen, partly because it probably didn't matter very much at this point, and also because she was fairly certain Caleb wouldn't tell her the truth anyway.

"Clever," she said, in tones that indicated she thought pretty much the opposite. He didn't seem to take offense, however, but merely lifted an eyebrow. Before he could respond to her remark, she went on, "I don't suppose you're going to tell me why you bothered with such a charade."

"Oh, sure," he responded easily. "But first, let's sit down and discuss this like adults."

"I'm not sitting down with you," she told him, arms crossed.

"Suit yourself." Caleb went over to the sofa

and took a seat. A moment later, a pint glass filled with amber liquid appeared in one hand. "You sure you don't want a beer?"

While a drink to steady her nerves sounded kind of great right about then, Rosemary knew she'd never admit to such a weakness. "Positive."

He shrugged and took a large swallow from his pint glass. "Being dead served two purposes. First, it caused trouble for you—"

Somehow, she wasn't the least bit surprised by that revelation. "So, you wanted me to get arrested for murder?"

"Oh, I knew you'd get off eventually, just because there wasn't anything except the most minor circumstantial evidence tying you to the crime." Caleb drank some more beer before continuing. "But it sent you off-balance, occupied your mental energy for a time. Also, it helped me to be dead because that way 'Caleb Dixon' was effectively removed from the board. No trouble with breaking my lease, or leaving my job—"

"Your job was real?" Rosemary cut in, surprised. Not that it really mattered anymore, but she'd just assumed he'd made up his P.A. job on a Netflix show as a ploy to give him time away from her to do, well, whatever demonic skullduggery he was up to at any given moment.

"Yes, it was real." He leaned back against the sofa cushions, the amused expression returning to his face. Looking at him, she found it hard to believe that she'd once found him attractive. He looked like…well, he looked like a total asshole. An asshole demon. Before she could respond, he went on, "Should I be offended that you think I couldn't hold down a real job?"

"You can be offended, or not," she said. "I honestly don't care."

Caleb crossed one leg over the other, ankle resting casually on one knee. He definitely had the appearance of someone who didn't have a care in the world…which was probably why Rosemary could feel herself growing tenser with every passing moment. What was he playing at, anyway? If he was here to recover the hard drive, why the whole devil-may-care act, so to speak? He'd already proven that he could overpower her without any problem, so it wasn't as though he had to be worried about her trying to stop him.

"Oh, I think you do care," he replied. "If only because you still can't quite figure out why I needed a job."

"Well, your daddy is rich, isn't he?"

"Yes," Caleb said without hesitation. "But you knew that already. You've been to the house and met him, after all."

She wasn't quite sure why such a comment made a cold trickle of fear work its way down her spine. After all, it seemed obvious enough to her that of course father and son must have been communicating, or Caleb wouldn't have even known that the hard drive had been taken from his parents' home in Greencastle. "And your mother," she said lightly. "She seems pretty wrapped up in your father's money and position."

That remark wiped the remainder of the smug smile off Caleb's face. His brows drew together as he growled, "Leave my mother out of it."

Ah, apparently she'd struck a nerve. Rosemary couldn't be sure if that was because he didn't like to be reminded that his parents' marriage wasn't exactly founded on love, or whether he would prefer to forget that he was actually more human than demon. The latter, probably; she doubted that Caleb possessed enough finer instincts to be offended by the mercenary basis for his mother's supposed "affection" for Daniel Lockwood.

"Sure," she said easily. "So, what, you got the job to prove what a good, upstanding citizen you were?"

"It provided good cover," Caleb replied. "I needed to work in the entertainment industry to maintain the masquerade, and I also wanted the kind of job where I wouldn't have to worry about anyone trying to visit me while I was working."

Unlike her own job at the bookstore she owned with her sisters, where Caleb had sought her out. It definitely would have been a lot easier to avoid him if she'd been stuck behind a desk somewhere in a big office building...or on a film production somewhere.

"Fair enough," she allowed. "And now we've gotten that out of the way, why are you here?"

Another swallow of beer, and then he set his glass down on the coffee table—ostentatiously avoiding any of the provided coasters. "I should think that would be obvious."

The cold trail of dread down her spine seemed to spread out so it enveloped her entire body. Rosemary swallowed and then made herself lift her chin and reply, "You're not getting it back."

"Getting what back?"

She planted her hands on her hips and matched him stare for stare. "Don't try to play innocent, Caleb—it doesn't work when you're part demon."

"No, I suppose not," he said easily, then got to his feet. To her relief, however, he remained standing by the couch and didn't attempt to make a move toward her. "Yes, of course we want the hard drive. But I also wanted to talk to you, to disabuse you of a few notions you might be harboring."

"Such as?" Rosemary responded, doing her best to sound unconcerned. Her gaze slid toward the clock on the mantel. Fifteen minutes until five, which meant Will should be home in less than half an hour…unless he got hung up at the church. However, she honestly didn't know how much he could do to help her, although she thought he might be able to catch Caleb off guard by simply coming in through the front door. Normally, he would have entered the house via the back door off the kitchen, since the property had a detached garage, but they'd been tandem parking in the driveway.

However, that was a long shot, and probably not anything she could count on. Instead, she found herself mentally flipping through the book of spells Will had given her and wondering if she recalled enough of any of them to use them against Caleb Lockwood. Probably not; most of what she'd seen had been defensive in nature, and besides, the wards she'd put in place didn't seem to have done diddly squat when it came to keeping him far away from the property.

So much for those supposed powers of hers.

Caleb was silent for a moment, surveying her in a fashion that seemed almost pitying. That stare made her go cold all over, mostly because she guessed if a demon—or part-demon—was looking at you in such a way, you were probably about to get some spectacularly bad news.

"You sure you don't want to sit down?" he asked.

"Yes," she said icily.

A shrug. "All right. So, it seems you met your father in Indianapolis?"

If her body had felt cold before, now it seemed as though liquid nitrogen was being pumped through her veins. How the hell had Caleb found out about her father? Those meetings had been, if not secret, then definitely held in places that were far away from the watchful eyes of the Greencastle, Indiana, demon horde.

However, Rosemary realized there was no point in expending mental energy on the "how" of it all. What mattered was that Caleb seemed to know about John McGuire and the way he'd reached out to his daughter after allowing her to think he'd been dead for the past ten years.

"What if I did meet him?" she asked, her voice guarded. There didn't seem to be much point in denying the meeting had occurred, not when Caleb already knew about it, but on the other hand, there was also no reason to go volunteering information.

For a moment, he didn't reply, only stood there, still with that almost sympathetic expression in his dark eyes. Then he said, "He's not who he says he is."

"Oh?" she responded, doing her best to indicate with her tone that she wasn't about to believe a single word Caleb said. "Who is he, then?"

"One of us," Caleb said simply.

Rosemary didn't bother to ask him what he meant by that phrase. Instead, she let out an incredulous laugh and said, "A demon? Give me a break."

"It's true."

Once again, she looked over at the clock. Five minutes until five. *Please, Will,* she thought. *Please come home and stop this so I don't have to listen to anything else Caleb Lockwood has to say.*

But there was no sign of Will, and so Caleb went on, "I know you don't want to hear this. But how else do you explain these powers of yours suddenly manifesting out of nowhere?"

Even though she knew she should have kept her mouth shut, shouldn't have allowed Caleb to goad her into a response, the words tumbled out anyway. "There is an explanation. But it's not because my father is a demon."

The smirk returned to Caleb's mouth. "I suppose he told you he was an angel."

Her knees suddenly felt weak. How could he have known about her father's true origins? Unless....

No, she told herself, *these demons obviously have ways of digging up all kinds of information. It would be easy enough for them to find out about Dad, especially when he's apparently been watching them for decades. Know thy enemy, and all that.*

Apparently, Caleb was able to guess the reason behind her lack of response, because he said, "I know you want to think that I'm lying. It would be a lot easier for you, wouldn't it? But I'm not. You're not some magical half-angelic being. You're a quarter demon, same as I am."

Although her mouth was parched, dry as desert sand, somehow she was able to make herself reply, "That doesn't make any sense. Why would my father be working against the rest of you if he was supposedly on the same side?"

"Don't be so naïve, Rosemary. What makes you think he's working against us?"

She stared at Caleb, wondering what sort of game he was playing now. Something crooked and completely rigged, as befitting a demon, no doubt. In fact, she was starting to believe that he'd initiated this entire conversation in order to continue messing with her head. "I don't know... because he basically gave me everything I needed to go into your house and steal that damn hard drive?"

Caleb grinned. "Did you ever stop to think he might have done that precisely so you'd have a reason to be in my house in the first place?"

None of this was making any sense. Even though she'd adamantly insisted she didn't need to sit down, she realized then that she really did need to take a seat. Otherwise, her rubbery knees might have given way completely. Without responding to his question, she went over to the chair next to the couch and lowered herself onto it, then perched at the edge of the seat cushion, hands grasping the arms so they'd provide some additional support.

Staring at Caleb, at the satisfied smile that tugged at his lips, she made herself say, "So…why *did* you want me in your house?"

"Actually, it was my father who wanted you there. He wanted to see you in person, to have a chance to find out how strong you actually were. I'd told him about the way you warded off my attack, and he needed to know whether that was a fluke or whether you really were as strong as I'd said."

As much as Rosemary hated to admit it to herself, she had to recognize that Caleb's explanation made some sense. She couldn't help thinking that hers and Will's getaway from the Lockwood mansion had seemed almost too easy, even though she'd done her best to tell herself she was being paranoid and that it had been a simple case of her angelic powers being stronger than Daniel Lockwood's demonic ones.

But if he'd always intended for her to get away….

She swallowed, then said, "And was I?"

Caleb's smile broadened. "Oh, yes. He was

quite impressed. That was why he sent me here to talk to you, to make you understand what your true place in the world actually is."

That comment sounded ominous. Rosemary had thought she'd finally begun to figure out that very thing, knowing the truth of her feelings for Will Gordon, realizing how right and good it felt for the two of them to be together in this house, planning a shared future. But if Caleb was telling her the truth…if demon blood really did flow in her veins…then how in the world could she possibly be involved with a man of God?

Her hands were shaking. She knotted her fingers together and hoped Caleb hadn't noticed. "Why should I believe a word you're saying?"

"I know you don't have any reason to," he said, his tone casual. He sat back down on the sofa, this time at the end closest to the armchair where Rosemary was perched. In that position, his knee almost brushed hers. Almost. If either of them moved, they'd definitely touch.

She resolved to sit as still as a statue. It was hard enough to even have Caleb that close to her; the last thing she wanted was any physical contact with him.

"But," he went on, "although I know I haven't been entirely truthful with you in the past, I am telling you the truth now."

He sounded sincere. He even looked sincere…

which meant absolutely nothing where Caleb Lockwood was concerned.

"It doesn't make any sense, though," Rosemary protested. "How could my father be a—a cambion? And if we're all part demon, why don't my sisters have the same powers I do?"

For a few seconds, Caleb didn't reply. His silence seemed ominous, since during their entire conversation, he'd appeared only too happy to answer her questions. He released a breath, eyes not quite meeting hers. True reticence, or more play-acting? She couldn't begin to guess, although something in her gut tightened, as if anticipating yet another terrible revelation.

When he spoke, his tone was gentle...too gentle. That couldn't be good.

"Because they're only your half-sisters," he replied. "Their psychic powers are purely human powers, the ones that were passed down from your mother and grandmother. As humans go, they're very strong. But they're not like you."

"That's impossible," Rosemary told him, forcing herself to make the argument because to do otherwise was to accept the unimaginable things Caleb was telling her. "Our father wasn't a half-demon—he was just someone who worked in finance!"

Her protest elicited an ironic eyebrow lift. "And yet you were only too willing to believe he was an angel. You can't have it both ways, Rosemary."

As much as she wanted to argue that point, deep down, she knew Caleb was right. She hadn't made that same argument when told her father was an angel. Learning he wasn't quite human had been unnerving, but it wasn't the same as having to acknowledge that the same black blood flowed in her veins as the beings she and Will—and Michael and Audrey—had been fighting for the past six months.

But something in her forced her to continue the debate. "That's different. Not because he was an angel, but because he never claimed not to be Isabel and Celeste's father. He's been the same man all along—I mean, how could my father be one of you? The whole thing is impossible."

"Oh?"

And before Rosemary could reply, Caleb's appearance shifted again, this time to that of his own father. The change was so abrupt—and so frightening—that she began to launch herself from the chair where she sat, only to have his hand close on her wrist and pull her back down. As he did so, his face became his own again.

"That's how," he said quietly. "Your mother had no idea the man in her bed wasn't her husband. John McGuire traveled a lot for his job, didn't he?"

Mutely, Rosemary nodded. She wasn't sure she could trust herself to speak.

"And sometimes he came back early from those business trips?"

Again, all she could do was nod.

"Well, then," Caleb said, as if he knew he'd proved his point. "One of those times when he returned sooner than expected, that wasn't your mother's husband. Or I guess, several of those times. I don't have all the details. I just know that the man she was married to wasn't your biological father."

This was a nightmare. No, not a nightmare, but a night terror, one of those horrible dreams where you felt as though you were immobilized and couldn't move, couldn't do anything except lie there helplessly as horrible visions bombarded you and every limb in your body felt as though it had turned to lead. Rosemary clung to the armchair, cold sweat trickling down the back of her neck. She wanted to argue with Caleb, only she wasn't sure whether her protests would be of any use. Everything he'd said had sounded completely, horribly plausible.

But still, she had to try.

"Why my mother?" she demanded. "Why her, out of all the women in the world?"

"Because she was so psychic," Caleb said simply. "We—or rather, the other demons of my father's generation—wanted to see what the child of such a pairing would be like. I guess they were kind of surprised when your mother had a girl, though. That was unexpected."

Somehow, Rosemary was able to force out the words past the dryness in her throat. "Because all of the Greencastle demons are male."

"Exactly."

This had all been horrible, but an even more terrible thought had begun to surface in her brain. If this was some sort of demonic eugenics experiment, then it made sense that they would have used the strongest half-demon to stand in as her father. And that would mean....

She stared at Caleb in horror. "Is...is your father...my father?"

To her relief, he shook his head. "No. I think the thought crossed his mind at one point, but he decided he didn't want to be unfaithful to my mother."

"How noble of him," Rosemary remarked, her tone acid. Although she was very, very glad that Caleb hadn't turned out to be her long-lost half-brother, she wasn't sure she entirely believed Daniel Lockwood's reason for not being an active participant in their little breeding experiment. However, she didn't bother to argue. Maybe Daniel had told his son that because he wanted Caleb to believe that his parents actually did care about each other. Their messed-up family dynamic was their problem, not hers.

Because she hadn't gotten a response to her comment, she went on, "So...who *is* my father?"

Caleb smiled, a genuine one this time...or at least, a smile he wanted her to think was real. "Why don't you come meet him for yourself?"

"'Come....'" Rosemary repeated, then let the word trail off as she realized what he was asking. "You want me to come to Greencastle with you?"

"Yes." He rose from the chair and extended a hand to her. "It's time for you to meet the other half of your family, don't you think?"

Her head was swimming. Rationally, she knew she should refuse, should either keep him talking until Will showed up or, failing that, get rid of Caleb before she did something really stupid.

But...so much of what he'd said sounded so plausible. In a way, it made far more sense than the original story the man she thought was her father, John McGuire, had handed her, although she had to remind herself that the man she and Will had met in that Indianapolis restaurant hadn't been John after all. Just a cambion wearing a dead man's face, albeit one that had been cleverly aged to make it seem as if he really was the man she'd known as her father.

"I'm not giving you the footage," she said, and Caleb smiled, as if he'd realized the comment was a signal for her capitulation, even if she hadn't intended it as such.

"I'm not asking for it," he told her. "I just want you to come with me. And you can come straight back here after you've met your father. Will doesn't even have to know that you've gone."

Will. How in the world was she ever going to explain this to him? She didn't know, but she supposed she could figure that out later. For the moment, though, she needed to get to the truth… no matter what.

"I need to leave a note for Will," she said, and Caleb gave the slightest lift of his shoulders.

"Go ahead. Just don't be too specific. You don't want to frighten the guy."

No, obviously not. Rosemary sort of doubted that Caleb's solicitude had anything to do with actual concern for Will, though. Most likely, he just didn't want her to say anything that would send Will chasing after her. And there was no reason for that, right? Caleb had said this would be a quick trip…if she could even believe him at all. That was a pretty big "if." On the other hand, she needed to know the truth. If there was even the smallest chance that the man who'd approached her in the restaurant in Indianapolis wasn't an angel at all, but a half-demon cambion, then she needed to find out, needed to confront him and have him tell her to her face why he'd thought it was okay to hand his daughter so many lies.

This could be a trap. But if that turned out to be the case, at least she was only endangering herself.

As Caleb watched, she went over to the antique table by the door and pulled out the notepad and pen Will kept in one of the drawers. *I decided to take a walk,* she wrote, figuring that would explain why her car was still in the driveway. *Be back soon. Love you.* Then she tore the piece of paper off the pad and laid it on top of the table, and placed one of the ubiquitous books that were scattered around the house on one edge of the note so it wouldn't get blown off by a stray breeze. That way, Will should see it the minute he walked in the door.

"All right," she said as she turned back toward Caleb and pulled in a breath. "Let's go."

Chapter 2

WILL HELD BACK AN UNGODLY CURSE AS HE glared at the line of cars in front of him. Usually, the drive from All Saints Church in Old Town Pasadena to his house in the Bungalow Heaven section of town took him fifteen minutes at the most. This afternoon, though, there had been an accident on Orange Grove Avenue, his usual route home. And although he knew the area well and had decided to drop down to Villa Avenue to head east that way, apparently all the other Thursday afternoon commuters had decided to do the same thing, and traffic on the residential street was bumper-to-bumper, probably no better than the traffic on the eastbound 210 Freeway less than half a mile away.

Even though he'd only told Rosemary that he'd be home somewhere a little after five and therefore didn't have a hard-and-fast deadline for his arrival, he hated the thought of being late with no explanation. He pulled his phone out of his pocket and pressed her entry on his contacts list. Her cell phone rang and rang, and then went to voicemail.

Hey, it's Rosemary. I really want to talk, but something else has me tied up right now. Leave me a message, and I'll call you as soon as I can.

It felt a little foolish for him to leave a voice-mail when he'd probably be home in about ten minutes or so, but he went ahead and did it anyway.

"Hi, Rosemary. I'm stuck in traffic, but I should be home by five-thirty...I hope. Just wanted to let you know so you wouldn't worry. Love you."

He ended the call there and slipped the phone back in his pocket. It still felt new and a little strange to be declaring his love so openly, but they'd both said "I love you" several times to each other by that point, so he didn't see why he should dance around the issue. After all, he did love her, more than he'd ever thought he could love some-one. She was bright and strong and lovely, and something that had been sorely missing from his life.

As to why she hadn't answered her phone, well, he supposed there were any number of reasons for that. She could have gone out to collect the mail—it was delivered very late in the afternoon in his neighborhood—or she could have been in the bathroom, or next door at his neighbor Lucille's. The two women had hit it off right away, even though more than forty years separated their ages. Will suspected some of the attraction could have been Lucille's dogs, a pair of lively little terrier mixes, but he was glad of the women's acquaintance nonetheless. It made Rosemary feel even more connected to his life, to the world he'd built around himself over the past decade. He was profoundly grateful that she'd chosen to be a part of it.

He finally pulled into the driveway and saw Rosemary's little pale green Fiat parked up close to the garage. Clearly, she hadn't run out to the grocery store or gone on some other errand. Then again, he didn't see why she would have, since they'd already discussed going grocery shopping together, as the cupboards were starting to look a little bare.

Well, he supposed he'd figure it out soon enough. He parked behind her Fiat, then got out of the vintage Dodge Challenger that was his daily ride and locked it behind him. Satchel with his work papers slung over one shoulder, he went to the front door and let himself in.

"Rosemary!" he called out, figuring she must

be back in the kitchen, or maybe in the small bedroom he used as an office.

Only silence met his greeting, however, and he found himself frowning. He supposed she could also be out in the backyard, although it was getting on toward dusk, and the day had been just cool enough that it wouldn't have been all that comfortable to sit outside for any length of time.

Even so, he set his satchel down on the dining room table and went through the kitchen and out the back door, then paused on the stoop to take a quick look around. The backyard was as empty as the house, though, and he found his frown deepening. There was no point in calling her name again; the yard wasn't big enough that she could have been out of eyeshot somewhere.

He went back inside and glanced at the refrigerator, thinking that maybe she'd attached a note with one of the magnets on the door. However, he didn't see anything, so he went back through the house, checking all the likely places where she might have also left a note—the dining room table, the little table by the door, even his desk back in the office. Every surface was bare, or at least, bare of notes, since the usual pleasant clutter of books and magazines kept things from being completely tidy.

Even though he had a feeling it would be a wasted effort, he got out his phone again and tried making another call. Just like the time before, it went straight to voicemail. Wherever Rosemary was, either the reception wasn't good, or she'd turned off her phone altogether. That didn't sound like her, though. With everything they'd been through together, she'd made a point of keeping her phone on and fully charged so there wouldn't be any issue with getting through to her. And although Southern California had pockets of bad reception just like every other region of the world, Pasadena certainly didn't have many of them.

Unease began to tighten the muscles in his shoulders and neck, although Will tried to tell himself there had to be a perfectly logical reason why Rosemary was currently unreachable. He pushed aside his worry as best he could, and decided to go next door and ask Lucille if she'd seen Rosemary anywhere. For all he knew, she was there with Lucille now, and hadn't heard her phone because they were playing with the dogs in the backyard.

The mental image was reassuring enough that he felt himself relax slightly. He slipped his phone back into his pocket and went outside, although he didn't bother to lock up the house since he was only going next door. The evening breeze was cool and ever so slightly damp, a sign that the winds had shifted and were once again coming in from the ocean. If the weather held like this, they'd have a cool Halloween.

Lucille Atkinson's house wasn't so very different from his, a smallish Craftsman-style home built around the turn of the last century. Unlike his home's more sedate paint scheme of cream and dark green, though, her place was a cheerful pink with accents of burgundy and white and deep blue. The flowers that bordered the front walk were also pink and burgundy and white, echoing the colors of the house. Usually, he found himself smiling whenever he looked at that pink house, but right then, he couldn't quite summon a smile. Yes, it was probably likely that Rosemary was over here…but what if she wasn't?

Will mounted the steps to the front porch and then rang the doorbell. At once, dogs began barking inside, sharp little yelps that were borderline yappy but not quite. A moment later, the door opened, and Lucille blinked up at him. She was in her middle seventies, with some of the thickest, snowiest-white hair he'd seen outside an actress playing Mrs. Claus. Her features were still delicate and pretty. Actually, the person she reminded him most of was that old silent movie actress, Lillian Gish.

"Will!" Lucille exclaimed, looking a bit startled. "What can I do for you?"

"Is Rosemary here?" he asked, and did his best

not to peer past her into the depths of the house to see if he could catch a glimpse of the woman in question.

"'Rosemary'?" Lucille repeated, clearly surprised. At her feet, her two terrier mixes, Daisy and Rosie, milled about, tails wagging, their barks silenced now that they knew who was at the door. "No, I haven't seen her at all today."

Damn it. If she wasn't here, then where in the world could she be?

"Is there anything wrong?" Lucille asked then. Obviously, she'd seen some kind of shift in his expression, something that told her he was worried by her reply.

"I don't know," he said slowly. "It's just— Rosemary isn't home, which I suppose wouldn't be that strange, except I know she wasn't working today, and she didn't tell me about any plans to go anywhere. Besides, her car is still parked in the driveway."

Lucille craned her head out the doorway, as if by doing so, she could somehow catch a glimpse of the car in question, even though Will's driveway was on the other side of his house and couldn't be seen at all from the porch where they stood. "That is odd. Do you think she went for a walk?"

"That's the most likely explanation," he said.

"I don't know why she didn't leave me a note, though."

"Maybe she did, and you just didn't see it," Lucille suggested, and he gave a slow nod.

"I suppose that's possible. I'll go back and take a look around."

His neighbor offered him an encouraging smile. "I'm sure that's what happened. But I'll keep an eye out for her as well."

"Thanks, Lucille." Will did his best to smile in reply, although he knew his expression probably looked a little forced. Still, there wasn't much else he could do at the moment, and he certainly didn't want to say anything that might alarm his neighbor. So far, she had absolutely no clue about all the strange doings he and Rosemary had been involved in lately, and he wanted to keep things that way. Dealing with the Greencastle demons was bad enough without dragging his neighbors into the whole mess.

He gave Lucille a wave as he went back down the steps and headed over to his own house. Before he turned down the front walk, he paused on the sidewalk for a moment, hoping against hope that he'd see Rosemary come around the corner at the end of the street and walk toward him, blissfully unaware of the worry she'd caused.

But there was still no sign of her, and after a moment, Will made himself go back inside the house. Once again, he scanned his surroundings, thinking that he'd see a note dropped on the floor, maybe sent there by a wayward breeze, since the side windows in the living room were still partway open. However, he didn't see anything that looked like a note, not even when he got down on his hands and knees and peered behind the couch, although he had to admit that was a very strange place for one to have fallen.

He got up and brushed at the knees of his trousers, wondering what to do next. If their circumstances had been at all different, he would have told himself to calm down and wait. But since they'd recently fled the home of a powerful half-demon with the stolen footage in their possession, this wasn't exactly a normal situation. True, there hadn't been any sign of Daniel Lockwood or any of the other cambions who'd made that small Indiana town their home, but what did that mean? Had they really given Lockwood the slip, or had he and his demon fellows merely been waiting for an opportunity to descend and spirit Rosemary away?

Stop getting yourself all worked up over what's probably nothing, he scolded himself, but that inner rebuke rang hollow. After all, it wasn't as if he'd manufactured their enemies out of thin air. They really did exist...and they probably had revenge on their minds.

However, Rosemary wasn't exactly defense-less. The house was warded, and so far there'd been no signs of any marauding demons, or even any attempts by the demons to come around the property at all. Also, her own innate angelic powers had proven that she was more than a match for Daniel Lockwood, even if he somehow had managed to defeat the wards she'd set.

And there was certainly no sign of a struggle. The house looked basically the same as it had when he'd left that morning. If the demons had come for Rosemary—if they'd somehow managed to overpower her—there would have been some evidence left behind.

Unless they cleaned up after themselves, he thought glumly. *It's not as though they would have left the equivalent of a big neon sign proclaiming what they'd done.*

That seemed plausible, although if they really had taken her away, Will didn't know what he could do to help her. He was just an ordinary man, not anyone who possessed otherworldly powers. Against a full-blood demon, his faith and his Bible—and some strategically deployed bottles of holy water—might be enough for him to prevail, but in a way, these part-demon men were a far more frightening adversary. Their human blood allowed them to treat holy water as a nuisance, not the acid equivalent it was for full demons.

Will's fingers brushed against the phone in his pocket, and for a moment, he wondered whether he should call Michael and ask for advice. Unfortunately, with his friend five hundred miles away in Tucson, there probably wasn't a lot he could do to help.

But maybe another kind of psychic....

Rosemary's gifts hadn't come to her solely from her father. Her mother was also very gifted, and had already proven herself to be the sort of person who wouldn't hesitate to offer assistance. Although Michael certainly didn't want to cause Glynis McGuire any alarm, he also couldn't think of who else to contact. If nothing else, she might have some suggestions for where Rosemary might have gone. While he didn't like to admit such a thing to himself, it was only the truth that there was still a great deal he didn't know about the woman he loved. This lack hadn't bothered him too much, since he'd thought they'd be able to learn about one another as time passed, but at the moment, he could only think that Glynis might be able to fill in a few gaps.

Her contact information was already in his phone, along with the numbers for Rosemary's sisters Celeste and Isabel, just as he'd given Rosemary the phone numbers of a few people at the church, in case she ever had trouble getting hold of him for some reason. Will hesitated for a moment more, then pulled the phone out of his pocket and swiped his finger over the entry for Glynis McGuire.

Her phone rang several times, and he found himself tensing, wondering if she was also going to be unreachable. It was now a little past six—maybe she'd gone out for an early dinner, or had a meeting or something else occupying her time. He vaguely remembered Rosemary saying something about a book club; maybe that was where she'd gone, why she wasn't picking up her phone.

But then the fourth ring abruptly ended, and a woman's voice came through the speaker, sounding uncertain. "Hello?"

"Glynis?" he asked.

"Yes," she replied. "Who's calling?"

"It's Will Gordon."

"Oh," she said, sounding relieved. "I didn't recognize the number, so I almost didn't answer. But then something told me I had better pick up."

Her psychic gifts at work, telling her this was no ordinary phone call? Maybe; he'd seen Rosemary's talents in action, and therefore knew it wasn't wise to ignore a McGuire woman's little impulses. "I'm glad you did," he said. "Have you heard anything from Rosemary?"

"No," Glynis replied, a note of caution entering her voice. "Why?"

Briefly, he explained the situation, although he did his best to downplay his concerns, despite the worry that seemed to thrum louder and louder along his nerve endings. It didn't seem as though he did a very good job of hiding his unease, because when he was done, Glynis sounded more troubled than before.

"Maybe I should come over," she said.

"I'm not sure that's necessary—" he began, but she cut in, overriding his protest.

"I think it might be," she told him, her tone firm. "If I'm there, I might be able to sense something of what happened to her."

"There's a very good chance that nothing has happened, and I'm blowing this out of proportion."

"Well," Glynis said, "if that turns out to be the case—if Rosemary shows up while I'm over there—then the three of us can all go out to dinner and have a laugh about it. But if not...." The words trailed off into silence, followed by a long pause. When she spoke again, the worry was clear in her voice. "If not, then it's better I know about it, don't you think? And I think I probably have a better chance of learning something, unless you have some psychic powers you haven't told me about."

"No psychic powers," Will replied, thinking this probably would have been easier if he did. At the very least, he'd have a little more to offer Rosemary than his very modest salary at All Saints and a house not much bigger than her own small two-bedroom home in Glendora. "Unfortunately."

"They can be a blessing and a curse," Glynis said. "Anyway, I'll be over in about fifteen minutes. With any luck, Rosemary will have shown up by then, and we can forget about all this and go out to eat."

"I'll hope that's exactly what happens," he said. "Drive safe."

"I will."

They ended the call there. This time, Will didn't put the phone back in his pocket, but instead placed it on the coffee table, thinking he didn't want to waste the few seconds it would take to fish the thing out if he did get a call from Rosemary.

As he sat down to wait for Glynis, however, he had a feeling that call would never come.

Chapter 3

DANIEL LOCKWOOD'S IMPRESSIVE HOME IN Greencastle's most exclusive neighborhood didn't look all that different from the last time Rosemary had been there, although of course on this particular evening, it wasn't crowded with people there to raise money for the town library, and the lavish flower arrangements that had adorned the side tables were gone. Caleb had brought her into the family room at the back of the house, rather than his father's study. She wasn't sure why, except that maybe he'd thought she would feel a little more relaxed here.

It was the sort of room that invited you to relax, with plump couches of unbelievably soft caramel-colored leather, the walls painted a pale slate blue, a fire flickering in the mahogany-framed fireplace. She supposed it must be much colder here in Indiana on this late October evening than it was back in California, although the inside of the house seemed warm enough.

Even so, she couldn't quite repress a shiver as Daniel Lockwood entered the room and smiled at her. Maybe it was merely the pale blue of his eyes, so unlike Caleb's, that made her feel so cold. Some people probably would have said they were striking, and such a contrast to his gray-streaked dark hair, but Rosemary couldn't help thinking there was something inhuman about them nonetheless.

"Welcome back," he said, still smiling. "A drink, perhaps? A martini, or—"

"Nothing, thank you," she replied.

"It might help," Caleb put in. He still stood next to her, although he'd moved away slightly once they were back on *terra firma,* as if he'd realized she didn't want him any closer to her than was strictly necessary. She'd had to hold on to his arm as they traveled here in the unnerving eye-blink way of both demons and angels, since he'd informed her that the house was warded against intrusion by any demons other than himself and his father, but she certainly didn't want him to think that she'd enjoyed the contact.

Help to what, put her off her guard? She might have been crazy in coming here, but she wasn't so crazy as to accept any drink they might give her. Besides, even if all she was offered was a harmless glass of chardonnay, something untainted by any demonic tricks, she still didn't think it was a good idea to meet this supposed father of hers while even slightly befuddled by alcohol.

"No, I'm good," she said firmly. Lifting her chin, she added, "I'm just here to meet my father."

"So, you did tell her," Daniel said then, gaze traveling toward his son.

Caleb shrugged. "She wouldn't have come otherwise."

Those icy, pale eyes narrowed for a second, and then Daniel's shoulders lifted, echoing his son's gesture. "I suppose I can understand that. I'll let him know you're here."

Rosemary had expected him to pull a cell phone from his pocket, or maybe walk over to the land line phone she'd spotted on a side table across the room, but all he did was shut his eyes briefly. Reaching out telepathically to contact his fellow demon? She supposed that had to be what Daniel Lockwood was doing, and a little shiver worked its way down her back. Although the cambions' actions seemed to indicate they had some way of maintaining contact that went far beyond phone calls and texts, the thought that they were all psychically linked creeped her out more than she wanted to admit.

Caleb must have noticed her unease, because

he said in an undertone, "Our generation can't do that. Only theirs."

Well, that was something of a relief. She really didn't want to contemplate what it would be like to have Caleb—or any of the other quarter-demons in town—be able to invade her thoughts whenever they felt like it. All right, she supposed she should have realized that of course he didn't have that particular talent, or he would have tapped into her mind long before this, but still.

"He'll be here momentarily," Daniel said. "Why don't you go ahead and take a seat while you wait?"

What was it with the Lockwood men wanting her to sit down? Did they think she was some kind of fragile flower or something?

Then again, she had to be an unknown quantity to them. After all, she was the only part-demon offspring who'd turned out to be female. What that meant, she didn't know. It was the male who determined the sex of a child, or otherwise, she would have said maybe it had something to do with her mother's strong psychic gifts.

Even though she'd spurned Daniel Lockwood's offer of a seat, Rosemary was starting to wonder whether her stubbornness was doing her any favors. Her legs had started to feel shaky again. However, she'd said she was going to stand, and so she would, damn it.

Caleb, on the other hand, didn't seem to have any reservations about going over to the couch and sitting down on the center cushion. He leaned back, a faint smile playing about his lips, as if he looked forward to seeing how she would react to meeting this father of hers.

He's not really your father, though, she told herself. *A sperm donor, and nothing more.*

If even that. They could all still be playing some kind of a terrible joke on her. Caleb's little game of pretending to be dead had already proved that they enjoyed messing with her mind. She certainly wouldn't put it past him—or his father, or any of the other Greencastle demons—to have concocted this whole story to put her off-balance, to get her into their clutches so they could…what? Kill her? Possibly, but something told her the situation wasn't quite that simple.

The doorbell rang. "I'll get it," Daniel said, and disappeared down the hallway. Because the house was so large, Rosemary guessed it would take a while for him to collect their visitor and bring him back here to the family room.

She glanced over at Caleb and asked a question that had been tickling the back of her mind. "Where's your mother? Is she in on this little game of yours?"

Naturally, he didn't rise to the bait, but only shrugged and replied, "It's not a 'game.' Anyway, you know that she doesn't know anything about all of this." He waved a hand, as if to indicate his father and himself, and the rest of the Greencastle demons. "To answer your question, though, she went to Indianapolis to have a spa day and go shopping. She'll have dinner afterward, so I doubt she'll be home before nine."

How convenient…and probably the reason why Daniel had asked Caleb to approach her today. Rosemary thought of the glitzy mall she and Will had gone to when shopping for clothes to wear to Daniel Lockwood's benefit cocktail party just the day before, and guessed that his wife could do some serious damage there with her black Amex Centurion card.

And yes, she knew she was probably thinking about such trivialities because she didn't want to pay too much attention to the male voices that even now drifted down the hallway, voices that were getting closer and closer. Caleb straightened and shifted so he was sitting on the edge of the sofa cushion, and Rosemary found herself standing straighter as well, her chin up. Whoever was coming down that hallway, she wanted to make sure she looked confident and unafraid when he entered the room.

Daniel Lockwood was tall, but the man standing next to him was taller still. He looked as though he was a few years younger, in his late fifties rather than his early sixties. And, just like the other part-demons Rosemary had met, he was very good-looking, with the sort of chiseled, aging movie-star features that would make women even several decades younger stop and take a closer look. His hair was brown, his eyes blue, but the deep blue of a mountain lake, not the icy pale blue of Daniel's eyes.

Those eyes met hers, and Rosemary forced herself to stand still, to stare back at him. She'd honestly never thought much about the minor differences in her appearance from that of her two sisters, mostly because all three of them looked so much like their mother. Now, though, as she stared at this half-demon who was supposedly her father, she saw elements in his features that echoed her own—the faint lift to the right eyebrow, the high cheekbones, more sculpted than those of either of her sisters. And she hated to see the resemblance, because it meant she might actually be this man's child.

"Rosemary," he said, and even though she'd never heard his voice before, it still sounded somehow familiar.

She swallowed. "Who are you?"

Gaze still fixed on her, he replied, "My name is Gerald Gates."

"And you're a demon?"

"Half-demon," he corrected her, although in a gentle tone.

She crossed her arms, trying to fight off the sudden chill she felt, despite the warmth of the room where she stood. "Why should I believe you're my father?"

One corner of his mouth lifted slightly. "I know it's hard for you to believe. But it is the truth."

"We can do a blood test," Daniel Lockwood put in.

Rosemary pulled her gaze away from Gerald Gates and stared at Caleb's father. "That sort of thing works for demons?"

"Yes," he said, now looking somewhat amused. "Or rather, for part-demons. The test looks at markers that have nothing to do with our demonic natures."

A blood test would prove whether they were telling the truth…or would it? Test results could be faked.

The problem was, once you mistrusted a certain person's motives, it was all too easy to believe that everything they did and said was a lie. And if she was going to take that stance regarding the Greencastle demons, then she shouldn't have come here at all. All right, they hadn't given her any reason to trust them, but she also realized that if she didn't take the blood test, if she demanded to be returned to Pasadena immediately, then she'd spend the rest of her life wondering if this might have been the one time Daniel Lockwood had been telling the truth.

She glanced at the clock that hung on the wall across the room. Ten minutes until eight—or rather, ten minutes 'til six back in Pasadena, since they were on Central time here in Indiana. Will would definitely be home by now, and it would be growing dark in California. There was only so long he would wait for her to return from her supposed "walk" before he became alarmed by her absence.

"How long does a test take?" she asked.

"A few days," Daniel said. "At least, that's what I've read." His gaze strayed to his son; even though their coloring was quite different, their features were similar enough that Caleb's parentage would never have been in doubt. "Obviously, I've never had any reason to have one performed."

It seemed the logical thing to do. Provide a sample—Rosemary vaguely remembered reading about cheek swabs in a book or an article somewhere—then go home and wait for the results.

And hope they hadn't been tampered with.

And also figure out how in the world to explain all of this to Will. She didn't even want to try imagining that scene. When he'd thought her father was an angel, he'd said it didn't matter that she wasn't completely human, but would he feel the same way if he discovered she was part demon?

"It would put your mind at ease," Gerald Gates said, and anger flared within her.

"Oh, I kind of doubt that," she snapped. "Why did you tell me all those lies at the hotel? Why not tell me the truth then?"

Gerald didn't seem perturbed by the flash of anger, but merely looked at her with a level gaze and said, "Because that wouldn't have suited our purposes."

"Which was to get me to come here and meet Daniel," she returned. "Although, if you'd already met me, then you would have known how powerful I supposedly was. Couldn't you have just told him?"

"No," Daniel broke in, looking similarly unaffected by her show of emotion. "I had to meet you for myself. Otherwise, I wouldn't have needed to involve Gerald at all, and could simply have relied on Caleb's report. I needed to make sure our powers had bred true in you."

"And have they?" Rosemary asked, even though she wasn't entirely sure whether she wanted to hear the answer.

"Oh, yes," he replied. "You are very strong... which is why you should be here with us."

Here with…. She let the thought trail off, mostly because allowing it to take hold in her mind seemed truly horrifying. "I am not 'here with you,'" she retorted. "I came here because I wanted to meet my father—if that's even what you are," she added with narrowed eyes as she glanced over at Gerald.

"That's easy enough to prove, isn't it?" he said. "Just a cheek swab. You wouldn't even have to go anywhere."

"Exactly," Daniel put in. He held up a hand, palm facing toward the ceiling, and on it appeared an honest-to-God home paternity test in its box, with a happy-looking man and young boy on the packaging. "We can do it right now and mail it to the lab tomorrow morning."

"And I'm just supposed to trust the results?" Rosemary asked. Her voice shook a little, and she hated herself for that outer betrayal of the turmoil she felt inside.

The cambion leader shrugged. "To be fair, this sort of test isn't legally admissible…but it is very reliable. However, you're also welcome to go to a lab in Indianapolis and have it administered there. That sort of thing is very difficult to tamper with."

"I can't go to Indianapolis," she protested. "I need to go home. I'm sure Will is already starting to freak out about where I am."

The mention of Will's name made Daniel and

Gerald exchange an unreadable look. However, even though Rosemary couldn't tell anything from their expressions, she doubted that weighted glance had meant anything good.

"Maybe you should put him off for a while," Caleb suggested, and she stared down at him in consternation.

"I don't want to 'put him off.'"

"Just for tonight," Gerald said, as if that was a perfectly acceptable scenario. "You can go back to the DePauw Inn and stay the night there. In the morning, we'll go to Indianapolis for the test."

"Or maybe I can just go home to California and meet you in Indianapolis in the morning," she countered, not liking the sound of that plan at all. "Since I have this super-duper demonic power of teleportation and everything, it's not as though I'd be holding up the process."

"I'm not sure that's such a good idea," Daniel replied. Now his blue eyes looked colder than ever, and another shiver worked its way down Rosemary's spine. "Your boyfriend"—he uttered those two syllables in a voice dripping with contempt—"would be sure to ask too many questions about where you were going and what you were doing."

Although Rosemary could feel herself bristling at Daniel's tone, she took a mental breath and told herself she needed to choose her battles. Really, it shouldn't matter at all to her what a couple of half-demons thought of Will Gordon. She knew his worth, and that was enough. "Not necessarily," she said evenly. "It's not as though he camps out at the house all day to see what I'm up to. He has a job and his own responsibilities, ones that keep him busy."

Once again, Daniel and Gerald looked at each other. During all of this, Caleb had remained where he was on the couch, eyes flickering slightly as he watched the back and forth. From what Rosemary could tell, he seemed to be secretly amused by the way she'd tried to stand up to his father.

"No," Daniel said at last. "I really think it's better if you stay here."

So that was how he wanted to play it. Fine. Had he forgotten that she had powers of her own, ones she could command to send her back to Will's house in California or anywhere else she wanted to go?

"Think what you want," she replied. "But I'm going."

She visualized the living room at Will's place, the mismatched antiques and the gleaming wood floor, the faint scent of vanilla from the candle they liked to burn while they were watching TV after dinner. Just that image, coupled with her desire to return there, should have been enough to send her traveling in that strangely magical way demons used to move themselves from place to place.

Except that nothing happened.

Rosemary blinked and concentrated again, wondering if she'd somehow messed up because she wasn't focusing enough. However, her efforts were interrupted by a chuckle from Daniel.

"No point in wasting your energy," he told her. "You're gifted, Rosemary, but your powers aren't strong enough to overcome mine and Gerald's when we work together."

Was it possible they were able to stop her from leaving? Since she was still standing in the family room at Daniel's house, she had to assume he was telling her the truth.

Her fingers clenched in the fabric of the long sequined-adorned skirt she wore. "So, you're going to make me your prisoner?"

On the couch, Caleb shifted, looking almost uncomfortable. "You never said anything about forcing her to stay here, Dad."

"Because you didn't ask," Daniel replied, his expression almost bland. Clearly, he wasn't too worried about what Caleb might or might not think about the current situation.

"I'm sorry, Rosemary," Gerald said. He actually did look somewhat contrite, although that might have been only an act. "But it's better that you stay here until you have the proof you need regarding your identity."

Better for the cambions, maybe, but not for her. Panic began to awaken inside Rosemary, sending flutters of unease through her stomach, but she told herself she needed to hold it together. The last thing she wanted was for either of the half-demons confronting her to know how frightened she was.

Instead, she raised her chin and glared at the two men. "Will is going to know right away that something is wrong," she said.

"And?" Daniel countered, still looking supremely unconcerned. "What exactly do you think he can do? He's only a mortal man. Even if he suspects that you might have somehow ended up back in Greencastle, he'd have to drop everything to take a flight here. And even if he did such a thing, so what? Without you, he can't accomplish very much, can he?"

As much as she wanted to vigorously defend Will's abilities, inwardly, she had to admit that Daniel Lockwood had a point. Will was only a man. A strong man, a man of integrity and great personal courage, but he didn't possess the sort of supernatural abilities that would allow him to mount an assault against a group of part-demons. Daniel Lockwood and Gerald Gates were strong enough on their own; she really didn't want to think what would happen if they called in the rest of their cambion brethren to mount a defense.

"All right," she said, not bothering to answer Daniel's question. "But I need to give him some sort of explanation for my absence, or he's going to assume the worst…especially since I already left him a note that said I was going for a walk."

Once again, Caleb shifted his position on the couch. "Well, actually, I kind of made that note disappear."

"You *what?*" she demanded, her tone sharp. So much for keeping it together.

A shrug. "I figured it was probably safer that way. Better to leave things open-ended."

Son of a…. Rosemary pulled in a breath and told herself to let it go. Getting in an argument with Caleb Lockwood wouldn't salvage the situation…more like the exact opposite. "Fine. Then it's even more important that I text him and give him some kind of plausible story."

"That's a good idea," Gerald said. "What are you going to tell him?"

Because she had a two-year-old nephew, Rosemary didn't have to think very hard to come up with a narrative that wouldn't invite too many questions. "I'll tell him that my sister Celeste and her son Tyler are both sick, and I volunteered to go over to her place and help out. That would explain why I need to be gone overnight, but it also would keep Will away—his job requires him to work with the public, and he wouldn't want to go someplace where he was consciously exposing himself to some nasty germs."

Daniel appeared almost impressed, as if he'd halfway expected her to come up with something half-assed, the kind of story it would be easy for Will to poke holes into. "Good. Then go ahead and send the text. But if you try to tell him what's really going on, your message will get scrambled faster than you can say 'AT&T.'"

She didn't bother to point out that she was with Verizon. "No worries," she said. "I don't want to drag Will into any of this."

As the others watched, she reached into her purse and got out her phone. Thank God for texts; she didn't know for sure whether she would have been able to maintain her composure during an actual phone call. But it was easier than she'd thought to compose the brief message, to let Will know that Celeste's husband Kevin was out of town and Celeste had her hands full with Tyler throwing up every hour on the hour, and so she, Rosemary, had gone over to help out.

I'm not sure when I'll be back home, she concluded the message. *I'll try to let you know as soon as I know. Love you.*

"Let me see it," Daniel commanded, and although her first instinct was to tell him to go to hell—even if that threat didn't have as much meaning for a demon as it did a regular human— she reminded herself she needed to choose her battles. Holding back a sigh, she handed the phone over to Daniel so he could see what she'd written. There might have been the slightest flicker in his expression as he read that casual "Love you," but he didn't comment, only gave the phone back to her and said, "Go ahead and send it."

This could all be an enormous mistake, but Rosemary knew she didn't have much of a choice. As long as she kept cooperating, Daniel would most likely think she was on his side. And while she loved Will and would never want him to be anything other than who he was, he simply wasn't equipped for this sort of fight.

So she touched her finger to her phone's screen to send the message, then dropped it back in her purse. "There," she said. "I know he'll reply, but at least now he has a good reason for why I'm not home."

"Excellent," Daniel said. He glanced over at his son. "Caleb, why don't you take Rosemary upstairs and show her the guest room? After she's settled, we can order some food in. Probably better not to go out," he added, a twinkle of amusement in his pale blue eyes.

No, it most likely wouldn't be all that smart to

be seen in public with her, considering her probable origins. What she'd seen of Greencastle so far seemed to indicate that the people there were fairly tight-knit, and there might have been questions as to who she was and why she was being entertained by two of the town leaders.

Maybe that was why Daniel had ignored Gerald's suggestion about having her stay at the hotel. Rosemary wondered about her supposed father's family—she knew that all the cambions were married and had one son each, so presumably she had a half-brother out there somewhere. If the blood test came back as a match, would she get to meet that half-brother? And how in the world would Gerald begin to explain her to his wife?

"Sure," Caleb said, and got up from the couch. Now his expression was almost neutral, as if he didn't want his father to guess what his own feelings about Rosemary's presence here in the house might be. "This way," he added, gesturing for her to follow him.

While she didn't much look forward to being alone with Caleb, she figured it would still be better than staying downstairs with Daniel and Gerald. Her father. If he really was her father. Whatever he was, she guessed that the two men would want to keep watch over her until she went to sleep, just to make sure she didn't try to make a break for it once Daniel was the only cambion in the house.

Then again, she supposed Caleb could also help to stand guard…if he was strong enough. As with so many other aspects of the part-demon world, Rosemary really had no idea how all this worked.

She followed him up the stairs to the second story. Because she'd been up there before in order to steal the hard drive from the dresser in the master bedroom where it had been hidden, the surroundings weren't entirely unfamiliar to her. This time, though, her destination appeared to be a room at the end of one hallway, meaning that it overlooked the quiet residential street where the house was located. It was quite large for a guest room, with a bay window and a window seat in addition to a queen bed and several dressers and side tables. Then again, she supposed that in a house this large, it wasn't that big a deal to have a guest room that was bigger than her living room.

"Here you go," Caleb said, rather unnecessarily.

She didn't bother to thank him. For what, showing her to what effectively was a jail cell? A very nice one, sure, but still, it wasn't as if she could come and go of her own free will. Finding her voice, she replied, "I don't have any overnight stuff with me."

"You won't need it," he told her. "There's a bathroom through that door with everything you might need, including a new toothbrush."

"Clothes?" she inquired, knowing she sounded annoyed at whoever had the forethought to make sure the guest bathroom here was fully stocked.

"I'll steal a few things from my mother's closet. She has so much stuff, she'll never notice."

Rosemary's encounter with Caleb's mother had been brief, but she thought the older woman was probably around her size, although several inches taller. Anyway, her clothes should fit, except....

"And what am I supposed to do about clean underwear?" she asked, trying hard not to blush.

He grinned, the familiar glint back in his dark eyes. In the next instant, a package of cotton bikini panties appeared on the embroidered duvet that covered the bed. "I figured you were a size small."

No point in asking how he'd managed that particular feat. Demons could make things appear and disappear at will, although she had to hope he'd left behind some sort of payment wherever he'd gotten the panties. She didn't much like the thought of wearing stolen underwear, although she had a feeling she had far more pressing things to worry about.

"Thanks," she said. The silence that followed

that one brief word felt horribly awkward, and she found herself adding, "Did you know about Gerald?"

A nod. However, Caleb didn't seem inclined to pursue that topic of conversation, because he said, "We should go back downstairs."

Having to sit down to dinner with Daniel and Caleb and her alleged father seemed like the easiest way to kill her appetite, but Rosemary knew she had to eat sometime. Still, she lingered by the door, wondering if she could somehow delay the inevitable. "Were you ever going to tell me?"

He didn't ask her about what. A pause as he glanced toward the open doorway, as if he expected his father to be standing outside and listening to their conversation. "It wasn't my place to tell you," Caleb said at last. "But...." Another obvious hesitation before he went on, "We can talk later. Okay?"

Rosemary reflected that she had come to a very odd place in her existence when the promise of a conversation with Caleb Lockwood felt strangely reassuring. "Okay," she said.

A nod, and then he left the room, giving her no choice but to follow him. As she went, she wondered how Will was going to react to the text she'd sent...and if he'd start asking questions she couldn't possibly answer.

Chapter 4

Glynis McGuire stood in Will's living room, eyes closed as she appeared to reach out with her special senses to detect what might have happened there earlier that afternoon. He stood quietly, not wanting to interfere with what she was doing...whatever exactly that was. When she'd arrived a few minutes earlier, she'd told him that she needed to absorb some of the energy of the place, and that, with any luck, it would convey to her some information on where Rosemary was and what she was doing.

It was hard to stand there and do nothing, though, especially since the day had fallen into dusk as he was waiting for Glynis to arrive, making Will painfully aware of how much time was passing. Even if Rosemary had simply gone out for a walk, she should have been home long before this. He tried not to jump to worst-case scenarios—a mugging, an out-of-control car leaping up on the sidewalk to knock her down—but it was difficult, especially because he knew Rosemary's powers should have been enough to protect her against those sorts of ordinary mishaps. Which meant she might have come up against something even her own remarkable talents couldn't save her from.

At length, Glynis opened her eyes. Her expression was troubled as she said, "Someone was here. I can feel just a little of their vibrations, someone who doesn't feel like either you or Rosemary."

Alarm sang its shrill song along his nerve endings. "Who?"

"I don't know," she replied, brows puckering faintly. "I can't see them clearly. They weren't here long enough to leave much of an impression. Male…I think. But nothing more than that."

That tiny piece of information was less than reassuring. A strange man had been here, and now Rosemary was missing. Will would never suspect her of cheating on him, but he found himself far more troubled that it had been a man here and not a woman. "Would you be able to feel if there was any kind of a struggle?"

"Maybe," Glynis said, still frowning. "Did you see evidence of one?"

"No," Will said. "But maybe it wasn't a physical kind of struggle."

"You think it was the demons."

She hadn't phrased the comment as a question, but he went ahead and answered it anyway. "Honestly, I'm not sure what to think. I just know it isn't like Rosemary to disappear like this. I checked with my next-door neighbor, and she hadn't seen her, either. So, either she's taking the world's longest afternoon walk, or someone or something has come along to spirit her away."

For a long moment, Glynis didn't reply, only stood there with her hands spread slightly, as though reaching out to touch the currents of air in the room and trying to read something of what they said. "I don't feel anything like that here, but I've never had an encounter with a demon before. I'm not sure what they're supposed to feel like."

"Nothing good," Will said grimly, although he wondered how different a cambion would feel from a full-blood demon…and whether a quarter-blood man like Caleb would feel any different from a human at all. Yes, Caleb Lockwood was dead, but the Greencastle cambions each had a son, meaning there were six more of that generation out there somewhere. For all Will knew, one of them had been instructed to take up where Caleb had left off, so to speak, and was now tasked with carrying out the demon clan's dirty work.

"Well, I'm not feeling that. Just the presence of someone here, although I can't detect whether they meant Rosemary good or ill."

He was about to reply that maybe that was a good thing, that if a truly evil presence had been here, surely Glynis would have been able to feel it, when his phone buzzed in his pocket. At once he pulled it out, and tried not to sag in relief as he read the text on the home screen.

Will, I'm so sorry to bail on you like this, but Celeste and Tyler are both sick, and I headed over to her house to help out. I left my car at the house and took a Lyft because the parking at her place is really tight. Hope that's okay.

I'm not sure when I'll be back home. I'll try to let you know as soon as I know. Love you.

Since Glynis was watching him with inquiring eyes, he went over to her and held out the phone so she could read the message on the screen for herself. However, she didn't appear relieved by what she saw, but instead seemed to frown that much more.

"Celeste never said anything to me about her or Tyler being ill," she said. "And I talked to her just this morning."

"Maybe it's something that came on this afternoon," Will suggested, and Glynis only shook her head.

"I suppose that's possible, but still…." The words trailed off, and she fidgeted with the heavy silver and turquoise bracelet she wore on her right wrist. "Something doesn't feel right. Let me call Celeste and check with her."

"A good idea," he agreed, although he could already feel his heart sinking. Something told him that Rosemary's text wasn't real—or rather, while she might have sent it from her phone, its contents couldn't possibly be the truth, that for whatever reason, the message had been sent under duress.

He waited as Glynis went over to her purse, which she'd set down on the dining room table, and got out her phone. She entered a number rather than pull it up from her contacts list, which seemed to make sense. Clearly, she had her daughter's number memorized and had no need to look it up.

"Hi, Celeste," she said after a brief pause. "How are you doing? I heard you weren't well." Another, longer pause, during which her finely arched brows—so like Rosemary's—pulled together in obvious confusion and worry. "You're fine? Tyler's fine? And Rosemary isn't there?" Once again, she appeared to wait as Celeste replied, although Glynis looked over at Will and gave a brief shake of her head, as if to confirm what he already knew.

Celeste and her family were fine, and Rosemary had vanished into thin air.

Worry knotted in his gut, but he made himself stand off to one side as Glynis did her best to let Celeste know that everything was okay, that it was just a misunderstanding, and she'd see Celeste the next day when she went over to help with Tyler's Halloween costume. That reassurance signaled the end of the call, because she pulled the phone away from her ear after that and sent Will a very worried look.

"I don't know why Rosemary sent you that text, but it's all a fabrication," Glynis said. "Celeste hasn't seen her, and the whole family is fine and healthy."

"Someone must have made Rosemary send me that text," Will said. He did his best to remain calm and focus on the problem at hand, mostly because he knew getting so worked up that he couldn't think straight wouldn't help any of them, least of all Rosemary.

"To keep you from worrying?"

"I would assume so," he replied. "And it might have even worked if you hadn't been here. After all, I wouldn't have any reason not to believe her, and I probably wouldn't have called Celeste to check to make sure the story was true." He hesitated for a moment, wondering if it was appropriate to say what had been in his mind, then decided the hell with it. "Things are still pretty new between Rosemary and me, and I wouldn't have wanted to come off as some kind of controlling, suspicious jerk."

"I understand," Glynis said quietly. "But I'm glad you followed your instincts and called me, because at least now we know something very strange is going on here." She paused for a moment, gaze moving toward the front window, where a pair of car headlights briefly backlit the heavy curtains there before moving on. "What should we do? Call the police?"

Maybe that would become necessary at some point, although Will honestly didn't know how much help the police would be. Not if the Greencastle demons were involved in all this. Anyway, Rosemary hadn't been missing long enough yet.

And thank God it was the Glendale P.D. who'd been working on Caleb's case, and not the Pasadena cops. At least if he had to make that call, they wouldn't already be harboring suspicions about Rosemary McGuire and the strange events she'd gotten mixed up in.

"Not yet," Will told Glynis, and she tilted her head toward him, waiting for him to go on.

"First, I need to call Michael Covenant."

Daniel Lockwood ordered dinner in from the same restaurant where she and Will had eaten breakfast when they'd come to town a few days earlier. Rosemary might have been amused by the coincidence, although she guessed it probably wasn't coincidence at all, but rather the small selection of eating establishments in town.

Anyway, the food was good, and she made herself eat the roast chicken and grilled vegetables she'd ordered, mostly because she figured that starving herself wouldn't help matters any. She needed to be fit and ready to face whatever happened next.

The conversation was surprisingly mundane; Rosemary had a feeling that Daniel Lockwood was trying to keep things light in an attempt to put her at ease. Like that was going to happen.

Still, while she couldn't exactly relax, she wasn't quite as tense as she might otherwise have been, especially since the three men didn't try to immediately involve her in the discussion, but rather talked about the Halloween carnival being held in a few days and which the bank was helping to sponsor, and about what Caleb planned to do now that his work in California was done.

"It's time for you to start working at the bank again," Daniel said, and Caleb frowned slightly.

"I was thinking about going back to school."

"For what?"

"To get my master's degree."

"A waste of time," Daniel pronounced, then took a bite of his grilled pork chop. "You don't need a master's to run a bank."

"Maybe I don't want to run a bank."

That comment made the half-demon send a displeased, pale-eyed glare at his son. "What else are you going to do with your life?"

Obviously, Caleb had been the recipient of many such stares, because he seemed singularly unaffected by his father's annoyance as he reached for the glass of merlot in front of him. "Get my master's degree in film studies."

"What about you, Rosemary?" Gerald inquired, clearly trying to deflect the conversation to a topic that was a little less fraught.

"What about me?" she replied, wishing he hadn't addressed her directly. It was hard enough being in the same room with him, knowing what he'd done to her mother, without having to act as if this was all normal and there was nothing strange about having a civilized conversation with a demonic rapist.

"Where did you go to college?"

As if he didn't already know all about her. Still, if he wanted to play this game, she'd go along...for now. "I didn't go to college," she told him. "I decided it really wasn't for me. And I don't regret my decision. I like being a small business owner. Co-owner," she amended. "My sisters and I all run our store together."

"Not much money in bookstores, is there?" Daniel asked with a curl of the lip.

She realized that even if he hadn't been a half-demon cambion who'd basically kidnapped her and had been making her life a living hell for the past week, she'd still think he was a raging asshole. "There's enough," she said evenly, then reached for her own glass of wine so she could take a sip. "Not everyone on the planet has bought into the capitalistic wet dream of amassing more wealth than any one person could possibly need."

Across the table from her, Caleb let out a snort that sounded suspiciously like a suppressed laugh. Even Gerald's mouth twitched a bit in amusement, although Daniel didn't look at all impressed by her reply.

"Typical millennial remark," he said, eyes still narrowed.

She shrugged. "Okay, boomer."

This time, Caleb didn't even bother to hide his chuckle. Grinning, he swallowed some more wine and remarked, "Not exactly your typical demon, is she?"

"No," Daniel said with a slight grimace. "I blame her mother."

Thanks, Mom, Rosemary thought, and realized she had a lot to thank her mother for. After all, for a family of psychics, the McGuires were pretty level-headed. Also, she knew she needed to remember that even if Gerald Gates turned out to be her father, she was still far more human than demon. Obviously, those with mixed blood here in Greencastle wanted to cling to their demon heritage. That was their truth, though; it didn't have to be hers.

"So," Gerald said hastily, "I was thinking we could head out to Indianapolis around ten tomorrow morning, if that's all right with you, Rosemary."

Was there such a thing as a demonic peacemaker? She wouldn't have thought so, but it seemed that Gerald Gates was doing his best to fulfill that role at the moment. "Ten is fine," she replied. "Or even earlier. Might as well get this over with quickly so I can get home, right?"

"You'll still have to wait for the results," Daniel said in repressing tones.

Gerald let out a breath—possibly of annoyance, although his neutral expression didn't change. "Yes, but we can expedite those. We'll have them in twenty-four hours."

Meaning she'd have to spend another night here. The thought made Rosemary feel more resigned than anything else; somehow, she'd known she wouldn't be able to get away after just one night in Greencastle. She'd brought her phone with her to the table, since she'd expected to get a text from Will in reply to the message she'd sent him, but so far, she hadn't heard anything at all. His silence seemed strange to her. Maybe he'd gotten hung up with something at work and had only been able to read her text without having the time to compose an answer. She supposed that was a possibility, especially since she knew they were short-staffed at All Saints at the moment.

"That's not so bad," she said, doing her best to keep her tone even. No point in giving Daniel the satisfaction of knowing how on edge she was. "I mean, with my cover story of my nephew being sick, being away from Will for two nights won't seem too strange. Anything more, and he might start to get suspicious."

"Oh, it won't take any longer than that," Gerald assured her.

She did her best to smile at him, still trying to maintain the illusion that she wasn't inwardly writhing at the thought of being in the same room with him, and they all lapsed into silence after that as they finished their meals. By that point, it was a little after nine o'clock, a little early to go to bed, but she pleaded weariness anyway and went upstairs. Daniel didn't try to stop her—probably because he figured he'd had enough of her company by that point, and it was safer to have her confined to the guest room upstairs than wandering around the house.

Even though she doubted it would do any good, she locked the door before going to check out the *en suite* bathroom. Just as Caleb had said, it was stocked with anything she might possibly need—a toothbrush still in its package, a tube of toothpaste, mouthwash, dental floss, face wash, moisturizer, and more. There was even one of those fluffy white terrycloth bathrobes, the kind you might find in a five-star hotel or spa, hanging from the hook on the back of the bathroom door.

And when she peeked in the closet, she saw a couple of sweaters and matching skirts hanging there, along with a pair of high-heeled boots. Definitely not the kind of clothes she was used to wearing, but she supposed if Caleb had pilfered those items from his mother's wardrobe, then he couldn't exactly have provided the sorts of flowy skirts and knit tops that filled Rosemary's own closet.

So you'll look like a lady who lunches for a couple of days, she told herself as she changed out of her own skirt and top and into a silky blue nightgown with the tags still attached. Something else Caleb had conjured out of nowhere, like the package of underwear, or an item taken from his mother, one he knew Rosemary wouldn't object to because it was brand-new?

Hard to say. Mrs. Lockwood definitely seemed like the type of person to have a lot of unworn clothing tucked away in her closet or dresser, so either explanation seemed equally plausible. While the nightgown didn't seem very substantial for a cold October night in Indiana, Rosemary had to admit that the house was kept fairly warm, and there were extra blankets stacked on the closet shelf, just in case.

She went into the bathroom and washed her face and brushed her teeth, then came back out into the bedroom and inspected her phone for what felt like the hundredth time, even though she knew she'd really only looked at it about five times.

Or maybe ten.

Obviously, the number of times she'd glanced at the screen didn't seem to make any difference, because no matter how often she looked at the damn thing, no messages from Will appeared. She unlocked the phone, thinking maybe she should try texting him again now that no one was looking over her shoulder. Shouldn't she let him know what was *really* going on?

Her finger hovered over the screen, and then, with a sigh, she set the phone down on the night-stand. Just because she was alone at the moment didn't mean Daniel Lockwood wouldn't still have some way of snooping to see if she'd sent any unauthorized messages.

Okay, she'd forget about that plan for the moment. Time to try something else.

She sat on the bed and visualized Will's house —the kitchen this time, just in case that might help her cause. Small but neat and laid out nicely, with butcher-block countertops and that lovely window in the wall above the sink, allowing whoever stood there to look out on the backyard as they were doing the dishes. Just the mental picture was enough to send a wave of homesickness washing over her, even though the place wasn't technically her home.

It sure felt that way, though.

A deep breath, and then she imagined herself standing in the kitchen. Imagined the faint scent of cinnamon on the air, along with the slightest trace of wood smoke from the fire they'd had the night before. Called to the powers that lay coiled within her.

Apparently, those powers were asleep, or had decided to take the evening off, because she didn't budge even a single inch. She still sat on the edge of the bed, mussing the elaborately embroidered duvet cover, and it didn't look as though she was going anywhere.

Rosemary sighed. It wasn't that her powers

were gone. They were just being blocked. Clearly, Daniel Lockwood wasn't going to let down his guard. She was stuck here until she got this blood test out of the way…maybe longer.

A shiver went through her, and she made herself climb under the covers, since sitting on the bed in that skimpy nightgown didn't seem like a very good idea. Like it or not, she was sleeping in this house tonight, and she didn't much see the point in making herself uncomfortable for no reason. Once she'd reached over and turned off the bedside lamp, she pulled the blankets and the duvet cover up to her chin, and hoped she'd soon be warm enough to find some sort of escape in sleep.

No sooner had her eyes closed, however, than she heard a whisper.

"Rosemary."

Immediately, she sat bolt upright, eyes straining against the darkness. It actually wasn't completely pitch black in the room; some light seeped in past the curtains. Because of that faint illumination, she was able to detect the shape of a man sitting on the window seat.

Caleb.

"What the hell are you doing in here?" she shot back in a harsh whisper.

He didn't move. "I told you we'd talk later. So…I'm here to talk."

Right. He had made her that promise, but she'd figured that he'd decided to postpone their discussion until the next day. Apparently not.

Cautiously, she sat up in bed, holding the covers against her so she could hide most of what the bare nightgown revealed. "Won't your father know?"

A slight movement that might have been a shrug. "Probably. But I don't think he would care if I talked to you, as long as I didn't help you try to get away. Which I won't," he added quickly, "so don't get your hopes up."

"No hope over here," she replied, and he chuckled.

"It's not as bad as that." He got up from the window seat and came over toward the bed, pausing for a moment to collect the chair that stood in front of the dressing table so he could place it at her bedside. Before he sat down, he reached for the lamp and switched it back on. Rosemary blinked at the sudden glare but didn't try to move, since she really didn't want him to get a good look at her in her borrowed nightgown. He was wearing the same clothes he'd had on at dinner—a pair of faded jeans and a crew-neck brown sweater with a white T-shirt barely peeking out from underneath—and looked as if he didn't have a care in the world.

Rosemary wanted to scowl at his relaxed,

friendly attitude but decided there was no point in telegraphing her feelings any more than she already had. Maybe it was useless to pretend, and yet she didn't want Caleb to know how upsetting it was for her to be in this house, surrounded by part-demons. "Why is it so important for them to prove to me that I'm one of you?"

"I'd think that was sort of obvious," he replied. He leaned back in his chair, but not so much that he was in any danger of tipping it over. "We want you on our side, Rosemary. You're one of us."

"So you tell me," she returned, not sure if she dared to say much more than that.

His shoulders lifted. "It's a fact. There's no reason for us to be at cross-purposes."

Actually, she could think of about a hundred reasons why she had absolutely no desire to be aligned with the Greencastle demons, but she thought it was probably a good idea not to enumerate them at that particular moment. "Don't even bother trying to convince me you're the good guys."

"I won't," he said. "We're just...us."

"You killed Colin Turner."

"No," Caleb said, his expression almost regretful. "Belial's demons killed Colin. We had nothing to do with his murder."

Rosemary hadn't even stopped to think that

possibly the part-demon group here in Indiana wasn't marching lock step with the demon who'd possessed Jeffrey Whitcomb and his assorted minions. "You didn't?"

"I just told you we didn't." He shifted on his chair and then leaned forward slightly, gaze fastened on hers, everything about his posture all earnestness. "I'm not saying that my grandfather didn't do Belial's bidding as necessary. But once he left this mortal world and went back to—"

"To Hell," Rosemary said distinctly. That was what Audrey had told her, anyway; that once the original group of demonic trustees were finished with their work here on Earth, they returned to Hell where they belonged, leaving behind half-human sons to continue their line.

"Yes," Caleb said, now looking a little annoyed. "Anyway, once the original demons were gone, everyone left here just sort of…lived their lives."

"Except for the part where they meddled with mine," she pointed out. All right, maybe it was only the truth that it had been full-blood demons straight from Hell who'd burned Audrey's house to the ground and murdered Colin Turner and infested the Whitcomb mansion, but it sure hadn't been any demons who'd placed a hex on Rosemary's own home…and it hadn't been anyone other than Caleb himself who'd confronted her in Colin's Glendale house and attacked her and Will with fire and flame. "And are you forgetting the part where you tried to kill me only a week ago?"

"I wasn't trying to kill you," Caleb said calmly.

She crossed her arms, and the covers slipped a little. For just the briefest second, his gaze slid downward, to the exposed curve of her breasts, but almost at once, he refocused on her face. As much as she wanted to pull the covers back up, she had a feeling that doing so would only draw more attention to herself, and so she decided the hell with it—she couldn't stop Caleb from leering at her body, but she could definitely act as if she couldn't care less what he did.

"It sure looked like you were trying to kill me."

He let out a huff of a breath. Exasperation? Frustration? It was hard to know for sure. However, his tone was even enough as he said, "It was a test. Your powers seemed to be waking up, just a little, but I hadn't seen enough evidence yet that you were really who my father claimed you were. I guessed that, in a pinch, they'd activate out of sheer self-preservation."

Oh, they'd activated, all right. In that moment of terror, Rosemary hadn't even stopped to think, had only tried to protect herself and Will in the only way she knew how. To her astonishment, the magical shield she'd summoned had actually worked.

"A test, huh?" she responded, not bothering to keep the skepticism out of her voice. "Was nearly killing Will part of your 'test' as well?"

Caleb's mouth pursed, and she thought she caught a glint of amusement in his dark eyes. "Well, actually, I wasn't too worried about hurting him. What do you see in that guy, anyway?"

Anger flashed through her, but she made herself sit still. She was in no position to fight back at the moment, and besides, even if she didn't yet know what she intended to do with the information he was currently providing, Rosemary understood that it was better to keep Caleb talking for as long as possible. "Nothing you'd understand," she said, "since I wouldn't expect a part-demon such as yourself to comprehend courage, or nobility, or, or—"

"I get it," he said with a grin, apparently not offended at all. "The ineffable Will Gordon is far beyond my base comprehension. On the other hand, since you and I have the same amount of demon blood flowing through our veins, I'm not sure what this all says about you."

"Alleged demon blood," she countered, and his smile only broadened.

"Oh, it's there." A pause, and then he added,

"Why do you think we got along so well together?"

Rosemary wasn't sure how she wanted to answer that question, mostly because she remembered with some mortification how she'd thought basically the same thing when she first met Caleb and started spending time with him. It wasn't until later that she began to have doubts. "As I recall, we got along well…until we didn't."

Her comment didn't seem to faze him, although she'd hoped he would remember the awkwardness at his house when he'd tried to initiate further intimacies and had been rebuffed, and that such a recollection might make him reconsider his belief that they were somehow intended to be together. Unfortunately, he only raised an eyebrow and said, obviously undaunted, "I was trying to move things along too quickly. I see that now. But I never stopped hoping you would give me another chance."

"Not going to happen," she said at once. "I can't—I could never—"

"Never what?" he cut in. "Be with someone who was part demon, when you're pretty much the same as me? I'd say that was a little hypocritical."

Rosemary opened her mouth to argue, then stopped herself. Maybe Caleb was correct on that one point…but he needed to know there could never be anything between them. "I'm in love with Will Gordon," she said, hoping her bluntness would be enough to convince him he was pursuing a dead end.

"For now," Caleb said cryptically. "Anyway, I just wanted to disabuse you of the notion that we're up to anything nefarious here. You're safe… you can go to Indianapolis tomorrow and get your blood test done…and then you can go home and figure out what to do with the knowledge that you're a quarter-demon just like the rest of us Greencastle grandchildren."

"Just like that."

A nod. "Just like that."

"And all that chasing around after the *Project Demon Hunters* footage was just a game." She spoke lightly, but Rosemary honestly wasn't quite sure how she'd react if he told her the footage was only a red herring, an excuse for him to get closer to her and see if she really measured up to the rest of the part-demons of their generation.

"Oh, no," Caleb said, his expression abruptly sobering. "We wanted the footage. And we'll get it back."

"I'm surprised one of you didn't swoop down and take it once it was unguarded."

For the first time, his gaze shifted away from hers. "We're working on it."

Which meant they must have tried to take it,

and had been thwarted. How, she wasn't sure. Yes, she'd put extra wards on Will's safe, but, considering the way Caleb was able to come and go despite the magical protection she'd laid on the house, she didn't know for sure how effective those wards even were. The safe itself was small enough to pick up and tuck under your arm, so it wasn't as though another of the Greencastle part-demons couldn't have dived in and taken it away, even if they weren't yet able to open the thing.

The important thing, though, was that the footage wasn't back in their possession. She could hold that minor victory in her heart, even as she was trapped here in enemy territory. Because they were her enemies, no matter how polite they tried to be, how much consideration they showed her.

"Well, good luck with that," she said.

"Luck has nothing to do with it." Caleb got up from his chair and stood there for a moment, looming over the bed. Rosemary held herself still, wondering what she would do if he tried something…and whether any of her efforts would be successful.

After a painfully long pause, however, he sent her another of those grins that made her flesh want to crawl right off her body.

"Sleep well," he said with an obvious leer, and disappeared.

Even though he was gone, she made herself

remain where she was, absolutely unmoving, for another minute or two. At last, she slid down against the pillows, covers pulled up nearly to her chin.

She didn't know whether she'd be able to sleep a wink that night.

Chapter 5

THE SAFE STILL SAT ON ITS SHELF IN THE office closet. As soon as Will had called his friend to tell him what was going on, Michael had inquired in sharp tones about the hard drive with the footage. He'd said he would check and call back, and so Will had come here, Glynis McGuire trailing behind him, to make sure the drive hadn't disappeared along with Rosemary.

Will's hands shook a little as he reached up for the safe and lowered it to the desk, and he wanted to curse himself for his weakness. This was not the time to be losing it. If the footage was gone, well, they'd figure out how to get it back...after Rosemary was safe. Making sure she was all right superseded any other concerns.

Although he knew Rosemary had warded the safe, he also knew he wouldn't have any problem getting inside. The safe and its contents had been protected against those who might wish him ill, not against someone who only wished to keep those items secure. He rotated the dial to key in the combination—14-22-49—and then lifted the lid.

A relieved breath escaped him as he stared down at the hard drive. It appeared to be untouched...but what if the real hard drive had been taken and a dummy left in its place? He supposed he'd better check to make sure the precious footage was still intact. With everything that had been happening, he hadn't had the chance to go to Best Buy and get a drive large enough to back up the files, and he silently prayed that the blunder wouldn't prove to be a fatal one.

"What is that?" Glynis asked as he lifted the drive from the safe and began to rummage around in his desk drawers for a spare mini-to-USB connector. "Is it the footage?"

He didn't bother to ask how she knew about the *Project Demon Hunters* tapes, since he assumed Rosemary must have told her mother about them at some point or another. Without looking up from his work, he nodded and replied, "Yes. The drive looks all right, but I want to make sure all the files are intact. Luckily, they're .mp4 video files that I can play though QuickTime on my laptop. If they were still the native Premiere

Pro files, then I'd be in trouble, since I don't have that application on my computer."

Glynis nodded but didn't ask any further questions, seeming content to watch while he hooked up the portable hard drive to his laptop and then clicked on the drive's icon to look at the files it contained. As far as he could tell, they all seemed to be there. Just to be safe, he clicked on one of them and waited as QuickTime opened. Within a few seconds, the video started to play, showing Michael Covenant and Audrey Barrett standing in what appeared to be someone's bedroom, albeit a bedroom so large it would have swallowed up his own much more modest space several times over. Strange, ghostly tendrils began to reach out of the mirror, and Glynis let out an audible gasp. At once, he clicked on the player to pause it.

"Sorry about that," he said. "Some of this footage is pretty disturbing. I suppose I should have warned you."

"It's all right," she replied quickly, although he noticed the way she reached up to push a tendril of curly hair—so like her daughter's—away from her face with a shaking hand. "It's just...." The words trailed off into silence, and she shook her head. "I suppose I wasn't expecting to get such a sense of evil from merely watching a video."

He swiveled his office chair slightly so he

could face her more directly. "You could feel it just from that?"

"Yes. Probably not as bad as it must have been when it actually happened, but still...." Again, she lapsed into silence, as though searching for the best words to describe her reaction. "I don't want to think about my daughter being mixed up in anything so terrible."

"She's not," he said quickly, then added as Glynis looked at him in some surprise, "What I mean is, those were actual demons Michael and Audrey faced in the Whitcomb mansion. What we're dealing with now is something different. I'm not saying they're not capable of doing some very bad things, but they're still part mortal."

That explanation didn't seem to reassure Rosemary's mother, because she pressed her lips together and gave another look at the terrifying image on the screen before saying, "People do a lot of terrible things. Your enemies being part human isn't enough to guarantee my daughter's safety."

No, he supposed it wasn't. And although he wished he had some reassuring words to give Glynis, the truth of it was, he didn't know what the Greencastle demons even wanted with Rosemary. Revenge for stealing the footage, even though it wasn't theirs to begin with? Some kind of retaliation for Caleb Lockwood's death, even though she didn't have anything to do with it? Either explanation seemed plausible, although Will didn't pretend to understand anything of the part-demons' thought processes.

"If they really did take her, it was for a reason," he said. "And I doubt that reason involves hurting her, or...." He stopped himself there. No point in making things any worse than they already were.

Glynis seemed to understand where he'd been heading before he cut himself off, because her already fair skin paled visibly, and she took in a breath as though to steady herself. "Let's hope so. What's next?"

"I need to call Michael back and let him know the footage is still intact," Will replied. "After that...I suppose it depends on what Michael has to say."

Before he'd called Michael the first time, he'd almost responded to Rosemary's text, thinking there had to be some way to answer without letting slip that he knew the entire thing was a lie. However, he'd decided to wait until he spoke to his friend—and when he'd mentioned the possibility of sending a reply, Michael had shot the idea down right away, saying it was too risky. Now, though, Will found himself staring at the message screen and wondering if he should dare. Yes, there was every possibility that someone was monitoring Rosemary's phone, but wouldn't it look even stranger if he didn't answer at all?

That seemed to decide things. He sent a quick text, explaining that he'd gotten stuck late at the church and his phone battery had died, and that he was sorry to hear Celeste and Tyler weren't doing well. Of course, he understood that Rosemary needed to look after her sister and nephew, and he hoped he'd hear from her soon.

Before he could stop to second-guess himself, Will sent the text, then went to his contacts list and located the entry for Michael Covenant. The phone hadn't even rung twice before his friend picked up.

"Were you able to access the footage?"

That was so like Michael—no greeting, no preamble, just cutting right to the heart of the matter. Despite the dire circumstances, Will couldn't quite keep himself from smiling. "Yes," he replied. "I have the drive, and, as far as I can tell, all the files seem to be intact. I don't know why the drive was left behind, but maybe whoever took Rosemary just didn't have the time to try getting past the wards she'd set."

"Maybe," Michael said, although he didn't sound all that convinced. "Anyway, with everything that's going on, I think it's better if I'm out there in California with you."

"I thought you said the demons were stopping you from leaving Tucson," Will replied.

"Yes, but that was when I was trying to leave on my own. I'm bringing Audrey with me."

"You are?" He couldn't help but be startled at that announcement. After all, Audrey was hip deep in her post-grad work. It wasn't as if she could simply drop everything and go running off to California for an indeterminate period.

"We're heading into the weekend. She only has one class to teach tomorrow, and she has someone who can cover for her. If it looks like we won't be back by Monday morning, then she'll make further arrangements. It'll be okay."

Will hoped that was truly the case, but he didn't offer any more arguments. If Audrey said she had it handled, then that was her affair. He had to admit that he'd feel better to have her along; she and Michael made a formidable team.

"And we're going to stop on our way in and collect Fred," Michael continued. "He lives in Redlands, so it's on the way."

For some reason, that piece of information surprised Will. Although of course he didn't know the man, he'd gotten the impression that the hacker lived in a big city, not an Inland Empire town known mostly for the university located there. "Fred's a psychic, too?"

"No," Michael replied, sounding amused.

"But the guy's a genius at digging up information and hacking computer systems, and since we really don't know what we're up against here, I figured it was probably better to have all the bases covered."

"Sounds good. When do you think you'll get here?"

"We're going to leave as soon as we can tomorrow morning, so I hope we'll make it to Pasadena by late afternoon." A pause before he added, "I assume it's okay if we all end up at my place, since Rosemary isn't there at the moment."

"Of course," Will responded. Should he say anything else? It wasn't as if he and Rosemary had made things official, but they'd both been working under the unspoken assumption that she would be staying with him for the foreseeable future. "It would have been fine even if Rosemary was here."

A short pause before Michael said, "Ah, got it. I'm happy for you guys."

Feeling a bit awkward, Will said, "Thanks. Anything you need me to do over here while you're en route?"

"Not that I can think of, except keep your eyes open."

"I will," he said.

Honestly, if he slept at all that night, he'd surprise himself.

A small, clear *bing* sounded in the room, rousing Rosemary from her sleep. She blinked in confusion for a moment, not recognizing her surroundings. Then she remembered that she was in the Lockwood house, locked in the guest room. A quick glance at the digital clock on the nightstand informed her that it was a little past eleven-thirty. She hadn't been asleep for much more than an hour.

Her purse sat on the dresser across the room. After pushing back the covers, she went over to her bag and extricated her phone, then glanced down at the phone and saw a message from Will on the home screen. On the surface, it seemed innocuous enough—as she'd suspected, he'd gotten caught at the church and had to stay later than expected, and his phone battery had died.

Only...Will was a very careful person. She hadn't been around him for very long, but she'd never heard him use the excuse of a dead phone for being out of contact. In fact, she'd seen one of those USB adapters for cell phone charging stuck into the cigarette lighter of his vintage car, so she knew he paid close attention to that sort of thing.

The nighttime air felt chilly against her exposed skin, and so she hurried back to the bed, phone still in hand, and wriggled back under the covers. Once she was more comfortable, she stared at the message again, wondering if she was missing something. It didn't seem so terribly strange that the battery in Will's phone had died if he'd been kept at work longer than he'd expected and the thing had simply run out.

Unless....

Had he figured out that the excuse for her absence was a complete fabrication? Maybe he'd called Celeste—he had her number, after all—and Celeste had told him everyone was fine at her household. Or maybe he'd checked in with her mother, although Rosemary honestly didn't know whether Will would feel comfortable doing such a thing. They'd only been seeing each other for a very short while, after all, and even though he'd met Glynis and it seemed as though they'd gotten along well, he still might have thought calling her to check up on her daughter would seem strange and controlling.

However, if he had, then again, he would have learned quickly enough that everyone in the McGuire family was doing just fine.

Well, except for Rosemary herself. All right, she hadn't come to any physical harm, was sleeping in a very comfortable bed after having a tasty dinner, but still....

She still wasn't quite sure what to make of Caleb's nocturnal visit. He'd seemed friendly enough, and yet there were undercurrents to their conversation that made her distinctly uncomfortable. At the time, it had seemed the best course of action was go to sleep and try to forget the things he'd said to her, but now all she could do was lie there with her phone clutched in one hand as she stared at the ceiling, thoughts roiling.

He hadn't said as much, but he'd hinted that he wanted to repair their relationship. What, did he think that if her demonic heritage was actually proven, she'd abandon Will and go running back into his arms?

Possibly. No way that was going to happen, however. She hadn't quite figured out what to say to Will if it turned out that Gerald Gates really was her father, but she'd come up with something. After all, he was the one who'd reassured her that he didn't care about her supposed father's angelic heritage. If that didn't bother him, why would learning she was a quarter-demon change anything?

All right, except for that little bit about him being an Episcopalian priest, and not the kind of guy who would generally be consorting with demons and devils. There was a very good chance that he wouldn't want anything to do with her.

Worry started to bubble up through Rosemary, even though she tried to tell herself that she was borrowing trouble. Right now, all she had to go on was Daniel Lockwood's word—well, and Gerald's—and she doubted that was worth very much. A couple of demons, beings who probably lied as easily as they breathed. And okay, they were technically only half-demon, but they were still not to be trusted. For all she knew, they'd cooked up this whole thing to get her and Caleb back together. Why, she didn't know, although she supposed if she really was part angel, maybe they were curious as to what would happen if angel and demon blood were to mix. Maybe they wanted her and Caleb to have some kind of super-supernatural baby together.

Not going to happen, she thought, even as fear began to knot up her stomach and she felt cold all over despite the warm blankets that covered her. Problem was, they'd as much as admitted that Gerald had slept with her mother because they wanted to see what the offspring of a half-demon and a psychically gifted human would be like.

If it had even happened.

She hated this. As someone who'd had to deal with psychic abilities for most of her life, Rosemary was used to being in a position where sometimes the boundaries of reality shifted, where it wasn't always possible to tell what was real and what wasn't, and yet this was somehow different. In all those instances, she'd still known who she was. Now, though, it was as if the bedrock beneath her feet had tilted suddenly, and she was doing her best to hang on and not fall off the edge of her world.

It's all right, she told herself, even though she was pretty sure it really wasn't all right. She needed the reassurance, false though it might be. *If Caleb was going to try anything, he would have done it while he was here earlier. You're safe—they're trying to be nice to you. All you have to do is get through that test tomorrow, and then you can figure out what to do next.*

Because if it turned out that she really was half demon—if Gerald Gates really was her father, and she was far more connected to the Greencastle demons than she'd ever thought or wanted to be—then there was a very good chance she wouldn't be going anywhere.

Chapter 6

ROSEMARY STARED AT HERSELF IN THE mirror, wondering if she should go for another coating of concealer under her eyes, or whether she should advertise to the whole world just how crappy her sleep had been the night before. The concealer—along with the rest of the cosmetics she'd used that morning—had magically appeared in the bathroom drawer overnight. Everything was still in its packaging, and just the right combination of colors to suit her fair skin. That might have seemed a little creepy, except that Mrs. Lockwood's coloring wasn't so different from her own, and Rosemary had a feeling that either Caleb or his father had pilfered it from her stash. Since she was used to wearing drugstore makeup and not the Lancôme and Chanel that had been provided for her, she wasn't going to argue too much over where it had come from. If it had been obviously used, that would have been one thing. But it wasn't, and she realized she should use it. No point in letting Daniel Lockwood know he'd gotten under her skin.

Actually, it wasn't the father who was the real problem, but the son. She didn't like the vibes she was getting off Caleb, not at all. He was being too friendly, and she didn't trust him.

She didn't trust any of them. And she was starting to have her doubts about this outing to Indianapolis, but she'd already agreed to it and didn't see any way to back out now. Not with the senior Lockwood making sure she didn't have a chance of getting away. Also, she honestly did want to know what the blood test would reveal. Better to learn the worst and then figure out how to deal with it than spend the rest of her life wondering.

Jaw set, she paid more attention to her makeup than she normally would, mostly because the clothes she'd been loaned seemed to require it than because she wanted to impress anyone. Blow-drying her hair straight and then using a flat iron to smooth it further would have taken way too much time, though, so she pulled it back with a fabric-covered elastic band and then tied a scarf around the elastic. A few curly tendrils fell around her face, but she still looked far more chic than usual, and wasn't quite sure how to feel about that.

She was just slipping her silver hoop earrings into her ears when someone knocked at the door. "Are you almost ready?"

Caleb. "Yes," Rosemary replied. She stepped away from the mirror and went to open the door, but he forestalled her by opening it himself, although he didn't step into the room. However, she couldn't allow herself to be too relieved by his apparent reticence, because he sent her an admiring smile.

"You look great."

"Your mom has good taste," she said, her tone deliberately casual. Better to deflect the compliment and make it all about the borrowed clothes she wore, rather than a comment on her actual appearance.

He didn't seem to buy it, though; his dark eyes assumed their familiar wicked glint, and his mouth lifted at one corner. "Sure."

"Speaking of which, how are you going to explain me to her?" Rosemary asked as she followed him down the hall and they began to descend the stairs.

Caleb's smile remained in place. "No need to. She stayed over in Indianapolis last night."

Rosemary paused, giving him a sideways

glance. "I thought you said she was just going there for a spa day."

"Sometimes she stays overnight. She always packs a bag, just in case." A slight quirk of his eyebrow, and he added, "I guess it depends on whether the procedures she's getting turn out to have more recovery time than she first estimated."

Ah, okay. So, Mrs. Lockwood's spa days were a little more intensive than just getting a mani/pedi and a seaweed wrap. Well, Rosemary had to admit that Caleb's mother looked great, so whatever they were doing to her during her trips to Indianapolis, it seemed to be working. She didn't have that stretched, "duck face" look of some women who went overboard with plastic surgery and injections, that was for sure.

"Convenient," Rosemary remarked.

"Oh, I would've come up with an explanation for you if I had to…like telling her you were my girlfriend from California."

By that point, they'd reached the bottom step. Rosemary stopped there for a moment, arms crossed. "Don't you think she would have wondered why your 'girlfriend' was at your father's party with another man just the day before yesterday?"

Caleb shrugged. "Maybe she would…if she could remember you being there at all. My father made sure she couldn't recall anything about you and Will. It seemed safer."

Safer for whom? Rosemary wished she could make a superior remark about not meddling with other people's minds, but since she'd done basically the same thing when Mrs. Lockwood caught her snooping in the master suite the night of the party, she realized she really couldn't get too sanctimonious.

Before she could reply, Daniel Lockwood called out from the other room. "Is that Rosemary?"

"Yeah, Dad," Caleb replied.

"Come in and get some coffee and danish. Gerald will be over in a few minutes."

Rosemary had been wondering about breakfast, since it was nearly ten and she hadn't eaten anything yet. Caffeine and sugar didn't seem like a great combination to her—she drank coffee but preferred eggs in the morning—but she guessed it probably wouldn't be a good idea to ask for something else to eat. She followed Caleb into the dining room, where a plate of luscious-looking pastries had been set on the massive mahogany table. A silver coffee service sat next to it, along with cups and saucers painted with an old-fashioned rose pattern. Clearly, Daniel Lockwood didn't subscribe to the "grab and go" Starbucks model of coffee drinking.

"You're looking very well," he said, giving Rosemary an approving glance. "Those clothes suit you."

She thought pretty much the opposite, and would have said she felt like a little girl playing dress-up in her mother's clothes, only Glynis McGuire didn't exactly dress like a lady who lunched, either. However, there was no point in protesting, since that would only succeed in letting Mr. Lockwood know how uncomfortable she was in her borrowed wardrobe. "Thank you," she said politely, then went over to the silver coffeepot and poured a measure into one of the fragile-looking porcelain cups. There was also cream and sugar, but she ignored the add-ons and lifted the cup to her lips so she could blow on the liquid inside.

Caleb did the same, although he didn't seem to have any scruples about adding a decent measure of cream and a bit of sugar to his drink. He also put a cheese danish on a plate and took a bite before asking, "Are we driving?"

"Of course," Daniel replied smoothly. "Gerald offered, but the Range Rover has more room than his Cherokee."

It figured that he would drive a Range Rover. She wondered what the good people of Greencastle thought about the president of their local bank driving a vehicle that wasn't made in America. Most likely, they'd drunk the Lockwood Kool-Aid and thought he walked on water. The delusions of the locals weren't her problem, though. She just wanted to get this over with.

Since Caleb had already snagged the one cheese danish on the platter—it figured—she took a blueberry one and hoped the sugar content wouldn't have her bouncing off the walls. A bite told her that it wasn't quite as sugary as she'd feared, was actually rich and buttery and obviously very fresh. She must have made an approving sound, because Daniel said, "Those are from a local bakery. I think you'll find that Greencastle has more to offer than you thought."

"Mm," Rosemary said, noncommittal because her mouth was full, and also because she didn't see the point in arguing with him. All right, she had to admit to herself that Greencastle was kind of cute, and if it wasn't infested with part-demons, then it might be a decent place to live. She didn't want to give him any ideas, though. His compliment earlier had unnerved her, and she didn't like the way his gaze now moved from her to Caleb and back again. This morning, his son was a little less casual than the day before, in khakis and a cream-colored button-down shirt. Father's orders for him to look more presentable for their trip to Indianapolis, or was Caleb trying to impress her?

If that was the case, then he really didn't know

her at all. Even putting aside her current relationship with Will, she knew she'd never be impressed
by a man wearing khakis.

She was saved from having to say anything by
the doorbell ringing. Daniel excused himself to go
answer it, and she continued to punctuate bites of
danish with sips of coffee, figuring she should do
her best to finish her makeshift breakfast before
Gerald appeared. Caleb did the same, although
even the act of consuming a breakfast pastry
couldn't quite hide the slight smirk he wore.
Funny how she'd never really seen him wearing
that expression back in California, whereas now it
seemed to be almost permanently imprinted on
his face.

Gerald came in with Daniel a moment later,
just as she was setting down her plate. "Morning,
Rosemary, Caleb," he said pleasantly.

"Good morning," she replied as Caleb
mumbled a greeting around a mouthful of
danish. Looking at Gerald, she thought that if
circumstances had been different—if she hadn't
loved her own father very much…if Gerald
wasn't a half-demon…if she'd been the result of
an extramarital fling rather than her mother's
unknowing coupling with an entity bent on
deceiving her—she might not have been horribly
upset to learn he was her biological father. He
seemed to be a much more pleasant person than

Daniel Lockwood, that was for sure, although she also had to admit that Gerald's friendly demeanor could be nothing more than a false façade.

"Ready?" Daniel asked then, and she nodded, even while Caleb munched down the last of his breakfast pastry. He put his empty plate on top of hers and brushed his hands against his pants to remove any crumbs, thus earning him a disapproving look from his father.

However, Daniel didn't say anything, only nodded toward the back of the house, apparently signaling that they all should follow him. Since there wasn't anything else she could really do, Rosemary fell obediently in line behind him and Gerald, with Caleb bringing up the rear. They went out through the kitchen to a large detached garage with four bays. As they approached the leftmost bay, the door opened, even though she didn't see Daniel press a remote. Demon magic, or did he simply have the remote hidden in a pocket?

Inside was a large black Range Rover. Daniel got in the driver's seat, while Gerald took the passenger seat and Caleb climbed in behind his father. That left Rosemary to take the place behind Gerald. She clambered in as well, a little awkward because she wasn't used to getting into a tall vehicle in a pencil skirt. Caleb's mouth twitched a little as she squirmed her way into her seat and fought with the seatbelt, but he didn't say anything.

You'd better not, she thought as she slid the buckle shut and heard it click into place. *Because I'd like to see you attempt that kind of maneuver in a tight skirt, wise-ass.*

On that Friday morning, the streets of Greencastle were busy but not crazy. It didn't take long for them to get on the interstate heading north and east toward their destination. No one seemed inclined to talk, which should have made her relax slightly; she hated being forced to make small talk, and it would have been even more awkward, considering the parties involved. However, the silence grated on her ears, and she wished Daniel Lockwood had turned on the stereo, even if his background sound of choice was sports or talk radio.

Also, she hated being stuck in a confined space with Caleb so close to her. Obviously, he wasn't going to try anything with his father and Gerald in the front seats, but it was still awkward. From time to time, his gaze would slide toward hers, and she had to pretend to be staring out the window at the scenery. Not that there was a lot to see, other than mile after mile of flat farmland. Growing up in Southern California with its mountain ranges on all sides, she wondered how people could live in a place that seemed so flat and featureless. It was probably pretty enough in the spring and summer when everything was green, but with November around the corner, some of the autumn color was starting to fade, and the grass looked a little yellow, too, as if it had been touched by frost and probably wasn't going to hold on for much longer.

Anyway, she knew it wasn't an accident when Caleb shifted and his knee brushed against hers for a moment. About all she could do was hold herself still and pretend not to notice, since she didn't want to give him the satisfaction of knowing how uncomfortable she was. All the same, she allowed herself an inner sigh of relief when they reached the outskirts of Indianapolis, signaling that it shouldn't be too long before they reached their destination.

In fact, another fifteen minutes elapsed before they reached their destination—a strip mall, of all places. For some reason, Rosemary had been expecting a multi-story medical building, something that looked a little more imposing.

Caleb must have noticed the shift in her expression, because he said, "This place has very good ratings and can give us a twenty-four-hour turnaround. Unless you'd rather we went with someplace a little slower? Maybe you'd feel better if you chose the facility."

The same thought had crossed her mind, but

the thought of any further delays was unappealing, to say the least. "I'm sure this is fine," she replied stiffly, and put her hand on the door handle so she could let herself out. A cold breeze hit her almost at once, and she tried not shiver. For some reason, it felt chillier here than it had back in Greencastle, although maybe the trickle of ice that seemed to move down her spine had far more to do with her worries about the results of the paternity test than because of the actual temperature outside.

Despite her discomfort, she tried to look unconcerned as Daniel and Gerard got out of the Range Rover and came to stand next to her and Caleb. "Do we have an appointment?" she asked.

"No need for one," Daniel told her. "I called to check, but they said you could just walk in. Go ahead—Caleb and I will be waiting out here."

Caleb raised an eyebrow at those instructions, leading Rosemary to believe that his father hadn't told him about this element of their plans. "Shouldn't we go in with them?"

"No, that would attract too much attention. We can walk down to that Peet's Coffee at the end of the mall and wait there."

Rosemary spied the coffeehouse in question, a storefront next to a Sally Beauty, with open parking lot beyond. For a moment, she wondered if Daniel was making a mistake by giving her a chance to escape, then put the notion aside. The Peet's shop wasn't that far away, and it was entirely possible he could still block her talents from that distance. Besides, she'd come here to get the paternity test done. She wanted to know the answer, and running away didn't make much sense.

Some of those same thoughts must have been tumbling around in Caleb's mind, because he looked dubious. However, he didn't argue, only gave a lift of his shoulders and said, "Okay."

Gerald touched Rosemary's arm. "We might as well go in."

She nodded and followed him inside, not looking back to see if Daniel and Caleb had lingered to make sure they really went in the clinic, or whether they'd headed straight for the coffeehouse. The lab's waiting room was fairly typical, with flat-weave brown carpet on the floor and a number of metal chairs with vinyl cushions. Gerald went ahead to the reception desk, and she followed him and waited as he told the plump blonde woman sitting there that they needed to have a paternity test done. She didn't seem too surprised that a grown woman and her father would be asking for such a thing, and handed over a pair of clipboards with some paperwork for them to fill out.

It was the standard stuff, and Rosemary went through it quickly enough, although she had to pause and ask Gerald for Daniel's address, since she didn't know it and she assumed that was where the lab results would be sent. After they were done with the paperwork, the receptionist instructed them to take a seat, so Rosemary headed over to an empty chair and sat down, feeling a little awkward as Gerald seated himself next to her.

"This must all seem very strange to you," he said, and she shrugged.

"Well, yeah, if someone had asked me a few days ago what I planned to do with my Friday, I'm fairly certain that getting a paternity test in Indianapolis would have been pretty far down the list."

He chuckled. "I would suppose so." A pause as he took a quick, surreptitious glance around, but the receptionist was on the phone, and the only other person in the waiting area—a man in his mid-forties, pale and tired-looking—was also occupied with his phone and didn't seem to be paying them any attention. Speaking in a slightly lower tone, Gerald went on, "I only want what's best for you."

"And what would that be?" Rosemary inquired, feeling an edge creep into her voice. "For me to come be part of your big, happy family? Does your wife even know about me?"

His jaw tightened, and he glanced away from her.

Well, there was her answer. "So, she doesn't. And I assume your son doesn't, either?"

"No," Gerald said. "Neither of them know anything. I didn't want to tell Laurie because this all happened before we were married, several years before our son was even born. That was part of the reason why Daniel convinced me to do it—I was the only one of…of us"—the words stumbled a little, and Rosemary had a feeling he'd almost said "half-demons" before realizing that probably wasn't the sort of phrase you'd want to throw around in a public setting—"who wasn't married and with a family yet. All of us are only children, you see, and Caleb's generation are only children as well. If I was going to have only one shot at this…so to speak…then Daniel said it should be with Glynis McGuire."

"But it wasn't your 'only shot,'" Rosemary replied, feeling her mouth curl in distaste even as she said the words. "Because you had your son."

"Yes, but a year later. None of us knew what to make of it. But Daniel said there was no reason for Laurie or Noah to know about you, so I kept the whole thing to myself."

Her fingers clenched around the strap of her purse, which currently sat in her lap. Without looking at Gerald, she said, "And do you always do everything Daniel tells you to do?"

"He's the leader of our group," her supposed father said simply, which told her everything she needed to know. Maybe Gerald wasn't as overtly evil as Daniel, but she couldn't count on him to take her side in any of this. If she went up against Daniel Lockwood, she'd have to do it alone.

"Got it," she said, still looking away from him.

"Rosemary—" he began, but didn't get any further than that, because a nurse came into the waiting room and said,

"Gerald Gates?"

He nodded and rose from his chair.

"This way," the nurse said. Her gaze moved to Rosemary for a moment, and she added, "I'll be back for you in a minute, hon."

The two of them disappeared down a hallway, and Rosemary sat where she was, fingers still gripping her purse strap. Maybe this was her chance. No, she couldn't blink herself out of here, not with Daniel exerting his influence from a few hundred feet away, but she could get up from her chair and walk out. She had her phone. She could call herself an Uber and have it take her someplace where she could safely send herself back to California. No harm, no foul.

Except then she'd never learn if Gerald Gates

really was her father…and she'd have a bunch of pissed-off half-demons gunning for her.

Damned if you do, she thought. She pulled out her phone, looked at Will's message, and again debated whether she should reply. Maybe something that sounded innocuous but would tell him that things weren't quite what they seemed.

Hi, Will. Sorry about the family issues. They always crop up when you least expect them. But I want to help, even though Celeste keeps telling me she's not a charity case. I'll call you when I can. Loves.

Would he understand the admittedly oblique message? Rosemary didn't know, but she felt better, for some reason, like she'd finally struck a small blow for herself.

She'd just barely put her phone away when the nurse reappeared with Gerald. He offered Rosemary a reassuring smile as he came back over and assumed his previous seat, even as the nurse said, "Rosemary McGuire?"

Well, there wouldn't be any backing out now. She got up from her chair and went over to where the nurse waited for her. A short trip down a hallway whose walls were hung with incongruous tropical scenes, and then Rosemary was taken into a spare little exam room that held a phlebotomist's chair and not much else.

"Just a cheek swab," the nurse said. She got

out one of the items in question, removed the wrapping, and then reached in and gently collected a few cells from the inside of Rosemary's cheek. "That's it."

Rosemary closed her mouth. Definitely much easier than giving blood—and without any lasting marks, either. The last time she'd had to provide a sample, she'd had a bruise on the crook of her elbow for almost two weeks. "And we'll really get the results back in a day?"

The nurse nodded as she placed the swab inside a plastic bag and then affixed a computer-printed label with Rosemary's info to its exterior. "That's what Mr. Gates is paying for. They'll be couriered to the address you specified."

"Efficient," Rosemary managed, although with a somewhat sinking feeling inside. Seeing the swab with its official label made all this suddenly real, made her realize that in less than a day, she'd know whether Gerald Gates really was her father.

And whether she was part demon.

"That's what we do," the nurse said cheerily. "Although I have to say, we don't usually test paternity in adult children."

"It's an inheritance thing," Rosemary managed, and the nurse gave a knowing nod.

"Ah, I see. Well, best of luck with everything!"

She made herself smile, although she certainly wasn't feeling very cheery at the moment. After thanking the nurse, she went back out to the waiting room, where Gerald sat on his chair. The other man who'd been there was gone, probably off getting his own tests done, whatever they might be.

"All set," she said, and Gerald rose from his seat.

"Good. I'd suggest us all having lunch here in the city, but we need to get back to Greencastle."

"Why?" Rosemary responded, wondering if he was going to tell her there was a meeting of demons slated for later that afternoon.

However, his reasons turned out to be far more mundane. As he opened the door for her and they went back outside, he said, "Daniel has a meeting at the bank at two, and I need to be present at a pep rally this afternoon."

"'Pep rally'?" she repeated blankly, not quite understanding why he would need to attend that sort of event.

A quick grin, and he said, "Didn't Daniel tell you?"

"Tell me what?"

"I'm the principal of the high school, and it's homecoming tonight."

For a second or two, she could only stare at him. Honestly, she didn't quite understand why she should be so surprised, since it was obvious that pretty much all of the Greencastle demons had some sort of important occupation in the town. Still, she'd never thought that one of them would be in charge of watching over vulnerable kids.

Human kids.

She found her voice. "Then I'm extra surprised that you would want to do this paternity test. Wouldn't it be kind of a scandal if news got out that you had an illegitimate child?"

Gerald looked remarkably unconcerned. "Maybe twenty years ago. My job is secure enough —several of us are on the Board of Education."

Of course, they were. The demons did whatever they needed to in order to ensure they were tightly woven into the fabric of their town. "How…convenient."

He smiled and patted her on the arm, and she forced herself not to flinch. "I suppose you could look at it that way. But let's go collect Caleb and Daniel. Maybe you can have him bring you to the game tonight. It would be fun."

Rosemary highly doubted that. "I'm not much into football."

"Too bad," Gerald responded. "Caleb was the quarterback his senior year. I'm sure he'd like to take you, show you off."

I'll bet he would, she thought, but she only shrugged and said as lightly as she could, "Wouldn't he have a hard time explaining me?"

"Not at all. Everyone knows he spent some time in California. They'd just think you came here to visit during homecoming."

Right. The handsome high school quarterback returning a decade later to visit the scene of his former glory, his new girlfriend from California on his arm. All right, that wasn't an entirely accurate picture, since Caleb would have graduated eleven years ago and Rosemary knew she sure as hell wasn't his girlfriend.

But she knew it was the picture Daniel and Gerald wanted to paint. They wanted her here, wanted her to be a part of their world.

A part of Caleb's world.

And she wasn't sure how she would be able to escape it.

Chapter 7

WILL HAD ALREADY GOTTEN A BARRAGE OF text messages early that morning, most of them from Michael as he and Audrey geared up for their drive to California. Since she had someone lined up to cover her morning classes, the plan was to leave Tucson by nine so they could be in Pasadena no later than five. They'd make a brief stop in Redlands to collect Fred Peñasco, but that shouldn't delay them too much.

At any rate, he was somewhat surprised to see a text pop up on his phone around nine-thirty, since by that time he assumed Michael would be on the road and not available for texts. However, he supposed it could have been Audrey, or maybe even Glynis McGuire checking in, although there honestly wasn't much she could do about the current situation except sit tight and wait to see what Michael and the rest of them could devise in terms of tracking down Rosemary.

And speak of the devil....

The text was from her. Still acting as though she was at Celeste's house, watching over a sick sister and nephew, but something about the wording of the message seemed off. He supposed that wasn't so strange, not if she really was being held somewhere against her will, and yet....

He scanned the message again. *But I want to help, even though Celeste keeps telling me she's not a charity case.*

Charity case....

Will gazed down at the phone without really focusing on it. Something about charity....

Of course. The message only confirmed what he'd already suspected, but it was a piece of information they'd actually be able to act on.

The cocktail party at Daniel Lockwood's house had been a charity fundraiser for the Greencastle library. Rosemary must have used that phrase to let him know that was where she was currently being held. Will supposed he should be at least somewhat relieved that she apparently possessed enough autonomy to send him the message, but cold fear still curled in his gut at the thought of her there alone, surrounded by the part-demon offspring of Belial's minions.

Will had to get her out of there.

How, he had no idea, but he supposed Michael would have some thoughts on the subject. Too bad that he was still hours and hours away, driving west on I-10. It would have been nice if they had the demons' ability—or Rosemary's half-angelic talent—for moving instantly from place to place, but unfortunately, as mere mortals, they had to slog along at a steady seventy-five miles per hour.

Will almost texted Michael anyway to let him know what was going on, but the cool voice of reason stopped him. Getting the news now couldn't change their current course of action, but it might make him that much more impatient to reach Southern California. He might speed and get a ticket, or get into an accident. Better just to wait it out, excruciating as that felt at the moment.

However, he didn't see the harm in reaching out to Glynis to let her know that Michael and Audrey were on their way, and that he had an idea where Rosemary had gone. Instead of calling, he sent a text, figuring that was the easiest way to get the information to her without getting embroiled in a long conversation. He'd come in to work because he was needed at the church, and therefore his time wasn't entirely his own while he was in his office. In fact, he was waiting for a couple of parishioners who were due to arrive for some marital counseling. In the past, he'd sometimes felt like a fraud when offering such advice, considering he'd never been married, had never had a relationship last more than few months since Lois dumped him back in college.

Now, though, he knew what it felt like to passionately care about another person, to want to do whatever it took to make sure she remained in his life. Even if it meant dropping everything to take another flight out to Indiana…assuming that was what they eventually decided to do.

One way or another, though, he'd make sure Rosemary returned safely. Now that he'd opened his heart to her, he didn't want to imagine his world without her in it.

His phone let out a soft *ping*, letting him know he'd received a text. Will fished the phone out of his jacket pocket, heart beating harder with the irrational hope that it might have come from Rosemary, even though he knew she probably couldn't risk anything beyond the single message she'd already sent.

But no, the text was from Glynis. Brief, but it made him relax ever so slightly.

What do you need from us?

At the moment, he didn't think there was much Glynis—or Rosemary's sisters Isabel and Celeste—could do. However, Will reminded himself that all three of them were powerful psychics, and maybe there was a way they could help without having to get directly involved in the fight.

Try to see if you can get any visions or impressions about what's happening to Rosemary, he texted back. *I'm only guessing that she's in Greencastle, so some corroborating evidence would be helpful. And I assume Michael will want all of us to get together once he and Audrey and Fred arrive, but I'll keep you posted on that.*

We'll do our best, Glynis replied. *Celeste is working at the shop today, but I'll get in touch with Isabel and let her know what she needs to do.*

Thank you, he typed, and a response came back almost immediately.

I wish we could do more. But I'm trying to stay positive.

It's going to be okay, he told her.

He only hoped he was right.

Just as Gerald had indicated, there was no lunch or sightseeing in the offing once they were done at the lab—not that Rosemary was in the mood anyway. The four of them piled in Daniel's Range Rover and headed back to Greencastle without saying much. At that point, it was more a waiting game than anything else. Maybe there had been a moment when she could have slipped away and made her escape, but if such an opportunity had existed at all, she hadn't recognized it for what it was. And although she supposed it might be somewhat easier to get away from Caleb than if she had his father and Gerald Gates keeping an eye on her all afternoon, she had a feeling that someone would be watching, making sure she didn't try anything.

Somewhat to her surprise, Daniel didn't take them back to the house, but dropped her and Caleb off in Greencastle's quaint downtown area, only a block away from the restaurant where she and Will had shared breakfast just a few days earlier. "I figured you two would want to get lunch," Daniel said pleasantly, sounding like a completely normal father instead of the part-demon creature he actually was. "I need to get back to the bank, and Gerald has his own duties at the high school."

Rosemary wanted to protest, but she was hungry. Might as well have something to eat on Caleb's dime, even though she didn't much like the idea of being seen around town with him. Doing so would only reinforce the false belief that she was his girlfriend or something.

"No problem," Caleb said easily. "I'll find something to keep her occupied."

That remark sounded ominous, but Daniel only smiled. "Sounds good. Have a nice afternoon."

Caleb nodded and closed the car door, and the Range Rover moved off in a direction Rosemary assumed was back toward the Lockwood mansion. She crossed her arms and gave him a skeptical look. "I'm surprised your father is okay with leaving me with only one babysitter."

"Do you need more?" he inquired.

She didn't answer right away, but instead tried once again to send herself back to California, back someplace where she would be safe. All right, relatively safe, but worlds better than being here in Greencastle.

Of course, nothing happened.

Sunlight flashed off Caleb's teeth as he grinned at her. "You're not going anywhere, Rosemary. Word went out to make sure the whole town was locked down."

Since there was apparently no denying what she'd done, she gave what she hoped was an unconcerned lift of her shoulders. "Can't blame a girl for trying, can you?"

"Nope," he said. "Come on—let me buy you lunch."

Acknowledging her momentary defeat, she nodded and followed him as he led her down the street, past the place where she and Will had eaten breakfast, and on toward what appeared to be a brewpub, in another of the ubiquitous brick buildings. Since it was past one by that point, the place wasn't quite as crowded as it might have been at noon, but there were still plenty of people enjoying a sandwich and a beer. However, they were still able to get a booth toward the back, which Rosemary guessed was probably a good idea. She kind of doubted that Caleb would want anyone overhearing the sorts of things they were going to discuss.

And while it probably wasn't smart to drink too much, she figured one beer couldn't hurt. They both ordered brown ales and got some beer cheese dip to start, then settled down to wait for their food.

In a way, it all felt so relentlessly normal that Rosemary found her situation almost surreal. She should not be sitting here with Caleb in a brewpub in Greencastle, Indiana. He was supposed to be dead, and she was supposed to be back in California with Will.

And yet, here they were.

"Is this all a ploy to keep your mother from finding out I'm here in Greencastle?" she asked, and Caleb's mouth twisted in amusement.

"Not really." He paused for a moment as their waitress came back with the beers they'd ordered and a promise that their cheese dip was on the way, then continued. "After all, my father can make her believe whatever he wants her to believe."

Rosemary stared at him. "That's horrible."

"Not as horrible as her finding out the truth about the man she's married to." A shrug, and he added, "She has a nice life. I don't think she'd even want to know. But anyway, I know it probably wasn't fun for you to be stuck at my parents' house. I convinced my father to let you go back to the DePauw Inn tonight, since the entire crew has been put on alert and will make sure you don't try to slip away under cover of darkness."

The thought of all those half-demons and quarter-demons watching her from wherever they lurked made a chill move down her spine, but Rosemary did her best to focus on the positive. At least she wouldn't be expected to return to the Lockwood mansion, could spend her evening of waiting for the paternity test results in the far more neutral territory of the hotel that was adjacent to the college.

"Should I thank you for that?"

"Only if you want to," Caleb replied, then went silent again as the waitress returned with their dip.

"Anything else?" she asked.

"Maybe in a little bit," he said. "Thanks, Cheryl."

She sent him a sunny smile, then headed back toward the front of the brewpub to check on another table.

"Do you know everyone in Greencastle?" Rosemary asked, trying not to sound too sour.

"Pretty much," he admitted. "It's not a very big place."

And clearly, Caleb was well liked; she couldn't miss the warmth in their waitress's eyes as she looked down at him. Younger than he was, and than Rosemary, too, probably in her early twenties, so too young for them to have gone to high school together or anything.

She had to wonder how Cheryl would react if she ever found out there was a little more to Caleb Lockwood—and his father—than met the eye.

"But it has to be like that for you in Glendora, doesn't it?" he said then, and Rosemary chuckled despite herself.

"Hardly," she said. "I know that downtown where the shop is located looks all quaint and cute, but Glendora's actually a pretty big place. At last count, the population was over fifty thousand people."

"Really? It doesn't seem that big." He lifted his beer and took a sip. "But okay, then yeah, it's about five times the size of Greencastle."

"I'm surprised you all have been able to blend in someplace that's so small," Rosemary remarked.

A shrug. "It's not as hard as you might think. Like I told you before, we're mostly just trying to live our lives."

"Just innocent bystanders."

That comment made him grin. "Right. But I can tell from your expression that you don't believe me, so we'll leave that aside for now."

"Okay," she responded, capitulating for the moment because she knew better than to argue with him in a public place. While it might have been satisfying to try to out the Greencastle demons and let everyone in this town know exactly who they'd been dealing with all these years, she knew that sort of thing sounded easier on paper than it was in real life. Any attempt to divulge the truth about Daniel Lockwood & Co. would probably only result in everyone thinking it was about time for her to go back on her meds. She was the outsider here, while the demons had been a part of this town for several generations.

Their cheese dip arrived, along with a basket of crostini for dipping, and although most of the time, Rosemary would have tried to avoid such obvious carb consumption, she had to admit the food was fabulous. Besides, all this stress had to have burned a lot of calories, right?

"Good?" Caleb asked, and she nodded.

"Really good."

"So, what are you going to do when the test

results come back and tell you that you're one of us?"

His question caught her with some drippy cheese on her lip. She licked it off, trying her best to ignore the way he watched her tongue, gaze far too intent. Were they back to that? He had to know there was no way in hell she'd ever be with him again.

Although the room was warm enough and the borrowed cashmere sweater she wore cozy against her skin, Rosemary couldn't quite prevent herself from shivering a little. She didn't want him to be attracted to her. The situation was complicated enough already.

"I don't know," she said honestly. "Anyway, the first thing would be to convince me those results were genuine."

Although he'd been wearing a halfway amused expression, one corner of his mouth lifted in a partial smile, he sobered abruptly, dark gaze focusing on her face while she did her best not to blink and look away. "Wasn't that the whole reason why we went to the lab?" he demanded. "I thought the point was that we couldn't meddle with those results."

"You can't?" she asked. "Why not?"

He hesitated for a second or two, gaze moving toward the main part of the restaurant, as though he wanted to make sure there was no one in earshot who could possibly hear what he was about to say. "We're not good with large-scale automated stuff, big organizations. Yeah, if you and Gerald used that at-home kit my father showed you, then we could have gimmicked that somehow. But something that went to a big commercial lab?" A shake of the head, followed by, "That's a totally different story. It's kind of the same reason why I spent some time in L.A. getting a few credits under my belt. My story had to seem plausible. It wasn't as if we had the ability to hack IMDB to make it look as though I was some sort of indie wonder or the director of the next Marvel movie or something."

In a way, Rosemary supposed that made sense. Actually, she felt strangely relieved by this confession, if only because she'd begun to wonder how far the demons' powers really extended, whether they truly had the ability to meddle in whatever they wanted, whenever they wanted. But they weren't omnipotent. They had their blind spots and their weaknesses, just like every other living creature.

"So anyway," he went on, "that means whatever those test results say is the truth. The courier can hand them directly to you, if you like. That way you can see them before anyone else, before anyone's had any opportunity to meddle with them or alter them or whatever."

"That might help," she said, wondering whether she should feel grateful, or worried. Yes, she'd come here because she wanted to learn the truth about her father and her past, but on the other hand, if the test results turned out to be something she really didn't want to see, then she wouldn't be able to convince herself that the demons had somehow interfered with the results and changed them to reflect what they wanted and not the actual truth.

"Then we'll do it that way," Caleb told her, then dipped another piece of crostini in the cheese and took a bite. "I'll let my dad know. I think the plan was to call me when the courier was about a half hour away, and then I'd come by and get you and take you to the house."

She looked at him, a little confused. "You don't live at the house?"

Her question got a derisive chuckle in response. "I'm twenty-nine years old, Rosemary," he said. "You seriously think I live at home?"

"Well, I—"

He waved a hand and continued, cutting her off. "I've got a loft above one of the businesses here in downtown." A familiar glint entered his eyes as he added, "I'd be happy to show it to you after we're done eating. It's only a few blocks away."

How about no? she thought. No way in the

world would she allow herself to be alone with Caleb in his loft. Being with him like this was just barely tolerable, mostly because they were in a public place and she knew he couldn't misbehave too badly.

"That's all right," she said, then sipped some of her brown ale. "I'll take your word for it. I was thinking that after lunch I'd go straight to the hotel and hang there for the rest of the day…and evening."

He didn't look terribly surprised by her plans, which clearly had been designed for maximum demon avoidance. "That's no fun. I was thinking I could take you to homecoming tonight."

It was her turn to lift an eyebrow. "What, are we suddenly back in high school or something?"

"The homecoming game," he amended. "The dance is tomorrow night. Obviously, I have no plans to show up there."

"Well, thank God for that. Anyway," she went on before he could respond, "like I told your dad, I'm not much for football. I think it's better if I just stay in the hotel. But feel free to go to homecoming and bask in decade-old glory if it floats your boat."

For a moment, Caleb didn't say anything. He ate another crostini well coated in cheese, washed it down with some beer, and then said, "You really don't like me, do you?"

She gazed back at him steadily. "Is that a trick question?"

"No."

For once, the mocking edge to his voice had disappeared. Likewise, he seemed almost earnest as he stared across the table at her. For just the barest second, Rosemary felt almost bad for her harsh comment…and then wanted to shake herself. This was Caleb Lockwood, after all, the man who had lied to her about who and what he was, who'd attacked her and sent Will to the hospital with a concussion. He could make all the puppy-dog eyes in the world—it wouldn't change the fact that he was a part-demon lying sack of shit.

"You haven't given me much reason to like you, have you?" She drank some more of her beer, wishing it could have a more relaxing effect on her nerves than it currently seemed to be doing. "Maybe once I might have felt a little sorry for you, but—"

"'Sorry for me'?" he cut in, expression now one of disbelief. "Why in the world would you feel sorry for me?"

"For being born into family of—" Rosemary stopped herself there as an older woman passed by their booth, presumably on her way to the restroom. Lowering her voice, she went on, "For being born into your family. I know it must suck to be put in a situation you really don't have any control over. But it's also not like you tried to rebel, is it? You never told your father to take his stupid plans for world domination and shove them, did you?"

Caleb leaned against the back of the booth, eyes narrowing. "He's not attempting world domination, for Chrissake."

She reflected on the incongruity of a part-demon swearing by the name of a man who should have been anathema to their kind but decided not to remark on it. Instead, she made herself shrug and say, "Then what's his whole deal with the footage? Why's it so important?"

"It needs to be hidden so no one ever sees what's on it."

Was that truly what Caleb believed, or was he only telling her what she wanted to hear? "That's not what you said when you first met me. I seem to remember a whole lot of blather about how important it was for the world to know what was on that hard drive, to see the truth of what Colin Turner captured at the Whitcomb mansion."

"I know what I said." He ran an exasperated hand through his hair, mussing it slightly. Once upon a time, Rosemary might have thought doing such a thing made him look rumpled and adorable. Now, though, she could only gaze at him and wonder if he'd done it on purpose in an attempt to make himself appear more attractive to her. "And yeah, it was a lie, okay? I was telling you what I thought you'd want to hear."

She should have been satisfied by such a comment, but right then, she found herself wondering if it was yet another lie. "So, if it was so important to you to make sure no one ever saw that footage, why didn't your father trash the hard drive as soon as he had it in his possession?"

"I don't know," Caleb said. "I know that sounds like a cop-out, but in this case, it's the truth. Believe it or not, he doesn't confide in me about every little thing. Maybe he wanted to watch it for himself first but didn't have the time. I know this may be hard for you to comprehend, but he doesn't spend 24/7 being some sort of criminal mastermind. He has a job and responsibilities."

"Is that supposed to make me feel sorry for him?"

Caleb reached for his beer and took a large gulp. Stalling tactic, or did he actually need the booze to steady himself?

"No, I don't expect you to feel sorry for him. I'm just trying to tell you what happened, and some possible explanations for that. Do what you like with the information."

Expression aggrieved, he picked up another piece of crostini and dunked it in the cheese. After a long pause, Rosemary did the same, although her appetite wasn't nearly what it had been when she'd first sat down at the table. She wished she could know if there was any point in believing a single word that came out of his mouth. A lot of what he'd said sounded plausible, but….

"Is he worried that someone will make a connection between the Whitcomb mansion and all of you here in Greencastle?" she asked.

"I don't know," Caleb said, in tones that seemed to indicate he wished she would just drop the subject.

"It's kind of a stretch, isn't it?" she persisted, not really caring whether she was annoying him or not. "I mean, Michael only discovered the connection after he had a hacker friend of his do some pretty deep digging. It's not the sort of information that's readily available for just anyone."

He slammed his hand down on the table. Some of her beer sloshed, and Rosemary couldn't quite prevent herself from jumping. Good thing none of the booths in the immediate vicinity were occupied, or Caleb's outburst would definitely have attracted some unwanted attention.

"I don't know," he said again. Red seemed to flicker in his dark eyes, a reflection of the anger he was trying to control. "Just drop it, okay?"

"Sure," she said easily. "I'll drop it."

She reached for her beer, acutely conscious of the slickness of the glass against her fingers, thanks to the beer that had just sloshed over the rim a moment earlier. However, she didn't use her napkin to wipe it away. For some reason, doing so felt like betraying a weakness, like showing that she was upset by his unexpected show of rage a moment earlier.

All right, she was unnerved, but she'd do whatever she could to make sure Caleb didn't know that he'd rattled her. The flash of anger seemed to have proved to her that he could act as casual and friendly as he wanted, but he would always be a demon underneath.

She'd have to make sure she never forgot that.

Chapter 3

COME OVER, HAD BEEN THE TERSE TEXT FROM Michael, which hit Will's phone at a little after five, just as he was preparing to lock up his office. There was supposed to be an Adult Children of Alcoholics meeting that night, but he'd asked Stan, All Saints' senior priest, to take over that evening, since Will knew that Michael would want to gather everyone together as soon as it was feasible.

On my way, he texted back, and then went ahead and messaged Glynis that she and her daughters should also meet at Michael's house if they were available. Isabel he wasn't too worried about, since he knew from Rosemary that her oldest sister was divorced and didn't have any children to look after. Celeste was more of a wild card, but Will figured that if at least Glynis and Isabel were there, they'd be doing okay.

Traffic was thick, but since he didn't have to get on the freeway to get to Michael's house, he figured it could have been a lot worse. As he was pulling up to the curb, a dark gray Volvo parked behind him, and Glynis and another woman got out. She had the same curly brown hair as Rosemary, but was a good deal taller, slim and elegant where Rosemary was delicate and elfin-pretty.

"Will, this is Isabel," Glynis said as they met on the sidewalk. He extended a hand, and Rosemary's sister took it and gave it a firm squeeze, accompanied by a friendly smile. "Celeste said she'd try to be over later if she could, but her husband had to work later than expected and she couldn't get anyone to watch Tyler."

"Not a problem," Will replied—and it wasn't, since he'd already mentally prepared himself for such an eventuality. "Did you have a chance to try to get a read on Rosemary, how she's doing?"

The two women exchanged a glance. Then Isabel spoke. Her voice was slightly lower than her youngest sister's, but otherwise sounded very much like Rosemary's. "I think we'd rather talk about that with everyone."

A frisson of fear moved down his spine. "Is she in trouble?" he asked, once again cursing the hundreds of miles that separated them.

"Not...exactly," Isabel replied.

He couldn't be relieved, not truly, but it was something to hear that at least Rosemary hadn't met with some kind of terrible calamity. Still, he could tell that whatever they'd seen or felt was something the McGuire women wanted to discuss with the whole group, so he didn't push it. "Okay," he said. "Let's go inside."

The three of them went up the front walk to the porch. Will had only just begun to reach for the doorbell when the door opened and Michael looked out at them. He was wearing jeans and a long-sleeved T-shirt rather than his usual black button-down and black trousers, but otherwise, he didn't appear much changed from the last time Will had seen him. If he was at all fatigued by the long drive he'd just taken to get to Pasadena, it didn't show.

"Hi, Will," Michael said, gold-gray gaze flicking past him to the two women who also stood on the porch. "Isabel...Mrs. McGuire."

"Glynis," she said firmly.

"Of course. Come on in."

They all went inside, then followed Michael into the family room. Although it had only been a few days since the last time Will was there, the time that had elapsed felt much longer than that. So much had changed—he and Rosemary had become intimate, had traveled to Greencastle and confronted the demons who lived there. He'd thought they'd eked out a victory in that particular instance, but even though the *Project Demon Hunters* footage was still in their hands, he couldn't be too glad of that circumstance, not with Rosemary still missing.

Audrey was sitting on the couch, her long brown hair pulled back into a sleek ponytail. She also looked fairly relaxed, although maybe some of that was relief at surviving the seven-hour road trip without any demon-created mishaps. On the chair next to the couch was a man Will had never seen before and guessed must be Fred Peñasco. Will wasn't quite sure what he'd been expecting, except that Fred definitely wasn't it. The other man was probably in his middle forties, with gray-streaked dark hair pulled back into a ponytail and strong, rather saturnine features. His olive skin was further tanned by the sun, and the arms beneath the rolled-up sleeves of his army-green shirt were tattooed and thick with muscle.

Michael made some quick introductions, then went on, "We're not going to stand on ceremony here. There's some beer and wine and bottled water in the fridge, and I figure we'd order pizza or whatever later. But I thought we'd want to get right into it."

"Sure," Will said. He sent a quick, almost questioning gaze in Glynis's direction, and she nodded. "We're pretty sure Rosemary is in Greencastle."

"Sure, sure, or just a feeling?" Audrey asked.

"Well, she sent me a text." He went on to explain his hunch about the message Audrey had sent him earlier that day, then added, "But I think Glynis and Isabel can probably elaborate on that."

Isabel spoke then. "My mother and I both tried to reach out and see if we could get a sense of what was happening with Rosemary. Sometimes we're able to see each other pretty clearly, while other times it's much more difficult."

"I didn't have much luck," Glynis said. "But Isabel thinks she saw something."

"What was it?" Fred Peñasco asked, speaking for the first time. His voice was deep, almost rough, the kind of voice that sounded as if it had gotten that way through smoking too many cigarettes or drinking too many shots of whiskey.

She met his eyes, her gaze steady. "Michael explained to you that my whole family is psychic?"

"Yes."

"And you're okay with that?"

Fred's mouth curled slightly. "I wouldn't be working with Michael if I weren't."

That reply seemed to reassure her; something about the set of her shoulders relaxed slightly, and she said, "All right. Well, I did my best to focus on

Rosemary, to see where she was, what she was doing. I got a sense of her in a large city."

"Not Greencastle, then," Will murmured.

"No. I have a feeling she was in Indianapolis. There were three of *them* with her."

"'Them'?" Audrey repeated. "You mean the demons?"

Isabel nodded. "Or part-demons, I guess, if what Will has been telling me is true."

"Oh, they're part demon," Michael put in. "Either half, or quarter, like this Caleb Lockwood person. Depends on the generation. Did you get a good look at them?"

"No," Isabel replied. "It was more a...a sensation of them. They didn't feel right, for lack of a better word."

"So, Rosemary was with these three part-demons in Indianapolis," Audrey said. "Was she afraid?"

"Not exactly. That is, what I was sensing felt more like nervousness, or some kind of strange anticipation, than outright fear."

That had to be a good sign, didn't it? Will wasn't sure. Of course, being nervous also wasn't exactly a desirable state, but better than being obviously afraid for your life. "Could you tell what they were doing in Indianapolis?"

"Not really." Isabel paused there, eyes half shut as though she was trying to concentrate and make sure she didn't forget even the smallest detail, the tiniest bit of evidence that might help them figure out what was going on. "I could feel that there was a reason for them being there, that they had a sense of purpose. I don't know what that purpose was, though."

Odd. What in the world would have made Rosemary accompany three demon-kind to the closest big city? Was there something they needed in Indianapolis that could only be found there? He supposed it was possible, although he couldn't think of anything that would have made Rosemary willingly go anywhere with three of the Greencastle demons.

"Anything else?" Fred asked. He was leaning forward now, eyes fixed on Isabel. And while Will could tell the other man was intent on Isabel's reply, he also got the impression that there was something almost admiring in his gaze, that he hadn't expected the missing woman's sister to be attractive but was damn glad to be proven wrong.

However, Isabel didn't seem to notice that possibly Fred's interest in her wasn't purely professional. "That was all I got from that one flash. Later, though…later, I got one very brief, very clear image. It was definitely Rosemary. She was sitting in a restaurant somewhere, and a man was in the booth with her. That is, he looked like a man, but he felt wrong."

This piece of information did nothing to reassure Will. If Rosemary was being held against her wishes, what was she doing sitting in a restaurant with one of the part-demons? "Did you see what this man looked like?"

"He was about Rosemary's age, with sandy blond hair. Good-looking." She paused before adding, "I just assumed it was Caleb Lockwood."

Except that was impossible, because Caleb was dead.

Unless he wasn't.

Audrey spoke then, sounding startled. "Michael, I thought you said Caleb Lockwood was dead."

"What?" both Glynis and Isabel cut in. They looked shocked, and Will realized that Rosemary must have kept that bit of information to herself —probably in an attempt to prevent them from worrying whether she was a suspect.

"I suppose I should have suspected something when Rosemary told me about Daniel Lockwood but never mentioned Caleb," Glynis went on. "But I didn't want to pry, just because I knew Caleb was a sore subject with her."

"Well, he's dead," Will said. "At least, he wanted us to think he was. I saw the body, but...."

"You did?" Rosemary's mother asked, now looking even more startled. "How—?"

"It's a long story," he said. "And probably moot, if Isabel is correct about the man she saw."

Isabel didn't look offended by his suggestion that she might not have reported her vision accurately. A slight lift of her shoulders, and she said, "It was very clear. A man around Rosemary's age, maybe a little older, with dark blond hair. Tall, I think, although that was harder to tell because he was sitting down."

"Sounds like him," Will replied, figuring there wasn't much point in arguing the subject further. After all, faking his own death sounded like exactly the sort of trick Caleb might pull. "What were he and Rosemary doing?"

"Just talking, I think. They were sitting on opposite sides of the booth."

Well, that was something. At least they weren't being extra cozy and sitting next to each other. A weird stab of jealousy went through him, and Will told himself not to be foolish, that he very much doubted Rosemary was in that booth with Caleb Lockwood out of choice. But if that were the case, why would she allow herself to be with him at all in a situation where it didn't look as though she was being coerced?

It all just added to the mystery, and Will found himself thinking that he didn't know what was worse—not knowing anything at all about what was happening to Rosemary, or seeing only these brief glimpses that didn't tell a full story and made him start to invent scenarios that might or might not be true. Still, he knew Isabel was only trying to help.

"Did you see anything else?"

She shook her head. Her height and some-thing about the way Isabel carried herself tended to give the impression of a woman who was confident in her abilities, but in that moment, she looked troubled, uncertain. "No. I tried, but visions like that aren't something I can really control. And I only had an image of them and didn't actually hear anything, so I have no idea what they might have been talking about."

"That's okay," Michael said then, seeming to sense that Will was bothered by these revelations but didn't want to say anything that would reveal his inner turmoil. "At least we know that Rosemary is all right and they're not torturing her or anything." Glynis made a muffled sound of protest, and he went on, "Sorry about that, but I think it's important that we don't try to ignore what these part-demons are capable of. For some reason, they seem to think Rosemary is useful to them, or I doubt she'd be getting wined and dined by Caleb Lockwood. What we need to figure out is why they'd believe that in the first place—and how we can get her out of there."

"Should I look into flights to Indianapolis?"

Audrey asked, her pretty features tight with worry. "I assume we'd fly—that would be a hell of a long road trip."

"I'm not sure we should do either," Michael replied, and Will stared at him in consternation.

"You're not proposing that we just leave her there, are you?" he demanded.

"I don't know yet." His friend paused, jaw tight, hands shoved into the pockets of his jeans. "Look, I don't like the situation any more than you do, but we have to be rational about this. We know there are fourteen of these part-demons in Greencastle. Some are half demon, some a quarter, but Caleb's shown that even the younger generation can be pretty dangerous. Even when we add Celeste to our little group here, that's only seven of us. And you and Fred don't even have any psychic powers…or anything else that might be of use in a fight against a group of people with demon blood. No offense," he added quickly.

"None taken," Fred drawled, and he leaned against the back of his chair, expression thoughtful.

"I may not be psychic, but I can throw a mean bottle of holy water," Will said.

That remark made Michael smile…but only for a moment. Sobering, he replied, "Yes, I know. But it's already been established that these part-demons aren't necessarily deterred by holy water, right?"

Yes, that was an unfortunate truth Will had discovered to his dismay the last time he'd gone up against Caleb Lockwood. He gave a reluctant nod.

"So," Michael went on, "we have to question the wisdom of trying to confront them openly, especially on their home ground, where they'll have even more of an advantage. It sounds as though Rosemary is all right for the moment. Maybe it's better to wait a little and see if Glynis or Isabel—or Celeste, even though she couldn't be with us right now—have any more visions that will give us more information."

Although all this was said in a reasonable tone, Will didn't feel like being reasonable. The woman he loved was more than a thousand miles away in hostile territory surrounded by demons, and he was supposed to just sit here on his ass and hope for the best? If that was the best plan Michael could come up with, why the hell had he even bothered to come here to California?

Audrey spoke then, her tone gentle. "I know what you must be thinking, Will. You were hoping we'd get together our posse and saddle up and go riding to Rosemary's rescue—if you'll forgive the metaphor. But until we can come up with a good way of extricating her without putting her in any more danger, it's probably better to wait. And at least we're all here together now, so when the moment does come, we'll be able to act immediately."

"I suppose so," he said, wishing he sounded a little more enthusiastic.

To his surprise, Glynis came over and laid a hand on his arm, gave it a reassuring squeeze. "I think if Rosemary was truly in danger, I'd know," she told him. "I haven't gotten any sense of that. While we can't guess at what the demons want with her, Isabel's visions tell us she seems to be okay for now." A pause, and then she added, a glint in her blue eyes that reminded Will far too much of her daughter, "And you never know— Rosemary might not even need us to rescue her. She might be able to do that all by herself."

Once she'd been left alone in the DePauw Inn— after their uncomfortable lunch concluded, Caleb had taken her back to the family home briefly so she could pack a few things for an overnight stay —Rosemary tried once again to will herself away from this place, to send herself back to California and the safety of Will's arms. But it seemed that Caleb had been right about her powers being blocked, because she couldn't do a damn thing.

No, she was definitely stuck in Greencastle until the paternity test results arrived.

Whether they'd let her leave after that still remained an open question. Of course, the easiest solution would be that the test revealed Gerald wasn't her father at all, but she had an uneasy feeling that they wouldn't be going to all this trouble if they weren't pretty damn sure what the results would be. No, this was all being done for her benefit, to prove that what they'd told her about her past was nothing more than the truth.

Well, she could tell herself that was the reality of the situation, but until she knew what the test said, she was only borrowing trouble and paying it back with interest. She sat on the bed and turned on the TV, scrolling past inane talk shows and repeats of sitcoms now ten years out of date, wishing desperately to find something that might occupy her. However, nothing caught her interest, and she wondered if part of their scheme was to drive her half-mad with boredom as she sat there and waited to hear the news that could change her life irrevocably.

To be fair—as much as she hated having to extend that consideration to the part-demon contingent here in Greencastle—it was partly her own fault that she was sitting in a hotel room and staring at the TV. As lunch was winding down, Caleb had suggested they go to a movie to fill up some time this afternoon, but she'd refused. Being around him made her uncomfortable, because she could tell he was hoping she'd realize that maybe the two of them were more compatible than she wanted to admit.

Fat chance.

Scowling, she got out her phone and went to the messaging app. Although she hadn't heard a peep out of the thing all afternoon, she still hoped that maybe a text had come in and she'd missed it, that maybe Will had responded to her, even though she knew doing so probably wasn't a very wise idea. Just because it didn't seem as if anyone had tried to snoop through her things didn't mean they hadn't. Sending that one message had been a big enough risk, but engaging in an actual conversation would have definitely invited unwanted attention.

At least she could tell her text had been delivered, that it hadn't disappeared into the ether. She hoped she hadn't been too oblique and that Will had been able to decipher the subtext of her message. What he would do with that information, she honestly didn't know. It wouldn't be safe for him to come here by himself, that was for sure. Possibly, he would have reached out to her family, but Rosemary wasn't sure how much they could do, either. Their psychic gifts were formidable, but clairvoyance wasn't exactly an offensive skill—you couldn't use it to bust into a place and rescue someone, after all.

Holding back a sigh, she reached for the remote and channel-surfed a bit more, hoping she'd find something to distract herself. In a few hours—well, okay, more like four or five hours—she could find a local restaurant that delivered, eat dinner, and go to sleep.

And then when she woke up, she'd find out whether or not she really was Gerald Gates' daughter.

Ugh.

One of the Indianapolis stations was playing the second *Pirates of the Caribbean* movie. Not exactly her first choice, but diverting enough that she hoped she could focus on the antics on-screen and not think about how much she wanted Will's arms around her. Actually, she would have settled for simply hearing his voice. The urge to pick up her phone and call him was almost physically overwhelming, but she fought it back and told herself to be Zen about the situation. Just wait and let the minutes pass, let time flow on, shortening the distance between now and the moment when everything in her world could change.

She was almost successful. Or at least, she achieved a measure of patience and detachment, enough for her to sit on the bed and watch the whole damn movie, along with the local newscast that followed. In a way, it was sort of fascinating to see news from such a different part of the country, to realize that not everything was as fast-paced and intense as life in Southern California sometimes seemed to be.

A little before six o'clock, someone knocked on her door. Since it was far too late in the day for housekeeping to be coming by—and since only a few people even knew she was staying there—Rosemary had a pretty good idea who was out there in the hallway. For a moment or two, she considered ignoring the knock. However, since he could probably pop right into her hotel room without waiting for her to answer the door, she realized there wasn't much point in delaying the inevitable.

She got off the bed and opened the door. Caleb stood outside, looking much the same as he had when they'd parted earlier that afternoon, although now he wore a leather jacket over his jeans and long-sleeved T-shirt. He grinned down at her and said, "Bored out of your mind yet?"

"No," she lied, and his smile only broadened.

"Liar."

"Did you drive all the way over here just to insult me?"

"No," he replied. "Anyway, I wanted to know if you'd changed your mind about homecoming."

Rosemary knew she should tell him that no,

of course she hadn't changed her mind. After all, she'd just survived what had been one of the dullest afternoons of her life. What was a few more hours? But then she wondered if she was making a mistake by sequestering herself like this. Maybe it would be smarter to get out and about, to get a better measure of her enemy by watching him interact with the locals. If nothing else, doing so would help her gain more understanding of how Caleb and the rest of the demon descendants had managed to fit in so well here. She knew what it was like to try to hide essential truths about yourself from the people in your school and your community—she'd done much the same thing about her own psychic abilities, with varying levels of success. What Caleb and the other part-demons had been hiding was an order of magnitude larger, though. They'd had to hide the very essence of their beings, whereas she'd never thought she was anything except a normal girl with some very abnormal talents.

Of course, the past few days had taught her she was anything but a normal girl. Even if it turned out that Gerald Gates wasn't her father, she still had that whole half-angel thing to deal with…assuming what her not-dead-after-all father had told her was the truth.

"Maybe," she said, then looked down at herself. She was still wearing the wool pencil skirt

—now a little rumpled from her lying on the bed for the past few hours—and slim-fitting sweater that had been "borrowed" from his mother's closet. "I don't think I'm exactly dressed for smoking under the bleachers or standing around a bonfire, though."

His dark eyes glinted with laughter. "No, but here's a peace offering." He held up one hand, from which dangled a reusable grocery store shopping bag. "Jeans and boots and a jacket. The sweater you have on should still work."

"Your mother actually owns jeans?" Rosemary asked in surprise. Somehow, she couldn't imagine the immaculate Mrs. Lockwood deigning to wear something so plebeian.

"God, no. I got these at a local shop. I hope they'll fit—I told the salesgirl the sizes of some of my mother's stuff, and we sort of guessed from there. Same with the boots."

It sounded as though he'd gone to a good deal of trouble for something that wasn't exactly a sure bet—she could have refused to answer the door, or shot him down the minute he reintroduced the topic of homecoming—but she supposed he'd decided it was worth the risk.

"All right," she said, taking the bag from him. "You can wait out in the hall while I change."

For a second, he looked as if he wanted to argue, but then he shrugged and said, "Okay.

Because loitering in a hotel hallway doesn't look inconspicuous or anything."

"I'm sure you'll think of an explanation if anyone asks," she said sweetly, then closed the door before he could reply.

It felt damn good to get out of that pencil skirt and the tights she wore under it—she'd long since taken off the high-heeled boots, since she wasn't used to wearing heels and they made her feet hurt—and into the jeans Caleb had bought her. They actually fit pretty well, except for being shade too long. That wasn't a big problem, since the boots he'd provided added just enough lift to keep the pant hems from dragging on the floor. And the jacket was much cuter than she'd expected, a pretty dark teal wool coat cut to fall only to her hips. It was the sort of thing she might have picked out for herself, although she doubted she would've needed anything that warm back in Southern California.

Well, Caleb's not doing any of this to be nice, she warned herself as she hung her borrowed skirt up in the closet. *I don't know why he's doing it, exactly, but he's got to have an ulterior motive. He always does.*

After grabbing her purse and reminding herself to stay on her toes, she went back to the door and headed out into the hallway. Caleb was leaning against the wall opposite her door, looking at something on his phone. However, he shoved the cell phone into his jacket pocket as soon as he saw her emerge from her hotel room.

"Better?" he asked, taking in her new outfit.

"Yes," Rosemary replied, then forced herself to add, "Thanks."

"No problem." He paused for a second, as if he wanted to say something else, then went on, "Let's go."

She followed him down the hallway to the stairwell and out to the parking lot. Waiting there was a big shiny red Dodge truck, much nicer than the beat-up Nissan Frontier he'd been driving back in California while pretending to be a poor working stiff, same as anybody else.

"Yeah, I figured I couldn't exactly plead poverty while driving this," he said, as if picking up on what she'd been thinking just a moment earlier.

"Probably not," she agreed. For a moment, she paused, fingers resting against the door handle. Was there any chance she could make a break for it now? Caleb was walking around to the driver's side and might be caught off guard.

And the boots he'd gotten for her had nice low heels, barely half an inch. Rosemary guessed she could run pretty fast in those.

Not fast enough, though. He had a good ten inches on her in height...and hadn't he been the quarterback on his high school football team? Most likely, he'd catch up to her without breaking a sweat.

These thoughts passed through her mind in a flash, quickly enough that Caleb probably hadn't even noticed her hesitation. She pulled in a breath, then tugged on the truck's door handle.

For better or worse, she was committed to this thing…no matter what happened.

Chapter 9

ROSEMARY HAD NEVER ATTENDED HER OWN high school's homecoming game; she hadn't been lying when she told Caleb that she didn't give a shit about football. But she had to admit there was something just the teeniest bit exciting about the glare of the lights overhead and the energy emanating from the packed stands. Greencastle was such a small town; it felt as if almost its entire population must have turned out to watch the game.

And it also felt as if the entire population of the town knew who Caleb Lockwood was, and was watching her with speculative eyes, trying to figure out how she fit into the whole equation.

They'd first gone and gotten some pizza—really good pizza, actually, much better than she'd been expecting—and then drove over to the high school. Even before they left the parking lot, they met up with two guys who were around Caleb's age, maybe a little younger.

"Sean Cooper and Kevin Bell," he said, then added, "Part of the Greencastle contingent."

Which she assumed meant they were quarter-demons, same as he was. She wouldn't have known otherwise; it wasn't as though she got a little twinge every time she met one of them. If she'd actually been fortunate enough to possess such a talent, then Caleb wouldn't have been able to fool her so spectacularly back in California.

"Nice to meet you," Rosemary said after Caleb had made his introductions, although she wasn't sure whether it really was nice or not. All right, she supposed it was useful to know the faces of two more of this generation. Like Caleb, they were tall and good-looking in a sort of all-American kind of way, and probably the last people you'd ever think had the blood of demons flowing in their veins, Sean with blond hair and Kevin mid-brown, almost the same shade as Rose-mary's hair. Otherwise, though, he didn't look at all like her, and she realized he couldn't be her half-brother, since he wasn't young enough. She didn't know how much younger this hypothetical half-brother was, but since he hadn't been born when Gerald Gates put on an assumed face and slipped into her mother's bed, she figured the guy had to be at least a year younger than she, maybe more.

"Nice to meet you, too," they replied, sounding pleasant enough, although she noticed the significant glances they cast in Caleb's direction, the way they seemed to nod to themselves, as if noting something special about her. Maybe they could detect demon blood in a way she couldn't.

After that, though, they bumped into more people who obviously had been in their year at high school, people who she could tell were just ordinary humans, a lot of them married couples, several of whom were pushing strollers or had small children with them. Rosemary blinked at them in surprise, even as she realized it wasn't that strange for a bunch of twenty-eight or twenty-nine-year-olds to have kids. Just because she'd delayed that part of her life didn't mean everyone else was doing the same thing.

However, she also couldn't help noticing how popular Caleb obviously had been and still was, the way people came up to him and said hi, and clapped him on the back and told him they were glad he'd bailed on California and come back to Greencastle where he belonged. Rosemary was introduced to most of them, but their names and faces started to blur after a bit, so she settled for smiling and saying it was very nice to meet everyone. At length, though, they made it up to the stands, with Sean and Kevin flanking them, and then a few more men came to sit on either side of the quarter-demons, guys she guessed were also part of the "Greencastle contingent," although Caleb didn't bother to make any introductions to these late arrivals.

Still, she had a feeling they'd come to help keep watch over her. Their presence definitely drove home the fact that she wasn't going anywhere without their permission, no matter how easygoing Caleb tried to act.

"It looks like the whole tribe is here," she said in a murmur to him in between plays. "So, when do I get to meet my supposed half-brother?"

"He didn't come," Caleb replied, looking slightly irritated. "He's not that into football."

That revelation made her raise an eyebrow. "Seriously? Maybe we really are related."

In response, Caleb only shook his head. "You'll find out for sure tomorrow, won't you?"

His response effectively dampened the slight amusement she'd been feeling. Frowning, she crossed her arms and directed her attention toward the field, although she really didn't understand what was going on, except that the play kept getting stopped at the strangest intervals, halting the clock on the scoreboard and making her realize that it was going to take hours to get through the game at the rate they were going.

Maybe Caleb had invited her along as a way of subtly torturing her. She didn't see how this was any better than sitting in her hotel room and channel surfing. Well, except for confirming first-hand that the current generation of Greencastle demons was tall and athletic and that even one of them was more than a match for her physically, let alone six. And that wasn't even taking into account their fathers, who had to be in their fifties or early sixties but were also probably in decent physical shape, if Daniel Lockwood and Gerald Gates were accurate representatives of the rest of the group.

The thought did nothing to improve her mood. Because it was a high school game, obviously no alcohol was being "officially" served—although she had her suspicions about the contents of some of the sports bottles people were carrying—but at one point Sean went down to the refreshment stand and brought back bottled water for everyone.

"Thanks," she said, knowing she needed to act polite even if every part of her being was wishing violently to be someplace else. While being around lots of people gave her a spurious sense of safety, the crush on either side also prevented her from saying what she was really thinking.

The Greencastle team ended up winning —"we pretty much always win," according to

Caleb—and Rosemary dutifully followed him down from the bleachers and toward the parking lot. She still couldn't quite see the point of this whole exercise, although it began to be a bit more clear when Sean asked, "After-party at your place?"

"Of course," Caleb replied with a grin. "See you there."

By that point, the two of them had reached his Dodge pickup. Rosemary shot him an accusatory stare as Sean and Kevin headed off toward their own vehicles, then said, "You didn't say anything to me about a party."

"Nope," Caleb said. "Because if I had, I wouldn't have been able to pry you out of that hotel room. Besides, it's harmless—just a few of us getting together at my place. No biggie."

"You're sure?" she asked, hands planted on her hips, irritation flaring. "No Satanic invocations? No drawing spell circles on the floor?"

"After what I spent to get those floors refinished?" he scoffed, looking more amused by her insinuation than anything else. "Not likely. Come on—we need to get going or people will show up before we even have a chance to arrive."

Still frowning, Rosemary did as he asked—mostly because she couldn't think of what else to do—and climbed into the passenger seat. A moment later, they were headed out of the parking lot and toward the downtown area of Greencastle. Since it was dark already and she didn't know the town very well, she couldn't quite keep track of where they were going, except that they left the suburbs and in less than five minutes, Caleb had pulled up to the curb on a side street and parked.

"Come on."

She followed him to a brick building that seemed to have a hardware store—now closed for the evening—on the ground floor. Around the back was a set of stairs that led up to Caleb's loft, which, after they entered the place, she realized was quite large, with about the same footprint as the store below. The floor was gleaming hardwood, as he'd said, the walls exposed brick. One side had been partially enclosed, presumably to house the bedroom and bathroom. Otherwise, though, the entire enormous space was open, with a conversation group of a couch and some chairs clustered around a coffee table on one side, and a dining area on the other. The dining room table was covered with trays of sandwiches and bowls of chips and other kinds of party food, while a smaller table set up against the wall had a large metal bucket filled with beer bottles and a cluster of large, two-liter-size wine bottles sitting on it.

"You set all this up before you came and got me?" Rosemary asked.

"Yes. I figured I wouldn't have time after the game." He went over and pulled off the cellophane that had been protecting the sandwich trays, then went to the refrigerator and got out a tub of salsa and dumped it into a waiting bowl. Apparently, her dubious expression was obvious even though the loft wasn't all that well lit, because he chuckled and said, "It's no big deal. Just your average Friday night post-game party."

"With a bunch of demons."

"Part-demons," Caleb corrected her. "And it's not like we're the majority here. Most of my friends are just normal people. You'll see."

She didn't try to comment, mainly because someone knocked at the door then, and Sean and Kevin came in. They weren't alone this time, though, but had a couple of girls with them, girls who were laughing and hanging on them in a way that seemed to signal they'd started partying a bit earlier.

Caleb introduced them as Tiffany and Shellie, and they both smiled and said they were happy to meet her. However, Rosemary couldn't quite miss the way they looked her up and down and then glanced back at each other, eyebrows lifted as if in astonishment that the sublime Caleb Lockwood would waltz back into town with someone so obviously ordinary at his side.

"I'll just go put my coat and purse on the bed," she said, and he nodded.

"Sure—bedroom's through that door."

She probably could have figured that out for herself; it wasn't as though there were many doors in the place. Still, it felt strange to walk into the room and realize this was where Caleb slept, his true bedroom, unlike the room in his rented house in Eagle Rock. It was a very spare space, with a platform bed and a dresser, and three walls painted pale gray, a striking contrast to the exposed brick of the wall behind the bed. No pictures, nothing to show he had any connection to the space at all except as a place to lay his head.

Rosemary unbuttoned her coat and then set her purse down on the bed, which was covered in a dark gray duvet. After laying her coat on top of her purse, she hesitated for a moment. Should she look around, try to see if she could find anything of any use in one of the drawers? But no, that was probably a bad idea, just because someone else could come in here at any moment. Besides, she got the feeling that Caleb wasn't so sloppy as to leave anything incriminating in a place where it could be easily found. The Greencastle demons had been hiding secrets for generations, and they weren't about to make that kind of beginner's mistake.

Doing her best to adjust her expression so she

appeared happy to be there and unconcerned about anything in particular, she left the bedroom and headed over to the dining area where the refreshments were laid out. More people had appeared while she was putting her coat and purse away, and now there were at least two dozen partygoers filling the space. Since she'd already met the majority of the younger generation of part-demons, it wasn't too hard to pick them out in the crowd. They were mingling and chatting as if they completely belonged here...which she supposed they did. This was their hometown, after all, no matter what their heritage might be.

In fact, Tiffany was hanging on Sean's arm, giggling as he appeared to regale the people clustered around him with some sort of amusing anecdote. Rosemary couldn't hear what he was saying—someone had cranked up the music, and Kanye West was currently blasting out of the speakers. She tried not to wince; the artist on tap wouldn't have been her first choice, or probably even her thirtieth, but she knew her musical tastes didn't jibe with that of a lot of other people her age.

"They're probably going to get engaged soon," came Caleb's voice at her ear, and she startled a bit before turning to face him.

"Sean and Tiffany?"

He nodded, and then handed her a plastic cup

half filled with what looked like red wine. "I figured you'd rather have wine than beer," he said.

A good guess, since even though she drank both, Rosemary tended to prefer wine. "Thanks," she replied as she took the cup from him. Might as well act polite and as if there was nothing strange about her presence there; she could tell that several people were watching them, obviously curious about the newcomer from California. While it might have been emotionally satisfying to toss the wine in Caleb's face and announce to everyone exactly what he was, she doubted her current audience would be too receptive to such a far-fetched tale. Either they'd laugh and think she must have been drinking all during the game, or they'd be on the phone to the local mental hospital, inquiring about a seventy-two-hour psych hold. She sipped the wine, which was mediocre at best. Still, she thought she could use a drink right about then, so she wasn't going to be choosy. "Does Tiffany know about Sean?"

Caleb didn't bother to ask Rosemary what she meant by that particular question. "Of course not."

"Don't you think that's a little dishonest?"

His shoulders lifted, and he sipped from the cup of beer he held. "What you don't know can't hurt you, right?"

She thought about the moment of truth she'd

extracted from Caleb's mother, of how the other woman had confessed she'd married Daniel Lockwood for his money. But even though their marriage certainly hadn't been a love match, Mrs. Lockwood didn't know the truth about her husband, even after decades of being together. The woman might have been mercenary, but one would think she still deserved to know what Daniel Lockwood actually was.

Before Rosemary could reply, Caleb went on, "We can't take that risk. And I think if you went and took an informal survey of all the wives"—he didn't bother to specify which wives, but she knew who he meant—"then they'd all say they were perfectly happy with their lives and didn't find anything lacking in their relationships."

"It's still lying," she pointed out, and his mouth twitched.

"Useful omission of information," he countered, then swallowed some more beer. He looked around at the people gathered in the loft, something that looked almost like pride flickering across his even features. "You're at a party, Rosemary. Relax and mingle. Have a good time. You do know what that is, don't you?"

"Of course," she snapped, even as she had to inwardly admit that she'd never been much of a party animal. Possibly, that was because she'd always felt herself to be so different from everyone around her, and so was always worried that she might say the wrong thing or make the kind of misstep that would take years to recover from. It had just been easier to spend time with her family rather than try to get involved in a social scene she really didn't understand.

"Good," he said, dark eyes dancing. "Then prove it."

He sauntered off to the group where Sean and Tiffany and several of the other quarter-demons were gathered, and soon was involved in their conversation. Feeling nettled, Rosemary headed over to the refreshment table and grabbed some chips. In general, she tried to avoid junk food, but at least snacking gave her a reason to be loitering near the refreshment table, and hopefully not look too awkward at the same time.

A few minutes passed. Then a woman around her own age, pretty and with light brown hair cut into a cute long bob, approached her, looking diffident.

"You're friends with Caleb?" the woman asked.

"Yes," Rosemary said. "I'm Rosemary—I met Caleb in California."

Something about the woman's expression relaxed slightly. "Oh, that's why I didn't recognize you. I'm Becca—I went to high school with Caleb."

"And everyone else here, I assume," Rosemary remarked.

A chuckle. "Just about. Small town, you know."

"I'm starting to figure it out."

Becca paused there, then sent Rosemary a sideways glance. "I suppose Greencastle must feel really different from Hollywood."

That comment made Rosemary give the other woman a reluctant smile. "I don't know much about Hollywood. I live about thirty miles inland from there."

"Oh," Becca said, looking a little confused. "I guess I just assumed you must have met Caleb on a movie set or something. That's where he was working, right?"

"On a Netflix show, I think." Rosemary hesitated for a moment, wondering how much information she should offer. But apparently people in Greencastle knew that Caleb had been working in the film and television industry, so she guessed it wasn't that big a deal to elaborate a little. "Actually, he was sort of between gigs when we met. He came into my bookstore."

"You own a bookstore?" Becca asked, her expression now almost impressed.

Rosemary thought she'd better disabuse her party companion of any notions of being some kind of mini-mogul or something. "Well, I own it with my sisters," she explained. "It's small, but we're proud of it. Anyway, that's how I met Caleb. I've never set foot on a movie set in my life."

"Oh." An embarrassed little smile, and Becca went on, "I suppose it's kind of silly to think that just because you're from California you work in the movie industry." Her gaze strayed to Caleb as she said, "We were all sort of surprised when we found out Caleb was working behind the scenes and not in front of the camera."

Since Rosemary had thought basically the same thing—well, back before she knew what he actually was—she couldn't fault the residents of Greencastle for making that kind of assumption. "He does look like an actor, I suppose," she said, her tone noncommittal.

"And you're…." Becca's words trailed off there, but Rosemary had a feeling she knew what the woman was asking.

"We're friends. He asked me to come back for a visit, so I said sure." What a lie. Still, she couldn't exactly tell Becca that she'd been coaxed here by the possibility of learning the truth about her biological father, who might just be a half-demon. Figuring her bare-bones story could use a little embellishment, she added, "It was probably the last chance for me to take some time off work before the end of the year, since it gets so crazy in retail around the holidays."

Rosemary paused and added, "So, what do you do?"

"Oh, I'm a loan officer at the bank," Becca replied. "So, I guess you could say I work for Caleb's dad."

Talk about the boss from Hell…literally. However, nothing in Becca's expression seemed to indicate that she was unhappy with her job, so Rosemary guessed she'd better keep that particular observation to herself. Something about the way Becca talked about Caleb prompted her to ask, "And you and Caleb…?"

The loft wasn't all that well lit, but a flush was still obvious along Becca's cheekbones. "Oh, we went out our senior year of high school. It wasn't a big deal. Even then, he was talking about wanting to leave, wanting to get into the movie industry, but no one really thought he was serious. But he majored in film studies and did some independent projects after he graduated, and then earlier this year he went off to California. I don't know what finally made him leave after all that time."

Rosemary did—*Project Demon Hunters* wrapped, and the demons sent their golden boy off to get his hands on the footage. However, she couldn't tell Becca any of that, obviously. "It's been a while since graduation, though. What was he doing in the meantime?"

"Working at the bank. He minored in finance,

so his dad gave him a job. But I could tell he wasn't all that into it." She shrugged, and reached for a chip and lowered it into the bowl of onion dip that waited nearby. "Maybe he was just saving up until he had enough to support himself for a while in California. I don't know for sure—I didn't ask."

"So, you two didn't...?"

"We didn't date after high school, if that's what you mean." Becca's expression grew almost wistful, and once again she glanced in Caleb's direction. "I went to school out of state, and when I got back, well, I could tell he was fine with being friends but didn't want anything else. Which was okay. I mean, we were working together for a while. It would have been weird."

Not as weird as it would have been if you'd found out the truth about him, Rosemary thought then as she helped herself to a few more chips. As far as she was concerned, Becca had definitely dodged a bullet. "I suppose so," she agreed, then sipped some more wine.

"Are you in town long?"

"No," Rosemary replied, wondering if she was shooting herself in the foot by being so emphatic. But then, she'd already done her best to reassure herself that she'd be able to leave once the test results came in. If something changed and she was forced to remain here past the weekend, well, she'd come up with a story to explain her actions. "Just for the weekend, I think."

Becca looked a little puzzled by that revelation, as if she couldn't quite figure out why someone would travel a few thousand miles to only spend a couple of days at their destination. But then she seemed to shrug, and said, "Well, have fun while you're here. Greencastle is a good town."

"I plan to."

Another lie, but Becca seemed to accept the words at face value. She offered a comment about several points of interest worth visiting, and then wandered off to join a group of people who were laughing and talking over by one of the windows. Not the group Caleb was in; Rosemary noticed that right away. Most of the partygoers were standing around and eating and drinking and talking, but a small group over by the table that held an iPad and an expensive-looking bluetooth speaker system had decided to start dancing. No one seemed to be paying any attention to her, and she was just fine with that.

In a way, though, it felt strange to stand there and observe the doings of the party without being involved in them, as if she was some kind of alien observer sent from a distant planet to watch the doings of these humans and take notes on them. Which was kind of silly, actually, because six of those partygoers weren't even human, or at least, not completely so.

She noticed a balcony outside one of the windows, although no one was currently occupying it. Pretending to be interested in what she might find out there, Rosemary wandered in that direction, then went outdoors. The chilly night air hit her immediately, and she began to think that maybe coming out on the balcony hadn't been such a good idea.

But she forgot her discomfort in the next moment as she realized that a set of metal steps headed upward from the far end of the balcony, sort of like a permanent fire escape. There wasn't anything above them but the roof, and yet she still felt compelled to go take a peek.

No one was paying any attention, so she went over to the steps, took firm hold of the handrails to either side, and began to haul herself up. She didn't know exactly why she felt compelled to go up there, except that she thought it might be fun to get a glimpse of Greencastle from that vantage point—and maybe, just maybe, the demons would have relaxed their guard a bit, and she could take the opportunity to get herself the hell out of there.

The roof was wide and flat, and completely open to the night sky. Up there, the air was even colder, but Rosemary hugged her arms against herself as she walked to the edge that overlooked the main street. A few vehicles were moving about, some forty feet below, but otherwise, Greencastle looked pretty damn sleepy on this particular Friday night. No clouds obscured the stars, and she tilted her face to gaze up at them, big and bright, looking as though she could just extend a hand and touch them.

Not that she would bother to try. She had other things to expend her energy on.

Reaching out with that sixth sense—or special ability, or whatever you wanted to call it—she thought of Will's house, of the well-worn but oh, so comfortable couch in his living room. She imagined herself sitting on that sofa, leaning back against Will's arm as they snuggled and watched TV. It all felt so real…and yet, she knew it wasn't. She could imagine such a scene, but she couldn't send herself back there. The demons were still clearly keeping watch.

"Like the view?"

Rosemary turned and saw Caleb move away from the ladder/steps and come toward her. Doing her best to swallow her disappointment, she responded, "There's not much to see, really. But I saw the steps and wanted to check out what was up here."

He paused next to her and stared out over the town. "When it's warmer, I bring a telescope up here sometimes. The roof is great for that. But no, if you were looking for bright lights, big city, you've come to the wrong place."

It was in her mind to tell him that it was his fault she was here at all, but she pushed the retort away. To be fair, she'd come to Greencastle on her own volition; it wasn't as though Caleb had thrown her over his shoulder and hauled her bodily to his hometown.

"I s-suppose so," she said, teeth chattering a little in the chill wind.

Expression now concerned, he moved closer. "It's really too cold to be up here without a jacket."

"I'm fine," Rosemary told him, even as she had to inwardly admit that he was right. Maybe someone who was used to Indiana temperatures wouldn't have a problem with this particular night breeze, but it felt positively arctic to someone from Southern California. "I'll go back inside in a minute."

He shrugged. "Okay."

For a moment, they were both silent, watching the cars move on the street below. A faint sound of music from the party drifted upward, and Rosemary wondered if someone had opened a window. Maybe some of the dancers had gotten overheated from their exertions.

"I saw you talking to Becca," Caleb ventured next, and she nodded.

"She seems nice."

"I suppose so." A pause. "She doesn't compare to you, though."

Great. She definitely didn't want the conversation to move anywhere near that direction. "I don't believe in comparing people."

"You wouldn't." He shifted so he faced her directly, dark eyes fixed on her face. "But it would be nice if you'd give me a chance."

Rosemary crossed her arms, hoping that might help to dispel some of the chill that was beginning to seep through her body. Or maybe the shiver that had just passed through her had absolutely nothing to do with the actual temperature outside. "Caleb, I already told you that I'm in love with Will. Leave it alone, okay?"

Obviously, leaving it alone was not something Caleb was particularly good at, because he only replied, "But *why* are you in love with him? What the hell do you two even have in common?"

"You wouldn't understand."

"Why?" he demanded. "Because the blood of demons flows through my veins, and that means I'm incapable of experiencing any good or pure emotions? I think you're forgetting that the same blood flows through your own veins."

"Allegedly," Rosemary said, wishing her voice

didn't sound so shaky. "Anyway, Will and me…it just works for us. I can't tell you why. Chemistry, I guess."

"You think you'll have that same chemistry when he finds out you're not the little half-angel he thinks you are?"

An edge had entered Caleb's voice, one Rosemary really didn't like. She didn't know for sure whether he actually harbored what he thought were true feelings for her, or whether he just hated the thought of a man ten years older than he—and an Episcopalian priest, to boot—coming out the victor in this particular romantic contest.

Not that it was a contest at all. Even if she wasn't with Will…even if he told her he wanted nothing more to do with her once he discovered her connection to the Greencastle demons…she knew she could never be with Caleb Lockwood.

"I don't know," she said. "But that's for Will and me to find out."

Caleb stepped closer to her, and she did her best not to flinch. "You liked being with me once."

"'Once,'" she repeated. "Not now."

One hand reached toward her. "I think I could change your mind."

Don't move, she told herself. *Face him down. Don't let him know you're afraid.*

"Would you really want me that way?" Rosemary asked quietly. "You keep trying to make me think you're a decent person, Caleb. If that's the truth, do you really want to force things between us?"

For a long moment, he didn't speak, only stared down at her. Once again, she thought she could see a tiny flicker of red flame in his dark eyes before it disappeared. Slowly, his hand dropped.

"You'll change your mind," he said briefly, then turned and stalked away from her, back to the steps so he could return to the balcony outside his loft.

Rosemary stayed where she was, the night air chill against her face. Then, very slowly, she let out the breath she'd been holding.

That had been too close.

Chapter 10

AFTER PASSING WHAT COULD ONLY charitably be referred to as a very restless night, Will woke up to a text from Michael.

Fred did some hacking and found out that Rosemary is staying at the DePauw Inn. We don't know what that means, exactly, but at the very least, it seems to indicate she has some autonomy. Come over to the house when you can & we'll discuss further.

The message was time-stamped 7:12 a.m., only about ten minutes earlier. Will scrubbed a hand over the stubble on his face and then responded, *I can be over around 8. See you then.*

He set down the phone and poured himself a glass of water, deciding against coffee even though he knew he needed it. Anyway, if Michael wanted him over that early, then there would probably be coffee on tap at his house.

A fast shower and a change into some jeans and a long-sleeved T-shirt, since the day outside was gray and gloomy once again. No rain, as far as he could tell, but the skies looked like they wanted to open up if given the chance.

Will was out the door a little before eight and arrived at Michael's house almost exactly on the hour. Audrey opened the door after he rang the bell and smiled out at him. She looked far more rested than he knew he did, although she was dressed almost as casually, except in a sweater rather than a T-shirt.

"We're having a council of war in the dining room," she said as she stepped aside to let him in. "Coffee and bagels are on tap."

"Good," Will replied, managing to smile despite his continued worry for Rosemary. "I was worried it might be doughnuts. Too much sugar for me."

"Michael's not big on sugar, either," Audrey told him. "But you probably already knew that."

Actually, he didn't. Although he'd known Michael for several years, it wasn't as though they'd really ever hung out socially. Michael called Will when he needed his friend's spiritual assistance, but they'd never eaten together or gone to a baseball game or whatever it was that men did when they needed to bond. He'd always thought of Michael as a friend, but he knew they weren't exactly friends in the usual sense.

Once this was all over—and once Audrey had gotten her Ph.D. and the couple had returned to California—it was nice to think of a time when the four of them maybe could go out together as couples, to dinner and the movies or whatever else sounded like fun. Of course, that particular scenario imagined a future where Rosemary was safely back from Indiana with no harm done, and at the moment, Will couldn't be entirely sanguine about such a prospect.

He followed Audrey into the dining room, where Michael and Fred Peñasco were seated at the long table, each of them with their laptop in front of them and a mug of coffee nearby. A plate piled high with bagels sat in the middle of the table, with a smaller plate with cream cheese and butter placed next to it, although it didn't look as though anyone had started eating yet.

"Coffee?" Audrey asked.

"Yes, thanks," Will replied.

Michael glanced up from his laptop's screen and rubbed at his eyes. He didn't look quite as rested as Audrey, and Will wondered how much sleep his friend had actually gotten.

"So, you've located Rosemary?" he asked.

"We think so," Michael said, while Fred kept

typing away at something, although, since Will couldn't see the screen, he had no idea what the other man might have been working on. "At least, her name is on the list of current guests at the DePauw Inn, although she didn't check in with a credit card."

"Who paid for the room?"

"Not sure," Fred put in. "It just says 'on account.' I assume that means someone has a standing account with the place, but there isn't that much detail as to whom. It might be the sort of thing they keep off the books, so to speak."

Will thought he had a pretty good idea as to who might be in a position to keep an account active at the local hotel for any visitors he might need to show some hospitality. "Daniel Lockwood?"

"Probably," Michael said as he reached for his mug of coffee and took a swallow. "I assume it's good news that Rosemary is staying at a hotel and not, say, at his actual house, but we haven't found much more than that."

"She definitely hasn't been using her debit card," Fred added. "No records at all. So, wherever she was having lunch in that vision Isabel had, she wasn't picking up the tab."

No, that duty would have fallen to Caleb Lockwood. Will found his mouth twisting, but was distracted by Audrey coming over to him with a mug of coffee. He thanked her and took a sip. Good and strong, and just what he needed. That one swallow was enough to make him feel much more awake.

"Has Isabel seen anything else?"

"Not that we're aware of," Michael said. "Of course, it's a little early to be calling her this morning, but I assume that if she or Glynis had seen anything, they would have reached out, no matter what the time."

"Are there any other annotations on Rosemary's account at the hotel?" Will asked. "Anything to indicate when she's going to be checking out?"

"Nothing like that," Fred responded. "That field has been left blank, which makes me think the Lockwoods must want her stay to be open-ended."

Of course, they did. Will felt the frown return to his brow, heavy, telling him that none of this news was particularly comforting. All right, he supposed it was marginally reassuring to know that at least Rosemary had her own hotel room and wasn't being held captive in the Lockwood mansion, but still, he didn't much like the idea of her inexplicable visit in Greencastle being one of indefinite duration. They needed to get her out of there.

"So, we don't have much more to go on than

we did before," he said, not bothering to keep the worry out of his voice.

"We have a better idea of where she is," Michael told him. "And we know that the Lock-woods extended her enough consideration to get her a hotel room. That's something."

"It's not much."

Audrey came over and sat down opposite her husband, then reached for a bagel and started to carefully cut it in half. As she began to spread cream cheese over one side, she said, "And we have Isabel's visions to tell us she's safe. If anything bad had happened, you know either Glynis or one of Rosemary's sisters would have felt it."

Will wanted to believe that. But, even though he wasn't psychic himself, he knew enough to understand that these women's talents—amazing as they might be—certainly weren't infallible. It could very well be wishful thinking to blindly accept that they would instantly be able to sense whether something had gone wrong with a fellow family member.

But he could tell from Audrey's expression that she needed to believe such a thing, and so he didn't offer any protests, only said, "Most likely. But how long are we going to just sit this out? Don't you think at some point we're going to need to go there and help her?"

"I've taken that possibility into account,"

Michael said calmly. "In fact, I've been checking on whether it would be viable to get a private plane to take us there if necessary. There's a general aviation airport three miles outside town, so it wouldn't be too difficult to get someone to take us from Brackett Field in La Verne to Putnam Airport outside Greencastle."

"El Monte would be closer," Fred commented, not looking up from his laptop.

"Yes, but I know someone with a plane at Brackett," Michael replied.

"You do?" Audrey said in some surprise. "Who?"

Michael shrugged. "A friend. Max Fraser—I met him at one of my seminars years ago. Anyway, he's got a Gulfstream III. It's big enough to accommodate all of us, including Glynis and Isabel."

"Must be nice," Audrey said with a grin.

"Actually, in some ways, it's nicer to have a friend with a jet than to own one yourself and be worried about all the upkeep," Michael replied.

That comment made Fred lift an eyebrow, although he continued to tap away at his keyboard without looking up. He remarked, "I'm pretty sure if you can afford to buy a Gulfstream III, upkeep really isn't an issue."

"Point taken. But anyway, if necessary, I can reach out to Max and have us in the air pretty quickly without hassling with commercial flights. I already confirmed that he was in town right now, and available in case of an emergency."

It was good to have friends in high places, apparently. Will supposed he had to be content with Michael's solution; short of blinking from one place to the next like Rosemary could do, a private jet was definitely the quickest and easiest way to get from here to there.

If it came to that.

"Well, if we're going to end up staging a commando raid on the Greencastle demons, we'd better know what we're up against," Audrey said. She set down the half bagel she'd been holding and gazed up at Will, who still hadn't taken a seat. "You've been there. What can you tell us?"

"It's a small town, probably around ten thousand people," he said. "As far as I can tell, absolutely no one knows anything about Daniel Lockwood's true identity, or the identities of the other part-demons who live there. If we try anything too overt, I'm sure we'll have the local police on us in a heartbeat for going after such upstanding citizens.

"Then we'll be covert," Michael put in with a grin. "Lockwood's house?"

"It's basically a mansion," Will told him. "I'm not very good at estimating this sort of thing, but I'm sure it's probably at least five thousand square feet. In a nice neighborhood to the southwest of the downtown area, on a big lot where the driveway access is actually off the street to the back, since there's nothing behind it."

"Nice and private," Michael observed.

"Exactly. But Lockwood's is the only house I know about in any detail. Rosemary and I drove around and sort of scoped out where all the other demons' homes were located, thanks to the information Fred provided"—Will paused to nod in Fred's direction, and the other man gave a shrug, a *just doing my job* kind of gesture—"but I can't tell you much about them."

Michael didn't look too concerned by this apparent lack of information. "I don't think they're important. It seems pretty obvious that Daniel Lockwood is the ringleader of the group, and so any activity is probably going to be centered at his house. Since you've already been inside, we have an advantage."

"Not much of one," Will said. "Considering we're outnumbered two to one."

"True, but they won't see us coming."

"You hope," Fred said darkly. "I know I'm coming late to all this, but from what you've told me about your dealings with these part-demons, they have abilities no human can hope to match."

No one said anything for a moment, probably because they'd all inwardly acknowledged that

Fred was right, even if they didn't want to admit to such a disadvantage out loud. Even in terms of sheer numbers, the Greencastle demons definitely had the advantage, and when you figured in all their assorted powers, well, it didn't take much effort to realize it would be an extremely lopsided fight.

After an uncomfortable pause, Michael said, "True, but they're not invincible. We need to keep that in mind, or we'll be dooming ourselves to defeat before we even get started. But for now, I think the best thing to do is just sit tight and see what happens. I know it's hard," he went on, before Will could begin to protest, "but I think it's the best thing to do. If Rosemary suddenly disappears from the hotel's records, or if any of the McGuires get a twinge, then of course, we'll act. All right?"

Will gave a reluctant nod. While he would have preferred to do something...*anything*...he understood that sometimes discretion was required in these situations. So far, nothing seemed to indicate Rosemary was in any real trouble.

Which created its own set of concerns. Because if the demons didn't intend to hurt her, why had they taken her at all?

Rosemary sat on the couch in the Lockwood mansion's living room, doing her best to ignore the knot of tension in her gut and failing miserably. Caleb had called her only twenty minutes before, telling her that the courier was on the last leg of his journey from Chicago, where the lab's headquarters were located, and should be in Greencastle within the half hour. She'd agreed to have him pick her up and take her to his father's house, although she was still annoyed at him for the way he'd acted the night before. In fact, after their confrontation on the roof of his building, she'd walked back to the hotel rather than stay at the party another minute. Luckily, her destination had been only a few blocks away, and Greencastle was clearly a very safe place, but still, she'd been irritated for being put in that position at all. He'd been all smiles this morning, acting as though nothing of importance had occurred, which only made her that much angrier.

However, she'd done her best to push aside her annoyance, since she didn't want him to see how he'd gotten under her skin. Also, she figured she needed to act cool and composed around Daniel Lockwood, no matter what happened. Something about him felt like nails on a chalkboard to her, although she couldn't say exactly why.

Well, except for the minor detail of him being the half-demon ringleader of a bunch of demon-kind who clearly didn't care about anyone's interests but their own.

A cup of tea sat on the coffee table in front of her, and she bent forward so she could lift it to her lips and take a sip. Caleb was drinking coffee, while Daniel didn't seem interested in any refreshments. And Gerald also had tea, but he mostly ignored the cup he held, his gaze continually moving toward the window as if he didn't want to take the slightest chance of any of them missing the courier's arrival.

"He's here," Gerald said suddenly, the words preceding the ringing of the doorbell by just the barest second.

Rosemary had startled when he spoke and just barely avoided spilling tea on the priceless antique carpet under her feet. Trying to compose herself, she set the tea back down, although she could feel the way her heart had started to pound, heavy and hard against the hollowness of her ribcage.

"I'll get it," Caleb said, and left the room to answer the door. A moment later, he came back into the living room, a bewildered-looking blond man in his early twenties at his side. "I told him he needed to hand the letter to you directly," he said, looking over at Rosemary. "Don't want you to think there were any shenanigans."

Too late for that, although she understood why Caleb didn't want to even touch the envelope the courier held. "Thanks," she said briefly, then got up from the sofa and went over to the courier. "I'll take that."

"Sign here," the man told her, handing her an electronic pad and a stylus. She signed in the indicated space, then gave the pad and stylus back to him. In return, he handed her the letter he carried. Still looking a little confused, as if he wasn't quite sure why he couldn't have simply given the envelope to Caleb, he said, "Have a good day."

Although her throat felt suddenly dry, Rosemary managed to respond, "You, too."

He nodded at all of them and left the living room. A moment later, she heard the front door close.

"Are you going to open that?" Daniel Lockwood asked, his tone dry. "After all, we've gone to a good deal of trouble and expense to get the results inside that envelope."

She wanted to tell him what he could do with his "expense"—like he couldn't afford all of this and much more—but instead she unsealed the thin cardboard envelope and slid out the smaller manila envelope it contained. Inside that envelope was a single piece of paper. There was some official verbiage at the top of the sheet, but her eyes skimmed past that to the really pertinent information.

Rosemary McGuire — Gerald Gates: 99.98% match

The knot that had taken up residence in her stomach seemed to pull itself even tighter, and for a few horrible seconds, she wondered if she was actually going to throw up. However, she gulped in a breath and stood very still, telling herself that she wasn't going to lose it in front of these three part-demons.

Only…it seemed as though she was part demon as well.

"You're very quiet," Daniel Lockwood said. He came over to her and took the piece of paper from her nerveless fingers, then briefly scanned its contents. A satisfied smile spread across his lips, and he looked up at Gerald, who'd moved closer to where they both stood. "She's yours, Gerald."

The other man smiled as well, although his expression was only one of sudden delight, not the near gloating Rosemary had seen on Daniel's face. "I knew it," he said quietly. "I just knew she was my daughter."

"'She' is standing right here," Rosemary remarked. In a way, she was glad of the chance to be annoyed with the two of them, because her irritation gave her a way to focus on something other than the enormous, horrible truth that had just been dropped on her like the proverbial ton of bricks.

"I'm sorry," Gerald said quickly. "I know this has to be a shock for you. But just know how glad we are to count you as part of our family."

"You're not my family," she retorted. "I have a family—they're back in California." Her mother's face appeared in her mind, and Rosemary could feel her throat clench at the thought of having to tell Glynis that no, her dead husband hadn't been an angel, had only been an ordinary man, and that her youngest daughter was the offspring of a half-demon wearing John McGuire's face so he could father a child with a psychic woman. Suddenly, the room felt as though it was closing in on her.

She had to get out of there.

Somehow, she managed to say, "I need some air," and turned away from the two men so she could stumble toward the French doors that opened on the patio and open one of them. Out of the corner of her eye, she thought she saw Caleb begin to move in her direction, but she ignored him and kept going.

A few clouds had moved in, but it was still a beautiful late autumn day, the air crisp, the sky a clear, deep blue. The oaks and sycamores and maples that ringed the yard blazed forth in shades of gold and umber and crimson, but Rosemary could barely take note of their beauty past the burning ache in her heart.

She was one of…them. A part-demon. Something inhuman, something that wasn't meant to be here, even if she looked as human as the rest of them.

A dead leaf crunched nearby, and she turned to see Caleb pause a few feet away from her. "I don't want to talk to you," she said.

"Probably not," he replied, not looking terribly troubled by the rebuff. "But I didn't think you should be by yourself."

Since she couldn't immediately think of a fitting retort, she settled for letting out a huff of a breath and shifting so she again stared at the trees that bordered the yard, and not at the big brick house behind her.

"It's not that bad," he said softly, much closer this time.

Rosemary didn't move. "It is. I'm not…I'm not one of you."

"But you are. The paternity test proves that."

"Leave me alone, Caleb."

His hand settled on her arm. She almost jerked it away, but she had a feeling he would have only tightened his grip if she'd tried that kind of a maneuver.

"I'm not going to leave you alone," he said, his tone reasonable. "You're family now."

Was he really going to try that angle? Jaw set,

she retorted, "I wasn't aware that all the demons who started this little coven were related."

"All right, not that kind of related. But still, we consider ourselves family. We have to. And you're part of that family."

"I have a family."

"So you said." He let go of her arm but remained standing close to her, close enough that she could smell the woodsy scent of his aftershave. "But you can't pretend we don't exist just because you don't like knowing you're also part demon."

She wished she could press her hands to her ears so she wouldn't have to hear those words, but acting in such a childish way wouldn't change the horrible reality of her situation. After all, she'd seen it right there on the report from the lab. Black and white. Kind of hard to argue with that sort of thing. She hugged her arms against herself and said, "It doesn't matter. Gerald hasn't been a part of my life. He wasn't there to attend my sixth-grade graduation or teach me how to drive. He's a sperm donor, nothing more. I have a real family, and he isn't it."

"You're upset," Caleb said calmly. "I get it. But he wants to be part of your life now that everything is out in the open."

"'Out in the open'?" she echoed, her lip curling. Was he serious? "Sorry to tell you this, Caleb, but you demons aren't exactly the most transparent people in the world."

Rather than take offense, he smiled in a lopsided way, shoulders lifting slightly. "Okay, point taken. No, we can't be transparent about who we are. What I meant is that there aren't any more secrets between you and Gerald. And I think he'd be willing to go to your mother and explain."

"That's a horrible idea," Rosemary replied. "What in the world makes you think she'd want to meet him? I mean, when you get right down to it, he basically raped her, didn't he? It's not as though she gave her consent to have sex with some half-demon who wasn't her actual husband."

Caleb's mouth thinned at the word "rape," but she didn't see the red flash of anger in his eyes. If anything, his expression grew more pleading. "I know what he did seems terrible, but still…you've met him. Come on—the guy doesn't have a mean bone in his body."

That seemed like a crazy thing to say about someone who was half demon, and yet Rosemary had to reluctantly agree, even if she would never have made such an admission to Caleb. If circumstances had been different—if Gerald had been just an ordinary man, maybe someone her mother had had an affair with—then Rosemary thought she probably could have accepted him as her biological father.

But of course Gerald wasn't an ordinary man, and Glynis McGuire was not the sort of woman to ever cheat on her husband. She would be horrified to learn that she'd been seduced by a creature wearing her husband's face, even though she hadn't done anything wrong.

"Well, he's nicer than your father," she allowed, then added, "although that isn't saying much. But I don't want him in my life. I don't want any of you in my life."

Caleb's eyes narrowed. "You can't pretend we don't exist."

No, probably not, although Rosemary thought she'd do her best to try. All she wanted was to get out of this place and never see Caleb Lockwood—or any of the other Greencastle demons—ever again. Not bothering to reply directly, she said, "Okay, I've held up my end of the bargain. I waited until the results came in. Well, we all know the truth now. And I want to go home. You told me I could leave once this was all done."

He didn't reply right away, and she noticed how his gaze shifted to the house and then back to her, almost as if he was trying to decide whether to call for reinforcements.

Icy fingers inched their way down her back. Were they going to renege on their promise, come up with some excuse for why they couldn't possibly let her go back to California?

"Or were you lying about that, too?"

"No," he said immediately, something in his voice telling her that the question had bothered him more than he wanted to let on. "That was the deal. I suppose…I suppose we all hoped you would want to stay once you knew the truth."

"'Stay'?" she repeated, and let out a derisive laugh. "Why would I want to stay here when my whole life is in California?"

His dark eyes met hers, searching. Somehow, Rosemary forced herself to gaze back at him, although she wanted to look away. It was too uncomfortable standing here like this, and yet she guessed if she did or said anything to break the contact, she'd only call more attention to her discomfort. "Is it, though?" he asked. "I mean, if you're going to go there and tell them all the truth about yourself, how do you think they're going to react?"

"They won't care," she said stoutly, although even as the words left her lips, she experienced a niggle of doubt. It was one thing to stand there and declare that this revelation about her true parentage wouldn't change anything, but did she know that for a fact? Celeste and Isabel loved her, but she would suddenly be *other*, no matter what they might say to the contrary. Her mother would be forced to acknowledge that the child she thought was the product of a joyful union between herself and her husband was actually the result of the demons' biological experiments.

And as for Will....

No, she wasn't quite sure she wanted to think about that at all.

"You're sure about that?" Caleb asked. "You're sure this won't matter to them, that everything will go on just as it always has?"

"Yes," she said. *He's just trying to make you question everything,* she told herself. *Don't let him. You know you can't possibly stay here.*

His brows lifted slightly, but he didn't throw the lie back in her face. Instead, he told her, "But we already know who you are. We want you here. You're special, Rosemary. You're the only female born to demon-kind. Don't you want to stay here and find out more, find out why that is?"

"Do *you* know?"

"No," he admitted. "I don't think anyone does. But we can work on it together. We made a good team, you and I. Don't say that we didn't, because that will be a lie."

She wished she could tell him he didn't know what he was talking about. Only...what he'd just said was nothing more than the truth. It had been fun working to discover where the missing footage was hidden...challenging to learn the truth about

Madeline Nash. Yes, that had all gone sour when Rosemary discovered Caleb wasn't who he'd said he was, but in the beginning, they had been a good team.

"We did," she said, then added quickly, before he could begin to smile or be at all relieved by her admission, "but that was then, and this is now. Everything's changed, Caleb. I don't—I don't want to work with you on this. I don't want to know anything more than I already do. I just want to go back and pick up my life."

"Back to him." Caleb's lip lifted in the beginnings of a sneer. "Do you really think Mr. Holier-Than-Thou is going to want a part-demon girlfriend?"

"I don't know," she said wearily, reflecting that Caleb's reaction told her all she needed to know; that any hint of understanding or kindness was something he'd put on for show, not because he actually felt those emotions. "But that's for the two of us to work out. I don't expect you to understand. All I know is that I've done what you asked, and so I expect to be shown the same consideration in return."

And then she stood there and waited to see how he would respond, her entire body tense with worry, with trying to figure out what in the world she would do if he laughed in her face and said that they'd never intended to send her back to

California, that the plan was to keep her here in Greencastle forever.

However, after a very long pause, one that knotted the tension in her neck even more and made her palms damp with worry, Caleb said, "All right. A deal's a deal. I think you're making a mistake, but…." The words trailed off as he lifted his shoulders. "Just know that we're here for you if things don't turn out quite the way you want them back home."

"Really?" she asked, staring up at him, not sure whether she could allow herself to feel the relief that wanted to spread all through her body.

"Yes, really." Now he looked amused again, eyebrow at an ironic tilt. "But get the hell out of here before we change our minds."

"Thank you," Rosemary said. "And—and I'm sorry I couldn't be what you all wanted me to be."

His eyes wouldn't meet hers. Staring off at some indeterminate point in the distance, he replied, "It's okay. We had to try. You should go inside and say goodbye before you leave, though."

Her instincts told her that wasn't a very good idea. "No, I'd rather leave from here. It would be awkward. I wouldn't know what to say." On a sudden impulse—maybe because he looked almost forlorn, although before that moment, she wouldn't have thought him capable of such an emotion—she extended a hand and squeezed Caleb's fingers. "Take care."

Before he could reply, she'd reached out with those strange demonic senses, imagining Will's house yet again. Only this time, she was able to see the living room and feel it simultaneously, and she realized it was going to work, that the Green-castle demons weren't going to prevent her from leaving this time.

A blink, and she was gone.

Chapter 11

WILL STARED AT HIS LAPTOP, KNOWING HE needed to finish writing his sermon for the next day, and finding neither the inspiration nor the inclination to do so. How in the world was he supposed to concentrate on such a thing when he had absolutely no idea what was happening to Rosemary? Michael had counseled patience, but Will knew he was desperately short of that much-lauded virtue at the moment.

Still, he'd already missed enough work as it was. Unless some emergency intervened, he was expected to put in a full day on Sunday—service in the morning, as well as overseeing the harvest potluck scheduled for the afternoon. Explaining that his new girlfriend had been kidnapped by part-demons and spirited away to Greencastle,

Indiana, probably wouldn't go over very well, even if it was the literal truth.

He leaned back in his office chair and stared at the screen. The subject for the sermon was supposed to be forgiveness, the quote from Matthew 6:14-15 —"For if ye forgive men their trespasses, your heavenly Father will also forgive you; But if ye forgive not men their trespasses, neither will your Father forgive your trespasses"—but his brain couldn't seem to come up with anything new and inspirational to say about it, probably because he wasn't in a very forgiving mood at the moment.

"Will."

Wonderful. Apparently, he was so obsessed with Rosemary's well-being that he was now hearing her voice in his head.

"*Will.*"

He swiveled the chair and stared, shocked, at the doorway to his office. Rosemary stood there, looking a little more sedate than usual in a pair of jeans, low boots, and a dark green cardigan over a high-necked T-shirt, but it was definitely her.

In the blink of an eye, he was out of his chair and going to her so he could pull her into his arms. Yes, that was really her, so delicate in his arms, and yet with a core of steel that he knew he would never take for granted.

"You're all right?" he asked, after he'd clung to

her for a moment and reassured himself that she wasn't some kind of vivid hallucination.

"I'm fine," she said, although he wasn't sure he believed her. There was a sorrow in her big blue eyes that hadn't been there before, and she looked pale and tired, although still beautiful. "But Will…there are some things we need to talk about."

"Of course," he replied. "Do you want anything? A glass of water, some tea?"

"Tea would be good. I still feel cold."

That comment did very little to reassure him as to her well-being, but he didn't press her for explanations, only went with her into the kitchen so he could get the water in the kettle boiling. She glanced around and let out a small sigh, as if relieved to find that nothing had changed in her absence.

"I love this kitchen," she commented, apropos of nothing, and he tried to smile.

"Me, too. It could be bigger, but—"

"It's perfect," she insisted, and he decided to let the matter go.

Speaking of which….

"How did you get away?"

Rosemary leaned against the counter and pushed up the sleeves of her sweater. It seemed a little big on her, and he guessed it wasn't hers, even though he hadn't been with her long enough to be familiar with her entire wardrobe.

"I didn't 'get away,'" she told him. "They let me go."

He stared at her, startled. "What?"

"They let me go. I—well, I'll tell you all about it once we sit down with some tea. Okay?"

"Okay," he agreed, wondering what on earth had happened to her in Greencastle. She didn't seem to have been physically harmed in any way, but something about her seemed almost defeated, her usual ebullience dampened somehow.

Worry stirred within him, but he made himself get busy with fetching mugs and bags of English Breakfast from the box in the cupboard, and soon enough the kettle was whistling. He waited a moment for it to stop boiling, then poured hot water into the two mugs he'd set out.

"There you go," he said, handing one of them to her. "Let's go and sit down."

She gave him a tired-looking nod and followed him out to the living room, where they both took a seat on the couch. However, he noticed the way she positioned herself nearly a foot away from him, as if she wasn't quite sure he would want her sitting any closer.

Which was ridiculous. He wanted her as close as possible...wanted to pull her into his arms again and hold her and have her tell him what had gone so terribly wrong. But something in her expression told him such advances would be unwanted, despite the hug she'd allowed him when he first saw that she was safely back from her ordeal.

For a moment, she didn't say anything, only held on to her mug of tea with one hand and methodically dunked the teabag inside, as if focusing on that one small task was the most important thing in the world. Eventually, though, she appeared to judge the tea ready to drink, because she let go of the tag on the teabag and took a small sip of the hot liquid inside the mug.

"What is it, Rosemary?" he asked, concern spurring him to ask the question even though he'd resolved to wait and let her speak first.

"It's…." That single syllable hung on the air for a moment, and she shook her head. "God, I don't even know how to say this to you."

Concern morphed into outright fear. What had they done to her? If Caleb….

No, he wouldn't allow his mind to finish that sentence, to take the final step toward the horrible possibility his brain had begun to manufacture.

But if he had, Will knew he would kill him. As God was his witness, he'd find a way to make sure that bastard stayed dead this time.

"Just say it however is easiest for you," he said gently. "It's all right. I'm listening."

She sipped from her tea again and then set the mug down on a coaster, the movement very precise, as if it was vitally important to her that she make sure the mug was perfectly centered. "I —I went with Caleb to Greencastle."

"I know," Will said, and she stared back at him, clearly startled by his casual acceptance of that statement. "Isabel had a vision of you," he added by way of clarification, and Rosemary relaxed slightly. "So, we knew you were there and that you seemed to be safe, but none of us could figure out exactly what was going on."

"Okay." She paused there and drew in a breath, fingers clenched on the knees of her jeans, which looked new and dark, as if they'd been purchased recently. "He had—he had something to tell me about my father."

"About John?" Will asked, a little surprised by that revelation. He'd gotten the impression that the demons couldn't exactly tell what their angelic observer was up to, or even knew of his existence. "Is he all right?"

"I don't know." Again, her fingers tightened on her knees, and she stared across the room, obviously doing her best not to meet his gaze. "About John, I mean. But the thing is…he's not my father."

Will stared at her, at the delicate profile she presented to him, jaw clearly clenched. "He isn't?

But he said—that is, you told me he was your father."

"I know. But he wasn't. He was…he was a demon pretending to be my father." Rosemary stopped herself there and gave a small shake of her head, as if chiding herself for getting the story wrong. "I mean, he was a—a cambion, pretending to be the man I thought was my father. Except it turns out that cambion—Gerald Gates—is my real father."

This pronouncement was delivered in such a brittle tone that Will wouldn't have been surprised if those words had somehow cracked and broken as they left her lips. For one agonizing moment, he could only gaze at her, searching the outline of her face for some hint that she was making a terrible joke. But of course, there was none. She seemed to be telling him the truth, or at least the truth as she saw it.

"How is that possible?" he asked, and her shoulders lifted.

"Cambions are shape-changers," she said simply. "My mother had no idea it wasn't my actual father."

The reality of what she'd said began to sink in, and a sort of numb horror began to take over. Will didn't know Glynis McGuire well, but he knew enough to see what a lovely and gracious person she was, but tough and smart as well. To think that such a hideous trick had been played on her....

Still, he forced his outrage aside as best he could. "How do you know the Lockwoods are even telling you the truth? They could have manufactured this whole story just as a...as a sort of psychological warfare."

Rosemary gave him a dreary little smile. "I wanted to think that, too. Except I met my father, and we went into Indianapolis to get a paternity test done at one of the big labs there. Priority rush, all that. The results came back as a more than ninety-nine-percent match."

"It could be a trick—" Will began, and she shook her head.

"I don't think so. I mean, I know they're capable of a lot, but I'm not sure even our Greencastle demons are powerful enough to meddle with lab results like that, especially since the courier handed me the letter directly. It's not as if anyone except the lab personnel could have had access to it before I did. After all, we're talking about a small group of part-demons, not some kind of vast underground network or something."

All this was related in a flat little voice, as if Rosemary was recounting events that had happened to someone else. While he could understand that manufactured detachment—it was a way of coping with a truth so terrible, her rational mind didn't want to accept it—he also didn't want her to force herself into acceptance of something that very likely wasn't true.

"I still think they could have meddled with the results," he began, and she only smiled again.

"You weren't there, Will. I told you, I met him. I saw some of myself in his face. I know I look mostly like my mother, but there was enough to make their story more than plausible."

On the surface...possibly...and yet Will found he had to do what he could to make her see that just because something was plausible didn't make it true. He said, "If this man could alter his appearance to look like your father, then what's to have stopped him from making subtle changes to convince you that you're his daughter?"

Rosemary shrugged. "Nothing, I guess. It's just...their story makes a lot more sense than trying to convince me that I'm half angel. So, let's take the results of the paternity test at face value for now. What I need to know is...how does this change things between us?"

In her face was a terrible fear. No matter what else, no matter who was telling the truth—if anyone—Will knew he needed to make sure she understood that he didn't care who her father was.

Even if he was the Devil himself.

"It doesn't change anything," Will said, the words quiet but with a firmness he hoped she could hear and accept. "That was the truth when I thought your father was an angel, and it's the truth now. Our parents don't have to define us—our actions, and who we are deep down, are far more important. You didn't want to stay in Greencastle when you saw the test results, did you?"

"God, no," Rosemary answered at once, her tone emphatic.

He reached over and took her hand in his. Her fingers felt cold, but he could understand why. Still holding her hand, he said, "You see? If you thought you had any kind of a connection to the Greencastle demons, you would have wanted to stay. Or at least, you would have entertained the notion before rejecting it."

"That was never an option," she said. Now she shifted on the couch, moving a little nearer to him. In response, he let go of her hand—but only so he could drop his arm around her shoulders and pull her close. She leaned into his chest, and he released a breath. Thank God. He'd been worried that she would reject his touch, wouldn't allow him to reestablish a physical connection, but that didn't seem to be the case.

"Because you belong here with your family. And with me...I hope."

For a moment, she didn't speak. However, Will could sense her silence came from an attempt to gather her thoughts rather than a rejection of him.

Then she said, "I want to be with you. This is all new, I know, but still…." The words faded away, and he could feel her let out a sigh of her own. "I don't think I'm what anyone expects from a minister's girlfriend. And that's ignoring the whole half-demon father issue."

He'd noticed how she'd carefully said "girlfriend" rather than wife. Yes, it was probably far too soon to be thinking about things like that, and yet he knew he'd already fantasized about sharing that kind of a future with her. And if she was starting to worry about how people would regard her if she became a more permanent fixture in his life, then he guessed she'd begun to consider such a thing as well.

"I don't expect you to be anyone except yourself," he said, then bent and placed a gentle kiss on the top of her head. "And neither will anyone else. I know you probably don't have a lot of experience with churches and their congregations, but the people at All Saints are very open, very accepting. They won't care that you're not some prim, conservative type in a cardigan and sensible pumps."

That description made her chuckle, and Will was glad she'd relaxed enough to be able to laugh about things. "No, I'm not generally a cardigan kind of girl, even if I had to borrow one from Caleb's mother."

So, that was where the sweater she was wearing had come from. He could tell it was something she wouldn't have chosen for herself, even though the color looked good on her. "And you don't need to be. Don't place expectations on yourself, since I know no one else—at least, no one from my church—will."

Rosemary's face was partly obscured by the fall of her thick, curly hair, but he could still see her expression, somber again. "And you really don't care that my father could be a cambion?"

"No...although I hope you don't mind if I say that I'd prefer to avoid inviting him over for Thanksgiving dinner."

She laughed again, a real laugh this time, not the muted chuckle she'd given a few minutes earlier. "I'm pretty sure we can avoid that. And Christmas, too."

"Deal." He held her for a moment longer, wanting her to know she was all he cared about, not who her father might or might not be, not what kind of blood might be blended with the human blood in her veins. In a way, he was a little surprised by how much he didn't care. Rosemary was Rosemary, the woman he loved. If she had a little demon mixed in, well, they'd manage. And since he thought they should try to get past the subject, he asked, "Hungry?"

"I guess I am, a little," she replied, looking somewhat surprised that such a mundane need might surface after the shocks she'd just suffered. "I was so nervous before I went over to the Lockwood house that I haven't eaten anything today."

"Then let me take you out for breakfast," he said.

She sent him a dubious look. "Are you sure that's safe?"

While he could understand her concern, he wanted to assure her that everything would be fine. She couldn't spend the rest of her life looking over her shoulder, even though he also wondered why the demons had simply let her leave. If they thought she was one of them, wouldn't they have tried a little harder to keep her in Greencastle permanently?

So many questions, and so few answers. He pushed aside his own misgivings and said, "Of course, it is. We've seen how these demons operate. They don't do anything in public, or at least, they actively work to avoid attracting attention. If I were going to take you out to a late breakfast in Old Town Pasadena, that would be about the last place where they'd try something, don't you think?"

"I suppose so," she said, still looking a bit

skeptical. But then she squared her shoulders and added, "No, you're right. I need to get past this, and breakfast in Old Town sounds great. Just give me a couple of minutes—I want to get out of this damn sweater."

"Take as long as you need," he told her, and watched as she got up from the sofa and left the room. Her chin was held high, and he thought she was probably telling herself that breakfast in a public place surrounded by regular people was the best way to get past her ordeal with the Greencastle demons.

He hoped she was right.

Rosemary was glad that she and Will had stolen an hour or so to go to breakfast, because once they were done, he said, "You really need to call your mother and let her know you're back. She's been worried sick over this whole thing—everyone has."

"I know," she replied. "It's just...I don't even know how to begin to tell her what happened."

"Tell her the truth," he said. "Or at least, the truth as you know it so far. Anything else wouldn't be fair."

He was right, of course, and yet she dreaded having to drop yet another terrible revelation on her mother. And this one was so much worse than the news that her dead husband wasn't quite as dead as she thought. "Will you—will you come with me?" Maybe it was cowardly to ask such a thing of him, but Rosemary knew she'd feel better with Will at her side. Besides, he was a minister; he must have been used to getting involved in sticky family situations.

"Of course," he answered without hesitation.

Warmth filled her, a rush of love for this man who'd come into her life and let her know that she wasn't destined to be alone, someone who didn't seem to get rattled by anything, no matter how crazy. She wasn't sure she deserved someone like him, but she was going to do her best to make sure he never regretted his decision to be with her.

She reached across the table and took his hand. "Thanks, Will. And I know we need to talk to Michael, but...."

"Your mother comes first," he said firmly, fingers tightening on hers. "She deserves to know what's going on."

"Also, I have a feeling that Michael is going to give me the third degree," Rosemary went on, deliberately lightening her tone, "and God knows how long that's going to take."

"A while, probably," Will returned with a grin.

The waiter came by with their check, and she tried to grab it, to no avail.

"Did you really think I was going to let you pay for breakfast?" Will asked. "After everything you've been through?"

"It's really not that big a deal—"

"And it's not that big a check, so there's no need to worry about it. Why don't you try texting your mother, make sure she's at home?"

Since it was Saturday, there was only a fifty-fifty chance of that being the case. Rosemary couldn't really keep track of her mother's schedule; she knew Glynis had a horticultural group she met with at the Arboretum in Arcadia once a month, but which Saturday that meeting actually fell on was a complete mystery. Plus, Halloween was less than a week away, and so there was a chance she might have been pressed into service to assist with the final touches on Tyler's costume. But no, probably not—since Rosemary was unavailable, presumably both Isabel and Celeste were working at the bookstore.

"Sure," she responded, and retrieved her phone while Will fished his wallet out of his pocket and pulled out his credit card.

Mom, I'm back, Rosemary typed. *Can Will and I come over in a bit?*

The reply was almost immediate, signaling that her mother was home—and apparently camped on the phone, considering her fast response time. Guilt over the worry she'd caused assailed Rosemary, even though she tried to tell herself that it wasn't really her fault. Yes, she'd agreed to go with Caleb, but she'd had no idea that the demons were going to make her stay in Greencastle for two nights.

You're home? her mother replied. *You're safe?*

I'm fine. But I need to talk to you. Are you available?

Yes. I'm home. No plans today. Come over when you can.

Be there in about 20. Loves.

Rosemary closed the wallet case for her phone and put it back in her purse just as Will was handing his credit card to their waiter. "She's home," she said. "We can go over there as soon as we're done here."

He looked pleased that they wouldn't have to wait. "Good."

Honestly, Rosemary didn't know for sure how "good" any of this was, but she tried to tell herself that it was important for her mother to know what was going on. After that, they'd have to figure out what to tell Celeste and Isabel, but that conversation could wait a little longer. It would have to, since they wouldn't even be done with work until after six.

Once the bill was settled, they left Green Street, the restaurant where they'd been eating, and went out to get into Will's car. "What is with this thing, anyway?" Rosemary asked. "I would have pegged you for a Prius or a Subaru. Something practical."

He gave her a pained look as he started up the Challenger. The big engine growled from under the hood, sounding similarly offended. "It's a classic," he pointed out.

"A classic that probably gets about ten miles to the gallon."

"Fifteen."

"Still."

"I'll admit, it's not the most eco-friendly car on the road," Will said, maneuvering out of the parking lot so they could head north on Lake and get to the 210 Freeway. "It was actually my father's car. He drove it in college and didn't want to part with it when he got married and started a family, so it sort of lived under a tarp in the carport until I started tinkering with it in high school. Had to rebuild the engine, do a lot of work on the suspension. When I started college, he said I'd put so much work into it that I could have it. And ever since...I guess I just never had the heart to part with it, even though the mileage stinks."

"I had no idea you knew how to work on cars," Rosemary said, impressed that he'd put so much of himself into the Challenger. No wonder he'd never wanted to get rid of it. "Is there anything you can't do?"

His head tilted to one side, as though he was seriously considering her question. "I can't carry a tune to save my life."

"I was serious."

"So am I. Major tin ear. They had to ask me to not sing in the choir back home in Brookline."

She smiled and shook her head, trying to imagine that particular scene. The smile didn't last very long, though, mostly because her thoughts kept slipping ahead to the coming conversation with her mother.

Maybe they should have gone to Michael's first. But no, that wasn't a good idea. While Michael and Audrey needed to know what was going on, Glynis was the person who really should hear the truth first.

If it even was the truth. For all Rosemary knew, this was the demons' real plan—to get her so harrowed up with doubt and worry that she couldn't function effectively. Why exactly they'd need to mess with her in such a way, she wasn't sure. If they were lying and she was just a normal person, then one would think she'd be beneath their notice. Michael and Audrey were the ones who really should have been on the demons' radar, considering the way they'd banished Belial to Hell.

All of this was beginning to make her head hurt, although she supposed the mild headache that had begun to pulse behind her temples might have more to do with the crappy night's sleep she'd had the evening before at the DePauw Inn. There wasn't anything really wrong with the bed, but stewing over whether you were some half-demon's bastard daughter was enough to screw with anyone's sleep.

In less than fifteen minutes, Will was pulling his big muscle car into the driveway of her mother's Craftsman house in Sierra Madre. The day had stayed cloudy, although there didn't seem to be any rain in the offing, and the house looked almost brooding under those gray skies, although Rosemary generally thought of it as a cheerful kind of place.

Then again, her current mood was probably the real reason for the home's current forbidding aspect.

They got out of the car and went up to the door. Apparently, Glynis had spied them as they walked up the path, because she opened the door before Rosemary even had a chance to knock.

"Come in," she said. "I put a pot of Darjeeling on, since this doesn't seem like a day for iced tea."

"Sounds great," Rosemary said, forcing a smile. Good thing she'd only had water with breakfast, or she would have been completely tea'd out.

Her mother gave her a quick glance, as if trying to gauge something of her daughter's mood. However, she didn't comment, only went on, "Let's all go into the living room, and I'll get that tea."

There wasn't much to do except follow and then sit down on the couch. Glynis offered them cookies to go with their tea, and Will and Rosemary both demurred, saying they were still full from their late breakfast. They waited while she went to fetch the tea, bringing it back on a tray with three cups, the same set with the hand-painted rose sprays that had once belonged to Rosemary's grandmother.

After Glynis had poured tea for everyone, she picked up her cup, although she didn't take a sip. "So…what happened?" she asked.

"I'm fine," Rosemary reiterated, just as much to reassure herself as her mother. Although she felt better the more time she spent with Will, she honestly didn't know whether she truly was all right. But she figured she'd have to accept the contents of those test results and move on, or she'd never have a moment's peace. "Isabel saw me in Greencastle, right?"

Her mother nodded. "Yes. Or at least, we assumed that was where you must be. Caleb took you there?"

"He did. I went voluntarily," Rosemary added quickly.

Surprise flashed in Glynis's eyes. "Why?"

"Because he had something to tell me. Or rather," she went on, seeing the question in her mother's expression, "He had someone he needed me to meet."

"Who?"

The moment had come. Rosemary looked over at Will, and he gave her an encouraging nod. "My father."

Her mother's brows drew together in apparent confusion. "Why would an angel be with the half-demons in Greencastle? I thought you said he was only supposed to observe them and not have any interactions."

Yes, that had been John McGuire's supposed role. Just a convenient lie Gerald Gates had told in his guise as the "angel" who had been tasked with watching the Greencastle demons to make sure they didn't get too out of hand. It made a plausible excuse for why he'd pretended to be dead for the past ten years, but the whole thing had been a fabrication.

Maybe.

"Because he wasn't an angel," Rosemary said. "He's a half-demon named Gerald Gates."

A heavy silence fell after she uttered those words. Her mother stared at her, openly perplexed at first, confusion turning to horror as her eyes widened.

"That's not possible," she murmured. Clearing

her throat, she went on, "I never—that is, I was always faithful to your father, Rosemary."

"I know," Rosemary replied. "You wouldn't have known. They—the half-demons—they can shape shift, alter their appearance. You would have thought it was Dad."

Glynis's hand went to her throat. Rosemary wasn't sure she'd ever seen her mother dumbfounded before, but clearly, she was now. She hated to see her mother so stricken, but she had no idea what she could possibly say to make any of this better.

"They told you that?" she said at last.

Rosemary nodded.

"And you believed them?"

"No. I mean, I didn't *want* to believe them. But…Gerald Gates and I did a paternity test. It came back as a near-perfect match."

Her mother's gaze shifted to Will, who had been quiet through their exchange, as though understanding that this was something they needed to work through together, even if Rosemary had requested his presence. "You believe this?"

He clasped his hands on his knee and leaned forward slightly, expression earnest. "To be honest? I'm withholding judgment. These part-demons aren't exactly known for their trustworthiness. I'll admit that it seems as though they'd have a difficult time faking a paternity test taken at a professional lab, but I suppose it's not beyond the bounds of possibility, even if I can't figure out how they could have done it."

Glynis absorbed this observation in silence, appearing to think over what Will had just told her. With a hand that shook slightly, she lifted her cup of tea to her lips and took a sip.

"It's not as if I *want* this to be true," Rosemary burst out. Something in her mother's lack of a response made her feel guilty, as though she was pushing a theory that no one with any sense could possibly believe. "But it also makes sense. If—if our father was really John McGuire, an angel pretending to be a human being, then why don't Celeste and Isabel have the same crazy talents I've started to show recently? Before a few weeks ago, I think we all would have agreed that we were basically the same kind of psychic. Now, though—"

"Yes, now," her mother cut in, but quietly, in a way that didn't seem like an interruption. "Why now, Rosemary?"

"Because my powers didn't come alive until I was around another part-demon," she said. "Simple as that. But you haven't answered my question, Mom. If Izzie and CeeCee are my full sisters, why are my talents so different from theirs?"

Glynis gave her a weary smile. "You might as

well ask why one child in a family plays the violin and another is a tennis star. Everyone has different levels of talents and abilities. Just because you and Celeste and Isabel are sisters doesn't mean you're going to be cookie-cutter versions of one another."

Rosemary supposed that explanation made sense, and yet she couldn't shake the feeling that her mother was dancing around the issue because she didn't want to acknowledge the horrific possibility that her youngest daughter wasn't quite what she seemed to be. "Being psychic isn't the same thing as playing tennis," she pointed out, and her mother only raised an eyebrow as she took another sip of tea.

"No, it isn't," she replied. "And I realize I have to acknowledge that this is a possibility. So many strange things have happened over the past week that I can't really pretend they don't exist. On the other hand, it's possible these demons are lying to you, for reasons none of us can comprehend. At the end of the day, none of this changes the fact that you're my daughter and I love you, no matter who your father might have been."

What, really, could she say in answer to such a statement? It was much the same thing Will had told her, and yet Rosemary couldn't help thinking this was still terribly different. Even though he loved her, he was something of an observer in all this; it wasn't his family being affected. And she realized that it didn't matter what she said—her mother needed to believe there was some chance that none of what Rosemary had witnessed in Indiana had been true.

And the horrible thing was, Rosemary couldn't be sure, either. Not completely.

"Okay," she said quietly. "I just—I just didn't feel as though this was something I could keep from you."

"And I would never have expected you to," her mother responded. She set down her teacup and reached over so she could pat Rosemary on the hand. "I can't exactly say I'm glad to have heard any of this, but I would have been more upset if you'd kept it all to yourself and I found out later. For the moment, though, I think we should all just be glad that you're back home and you're safe."

Safe…for now. Rosemary couldn't help thinking that this was only a pause, that the demons were still planning something she couldn't foresee. Her second sight had always come and gone at its own whim, or she would have tried to compel it now, done her best to make it tell her what Daniel Lockwood and the rest of them were plotting. But, because she'd made such attempts in the past and had failed miserably, she knew not to even bother. All she could do was hope that the closed book of the future might open itself to her, if only for a moment. Just enough to get a glimpse of what might be coming, and how to prepare herself for it.

Or failing that, at least brace herself for the inevitable.

Chapter 12

ROSEMARY DIDN'T WANT TO TALK ABOUT THE
conversation that had just transpired at her mother's house, and so she was quiet as Will pointed
the Challenger westward toward Michael's house.
And toward Will's house as well, although she
guessed it would be a few hours before the two of
them would be able to take sanctuary there.

There had been only enough time for Will to
send a very brief text, one that said Rosemary was
back and that they'd be over in about ten minutes.
His phone was assailed by a series of *bings* almost
immediately afterward, but since he was driving,
he couldn't pick it up to take a look at what they
all were.

Not that it really mattered. They'd be hashing
out all this at Michael's house in a few minutes
anyway.

They parked in front and got out of the car. A drop of rain hit Rosemary's hand as she and Will were walking up to the front door, and she slanted a glance up at the cloudy sky. It did seem a bit darker now than when they'd first set out. Well, the weather didn't matter all that much. They were going to be safely inside soon enough.

Extremely soon, since Michael opened the front door before they'd even begun to mount the porch steps. "You're all right?" he asked, staring at Rosemary. "What happened?"

"I'm fine, and it's a long story," she said.

He raised an eyebrow but seemed to understand that she was tired, because he moved out of the way so she and Will could step past him into the entry. "Family room," he said briefly. "Audrey's waiting for us."

"Where's Fred?" Will asked. Rosemary had been thinking much the same thing; she was surprised that he appeared to be absent.

Despite the frown that had previously furrowed his brow, Michael grinned. "Oh, he went to visit Rosemary's bookstore."

"He what?" she said, startled by his reply.

"He went to Sisters We. Said he wanted to check it out. Actually, though," Michael added, still smiling, "I got the impression that what he really wanted to do was check Isabel out. So to speak."

"'Isabel'?" Rosemary repeated. For some reason, what Michael had just told her didn't seem to have computed properly. Maybe she was a little more shell-shocked than she'd thought.

He shrugged. "Why should you and Will be the only ones to make a love connection in the middle of this mess?"

At last, the import behind his words got through, but she had a feeling he was misreading the situation. "I don't think Isabel's really interested in a relationship," she said.

"Have you asked her recently?"

"Well, no, but—"

"He's just teasing you," Audrey said. She'd been sitting on the couch, but stood up as the trio entered the family room. "Or rather, I don't think he's joking about Fred, because I could also tell that he was impressed by Isabel. Still, that's between the two of them. Can I get you something to drink?"

"Water is fine," Rosemary replied, deciding to leave aside the question of Fred Peñasco's feelings toward her sister for a time when she wasn't feeling quite so on edge. Actually, a glass of wine would have been great, but she guessed it would be wise to leave the drinking for sometime later in the day after they'd discussed what had happened to her in Greencastle.

"For me, too," Will added, and Audrey

headed over to the kitchen to get some glasses for them.

"So," Michael said as they sat down on the couch. "The demons let you go, just like that?"

"Apparently," she replied. "And no, I have no idea why."

Michael leaned up against the polished mahogany that framed the doorway and crossed his arms. "Tell me what happened."

Rosemary took in a breath, then launched into the story. By that time, she was less than happy to repeat it all over again, but she gamely went through the whole thing once more, from Caleb approaching her at the house to her trip to Greencastle and the paternity test that followed. Partway through this narrative, Audrey came over and handed the two of them their glasses of water, but refrained from comment, as if she knew better than to interrupt Rosemary in the middle of her account.

When she was done, she leaned against the back of the sofa and took a large swallow of water. "And that's all I know."

"'All'?" Michael repeated incredulously. "That's —that's—"

"Kind of mind-blowing," Audrey finished for him. Her gaze rested on Rosemary, sympathetic and more than a little worried. "Are you doing okay?"

"About as well as can be expected, I suppose." She drank some more water and then rested the glass on her knee. "I think I'm maybe a little shell-shocked. And also, like I said, I don't know if I can believe any of what they told me, or whether it's all some big con job."

"For what purpose, though?" Michael asked then, gray-gold eyes narrowed. "I mean, if it was some sort of ruse to get you to stay with them, it sort of backfired, didn't it?"

Rosemary's shoulders lifted. "I was thinking the same thing. The strange thing was, it felt as though Caleb was doing his best to convince me that I was one of them and so needed to stay in Greencastle, and then…he just sort of gave up, as if he'd decided it wasn't worth the effort anymore."

"That is strange," Michael said. He scrubbed a hand across his chin, which, as usual, was covered by a few days' worth of scruff. "You said it was Caleb doing the convincing?"

"By that point, yes." Rosemary rubbed a hand over the knee of her jeans; she'd gotten rid of the borrowed sweater, exchanging it for an embroidered jacket, but that was the only part of her outfit she'd changed. "After I saw the results of the paternity test, I was upset—"

"Understandably," Michael interjected.

Ignoring this interruption, she went on, "And so I went outside to get some fresh air. Caleb followed me out there, but Daniel Lockwood and Gerald Gates stayed inside the house. He kept trying to persuade me that they were my family and that I needed to stay with them, but I told him that was never going to happen. I reached out with my power and realized they weren't blocking it anymore. So, I told him goodbye and left, and went to Will's house."

"And no sign of any of them trying to stop you?" Audrey asked, and Rosemary shook her head.

"Nothing I could detect." She paused there, doing her best to focus again on the moment when she'd reached out with her extra senses in order to make sure she really was able to get away. There hadn't been even the smallest twinge to tell her that the demons were blocking her power to teleport. No, it had been smooth sailing. "It was as if they'd suddenly decided it wasn't worth keeping me there any longer."

Michael scratched his chin again, eyes narrowed. "Which in itself is more than a little suspicious, considering all the effort they'd gone to in order to get you to Greencastle and keep you there."

"I know." Something about the whole situation didn't smell right, but she was damned if she could figure out what the demons were up to this time. "I don't know what their plan is—even if they have one. Frankly, I'm just glad to be home."

"That's for sure," Will said, his fingers finding Rosemary's and holding on tight. His fingers were warm and strong, and she could feel the reassurance and love flowing out of him and into her. Everything seemed better when he was around. "And while I know we need to keep our guard up, there really isn't much more we can do other than that, right?"

"It seems that way," Michael replied, although he didn't look very hopeful that merely keeping an eye out would be enough to keep Rosemary—or any of the rest of them—safe.

She wasn't sure about that, either, but one thing she did know was that the Greencastle demons seemed loath to do anything that would attract too much notice. All right, faking Caleb's death had caused its own set of problems, but still, it wasn't as though he'd barged into her house and hauled her bodily from the place.

Although maybe that was because he physically couldn't do such a thing. Rosemary had noticed how he'd gotten close to her, had acted as though he wanted to lean in for a kiss but had never made the actual attempt. She sort of doubted his reticence was simply due to being a gentleman. Was it that he now respected her newly awakened demonic gifts and knew he might not be able to hold his own in a straight-up fight between the two of them?

She hoped that was the case. It would be nice to think she could kick his ass into next week if necessary.

"I agree with Will," she said, and felt his fingers tighten on hers. "I understand the need for caution, but I also have to get back to my life. I've left my sisters in the lurch enough as it is—I need to go to work, and I need to be able to cover Isabel's hours if she needs to go help Celeste with Tyler's costume. You know, regular stuff. I can't spend the rest of my life waiting for the other shoe to drop. That's no way to live."

"No, it's not," Audrey said. She went over to Michael and slipped her hand into his as she leaned against his shoulder. "Rosemary is right. None of us can be continually looking over our shoulders. Maybe there's a reason why the Greencastle demons let her go, and maybe there really isn't, except that they knew they'd never be able to convince her to join them, and they knew that if they kept her for too long, the rest of us would alert the authorities as to where we suspected our friend had gone. After all, they've spent all this time doing their best to escape notice, to pretend to be upstanding citizens. If we reported we thought they were involved in a kidnapping, that would open up a lot of questions they definitely wouldn't want to answer."

Rosemary hadn't even thought of that angle, but she realized Audrey had a valid point. Maybe Daniel Lockwood would be able to laugh off such an accusation...maybe not. Yes, they could say that she'd gone with Caleb willingly, that her presence at his party proved she was there as a guest and nothing more, and yet if she stood up and said that she'd been coerced into coming to Greencastle and kept there against her will, the police would be forced to at least interview her. And then all sorts of things the Lockwoods wanted to keep hidden would come to light.

Possibly, similar thoughts had passed through Michael's mind, or maybe he'd realized that not everyone was willing to put their lives on hold while they waited for the part-demons to make their next move. Whatever the reason, he gave a reluctant nod and said, "That makes sense. They're all about hiding in the shadows...or at least, hiding what they really are." He stopped there, gaze moving from Audrey to Will before coming to a rest on Rosemary. She did her best to meet his eyes, but she didn't even know what he was trying to see in her expression. Right then, she felt more tired than anything else. He added, "But still...don't take any chances."

"I won't," she said. "When I go to work, I'll go

straight there and back to Will's house, and I'll have my food delivered to the shop so I don't have to leave it for any reason during the day. But…." She let the word trail off, and gathered her nerve as best she could. "But I'm not going to do that forever, Michael. I understand the need to be cautious now, but sooner or later, something will have to give."

He didn't look thrilled, but he didn't try to argue with her, either. "I suppose that's about all I can ask. But unfortunately, Audrey and I can't stick around indefinitely and wait for the other shoe to drop. She has someone covering her classes, but obviously, she can't be gone for too long."

"I told Esther I might be gone for as long as a week," Audrey said then. "There's no need to go rushing back to Tucson right now. Anyway…." Her eyes went glassy, and her fingers tightened on Michael's, enough that Rosemary thought he made an involuntary wince. "It will be done by All Saints' Day," she said, her tone distant, almost as if someone else was speaking through her.

A shiver worked its way down Rosemary's spine. She knew that Audrey's own psychic powers had awakened when she came into contact with the ghost of her great-grandfather, but this was the first time she'd ever seen them in action, so to speak. Or at least, she guessed that her friend must be having a vision of some kind, judging by the faraway look in her eyes and the odd timbre of her voice.

At once, Michael shifted so he could look down into her face. He studied her for a moment, then asked quietly, "How do you know this?"

"I just do," she said in that same dreamy tone.

"All right," he said, voice calm and reasonable. "Is there anything else you want to tell us?"

A blink, and then she seemed to focus on him, expression growing confused, as if she couldn't quite understand why her significant other was staring at her so intently. "What's the matter?" she asked. "Is something wrong?"

"I think you just had a vision," he told her.

She blinked again. "I did? I don't remember anything."

"Has this happened before?" Will inquired. He didn't look too concerned by the way Audrey had just zoned out, but maybe that was because the episode hadn't lasted for very long.

"Not like this," Michael said. "I mean, she's had dreams that were definitely visions, but not anything while she was awake and conscious."

Audrey rubbed her forehead, as if she felt a headache coming on. "I don't know how conscious I was if I can't remember anything of what I said. What did I say, anyway?"

"That this would be over by All Saints' Day,"

Rosemary replied. Less than a week, since Halloween fell on a Thursday. She didn't know whether to be anxious or relieved that they might not have to wait very long to find out what their eventual fate would be.

"Well, then," Audrey said, obviously doing her best to look cheerful. "No harm, no foul, right? We make it to Friday, and then we can go back to Tucson. Easy."

About all Rosemary could do was summon a wan smile in response. She had absolutely no idea what the Greencastle demons were plotting, but she had a feeling none of this was going to be easy.

They didn't stay much longer at Michael and Audrey's house, partly because there really wasn't much else they could discuss with so little to go on, but mostly because Will could see the growing weariness in Rosemary's eyes and thought she needed to get back to his place so she could put up her feet and rest. He noticed that she didn't offer any protests when he said they should get going, only said that yes, she could use a little downtime.

When they entered his house, Will told her she should try to lie down for a while. At that suggestion, she cocked an eyebrow and said, with almost her old energy, "I'm not an invalid, Will. Yes, I've had a shit day, but I'll get over it."

He only smiled back at her and replied, "What, are you going to deny me a chance to fuss over you the way you did over me when I had my concussion?"

"I didn't fuss," she said sternly. "I only did what the doctor told me to do. But okay—I'll admit that I wouldn't turn down a chance to get on the couch and put my feet up for a while... especially if you bring me a glass of wine, too."

"Deal," he replied.

And so she went over the sofa, pulled off her boots, and grabbed the knitted throw that lay over the back so she could spread it across her legs. Satisfied that she wasn't going to fight him over giving herself a little of the rest she obviously needed, Will headed into the kitchen, got a bottle of wine from the small rack on the countertop, and opened it. Just a cheap merlot from Trader Joe's, but he figured it would do the trick.

When he returned to the living room, he saw that she'd picked up the remote and was aimlessly channel-surfing, although she'd turned the sound down so the quick turnover from channel to channel wouldn't be too annoying. "Saturday afternoon is sure a wasteland on TV," she remarked, then sent him a grateful smile as she took the glass of wine from him with her free hand.

"I wouldn't know," he said. "Usually, I spend Saturday afternoon working on my sermon for the next day."

At once, her expression clouded. "Is that what you should be doing now?"

"It's all right," he lied. "It's mostly done."

She cocked her head and gave him a sideways look which told him she could tell that was a bald-faced lie. "Will, this whole mess has already taken enough of your time. Go ahead and work on your sermon—I'm just going to be sitting out here watching TV and drinking wine anyway."

"I want to stay with you," he said, which was nothing more than the truth. After wondering if he was ever going to see her again, it felt just a bit anticlimactic to leave her alone with the television and her glass of merlot so he could go hack away at his sermon.

His words elicited another smile. "You're only going to be down the hall. This house isn't so big that you won't hear me call for you if I need something."

Well, he couldn't argue with that observation. And what she'd said earlier at Michael and Audrey's place was the simple truth—they needed to get back to their lives, and part of his was making sure he showed up on Sunday and delivered a message that was heartfelt and—he hoped —helpful.

"All right," he said. "It shouldn't take me more than an hour or so. And after that, we can think about what to order in for dinner."

"We never do seem to make it to the store, do we?" she responded ruefully.

"Maybe tomorrow after church."

The remark made her send him a skeptical glance, as if she wasn't quite sure what he'd been intimating by his comment. Then she said, "Are you asking me to come to church with you tomorrow?"

He honestly wasn't sure if that's what he'd meant, but once Rosemary had asked the question, he thought that it actually was a good idea. Not that he expected her to convert or anything, but if she truly wanted to be a part of his life, then she should at least make an appearance now and then, if only to learn a little more about what he did, as well as to meet his parishioners. Besides, he'd already begun to worry about what might happen if he left her alone again—the last time he'd done that, Caleb Lockwood had appeared and whisked her away to Greencastle. Better safe than sorry.

"Only if you want to," Will said. "But I know I'd feel better having you there with me rather than here by yourself."

For a moment, she didn't respond, only sat there with the untouched wine in one hand, the remote in the other. "I could go over to my mother's house if you're worried about leaving me alone."

"True," he replied, trying not to feel disappointed by this apparent rejection of his invitation. "I could drop you off on the way to church."

That suggestion made Rosemary shoot him a disbelieving look. "Um, my mom's house is in the exact opposite direction of All Saints, Will. Besides, I'm not an invalid. I can drive myself. I'm going to have to drive on Monday anyway, since I have to go to work."

All very valid points. He tried to tell himself that it was no big deal and that they'd have plenty of opportunities for her to come to church with him sometime in the future. Even so, the rejection stung a little.

Before he could say anything, though, she went on, "But I can tell it's important for you, so sure, I'll come. Just don't expect me to recite the Lord's Prayer or anything—I don't even know it."

He smiled in relief, then bent and placed a gentle kiss on her cheek. "Like I said before, I don't expect you to do anything but be yourself. Then again, the Lord's Prayer isn't a bad thing to have in your demon-fighting arsenal."

"Like holy water?" she said skeptically. "That

doesn't help so much with our particular brand of demons."

No, it didn't. Will didn't like dwelling on that particular fact, though, mostly because it only pointed out to him that the strongest weapon he had against demon-kind was pretty much nullified by the human blood that ran in the veins of the Greencastle demons. "True," he said, trying to keep his tone light. "But it's helped me in the past."

"With any luck, this all will soon be in the past," Rosemary replied. She finally lifted her glass of wine to her lips and took a sip. "I'd kind of like to know what it feels like to have a normal life with you."

He couldn't argue with that wish, because he held the same one in his heart. "Well, according to Audrey, we're almost there."

"Five more days." She let out a sigh, then glanced over at the television. Her channel-surfing had paused on a college football game, although Will doubted that had been done on purpose. "A lot can happen in five days."

"I know," he said. He'd kissed her before, but he bent and did so again, only this time placing his mouth against hers. Gently, so she'd know he didn't expect anything else from her, although he could feel desire rise in him at the sensation of her lips touching his, at tasting the faint tang of wine on her skin.

"Thank you," she said after he ended the kiss, and he sent her an inquiring glance.

"For what?"

"For kissing me. For…for wanting me, even knowing what I am."

His heart ached at the pain in her voice. He pushed a curl away from her lovely face and said, "Who you are is Rosemary McGuire. You're still the same woman I fell in love with. Nothing is going to change that. Okay?"

"Okay," she replied obediently. Then she forced a smile onto her lips and added, "Now, shoo. Go write your sermon. I'm just going to sit here and drink wine and watch a football game."

That he found difficult to believe. "You are not."

Her mouth twitched, and the smile suddenly looked much more genuine. "Okay, you got me. No football. But I am going to drink this wine."

He chuckled and left her to the TV and her wine, his heart feeling a little lighter. Yes, she'd suffered a shock, but she seemed to be coming back to herself, and he could only be grateful for that. And although he'd told her the truth when he said he didn't care who her father actually was, he still couldn't shake the belief that Daniel Lockwood and this Gerald Gates—whoever he might be—had been feeding her another lie, doing their best to manipulate her with their story that she was a quarter-demon, the same as Caleb.

Now if he could only figure out why. If she was important enough for them to attempt such a ploy in the first place, then why would they suddenly let her go without apparently even a backward glance? Something felt very wrong here, but as hard as his brain tried to pick at the problem, he couldn't come up with an adequate answer.

And he had to set it aside, because, as Rosemary had just pointed out, they needed to get back to their normal lives, and that meant he had to use all his mental focus to work on the sermon he'd just barely started writing when she miraculously reappeared.

Miracles. That was it.

He seated himself at his laptop, opened the file for his sermon, then copied the little he'd written so far on the topic of forgiveness and pasted it into a separate "Notes" file he kept for random jottings and scraps of ideas. Mind buzzing, he began to write a new sermon.

Funny how inspiration flowed once Rosemary was back in his life. He had to do whatever he could to make sure things remained this way.

Chapter 13

IT FELT STRANGER THAN ROSEMARY WANTED to admit to sit in the front pew at All Saints and pretend that she had every right to be there. Okay, in a way she did, just because she was there as Will's guest, but at the same time, she'd held her breath as she stepped over the threshold of the church for the first time, wondering if she was going to spontaneously burst into flames. Which she knew was probably silly, because even if she hadn't been in the chapel before this day, she'd been in Will's office on church grounds, and certainly nothing had happened then. She hadn't felt anything at all, except maybe a bit strange and fluttery just being around him, since of course, that had been back before she'd acknowledged her feelings for him, long before they'd kissed or made love. Everything was different now, and yet....

She was sitting next to a plump, friendly older woman whom Will had introduced as Gloria Jansen, one of the church's deacons. Probably, he'd asked Rosemary to sit with Gloria because he knew Gloria would take her under her wing and make sure her first experience here at the church was a positive one. And that was pretty much what had happened—even when Will had to excuse himself to go prepare for that morning's service, Gloria had taken Rosemary around and introduced her to a whole host of people, most of whose names she knew she'd never be able to recall. However, everyone seemed friendly, and no one seemed taken aback by her paisley sequined skirt and wild hair. Overall, despite the awkwardness of being in a social situation that was entirely new to her, she thought she survived the experience fairly well, although she was glad when it was time to sit down and she didn't have to worry about trying to keep track of all the new faces and names.

Still, Rosemary couldn't quite ignore how out of place she felt, sitting there and listening to the organist play a hymn that probably everyone else in attendance knew but which she couldn't begin to recognize. At least they weren't singing yet; she wasn't quite sure how she intended to handle that part of the service. Pretend to mouth the words? Stand there silently and hope no one noticed?

She'd need to figure it out soon, since the glance she'd taken at the printed program they'd been handing out as she entered the chapel seemed to indicate there would be an opening psalm, then a hymn, followed by various readings from the Bible, and the sermon, followed by more music.

The prelude music continued, and a procession began to make its way down the aisle. In the front was a man—well, boy, really, since he looked like he was barely out of high school, if even that —carrying a large wooden cross. Immediately behind him was Will, looking so different in the white robes of his office with the green drape of a chasuble over them that she hardly recognized him. It was hard to believe that someone who appeared so stern and almost otherworldly now was the same man who'd kissed her, held her, laughed at her quips and told her he loved her, no matter what. But this was another side of him, one she was seeing for the first time, and she knew she needed to understand it and accept it, just as he had accepted everything about her.

After he'd taken his position at the lectern on the altar, he spoke, his voice deep and quiet, calm. "Blessed be God: Father, Son, and Holy Spirit."

Everyone responded, "And blessed be his kingdom, now and forever. Amen."

Will went on from there, speaking a few more words before reading from a psalm she'd never heard before. Not so surprising—the only one she'd ever known more than a few words of was the twenty-third, but she knew this wasn't that. It spoke of strength, and love, and opening oneself to God, and although she wasn't quite sure she was ready to go that far, she had to admit that maybe—just maybe—Someone was out there helping her along. Otherwise, would she have survived all the ordeals that had been thrust in her path?

The thought was oddly reassuring. Or maybe it was just that she found it difficult to believe anything truly bad could happen when she had a man like Will Gordon at her side. Either way, even though she'd been sort of cajoled into coming today, she found herself glad that she had. Maybe this was just the pause before the hammer fell, or the deep breath that needed to be taken before the final leg of the race, but she allowed herself to take comfort in the things she knew she could count on—Will's love, the love of her mother and her sisters, Michael and Audrey's friendship. They were all so important, and she made an inner vow never to take any of them for granted.

When Will was done speaking, everyone rose from their pews. Rosemary did so as well, feeling a bit awkward because of the way she stumbled to her feet a bit later than everyone else. Then the music swelled, and everyone picked up their hymnals and opened them to a particular page—something specified in the program she'd been given, although since she hadn't known exactly what to expect, she hadn't committed the number to memory. Even so, she picked up the book, glanced sideways at Gloria to see that they were on page 382, and glanced down at the words.

Praise God from Whom all blessings flow.

She'd never heard the hymn before, but the music was beautiful, and she decided to relax and let herself simply read along as the rest of the congregation sang. In a way, even though she certainly wasn't religious and—at least not until recently—didn't actually believe in God, she could see why people would take comfort in participating in such a ritual. She thought of how Will had told her he had a complete tin ear, and wondered what he'd done growing up in the church if he'd had to sing along with everyone else. The image of a much younger Will Gordon, gawky and with his voice breaking, brought a smile to her lips, although she tried to smother it, thinking this probably wasn't the place to be standing there grinning like an idiot for no perceptible reason.

No one seemed to notice, thankfully. He spoke again, reflecting on miracles, of the everyday sorts of wonders that entered people's lives, often unnoticed. Several times, his gaze caught hers before it moved on to somewhere else in the congregation, and each time, Rosemary could feel her cheeks warm with sudden heat. She didn't want to be conceited, but she somehow knew that when he spoke of miracles, he was also talking about her, about the connection they shared, something that had come almost out of nowhere with the force of a river raging in flood.

Well, he was a miracle, too. And she had to make sure he knew that.

Eventually, the service wound down to the offering of the Eucharist, and Rosemary stayed seated at her pew, trying her best to ignore her discomfort as the members of the congregation came forward and were given the sacramental bread and wine. No, she wasn't the only person who remained sitting down and didn't partake, but they were definitely in the minority. Will had told her that you didn't have to be an official member of the congregation or even a practicing Episcopalian to take part, but a person did have to be baptized, and she knew she never had been. She wondered, with a wry twist of her lips, what would have happened during such a procedure if it had been attempted when she was a child. Probably nothing, considering that Caleb seemed to be completely unaffected by holy water.

And at last it was over, and Gloria was telling

her that they were having a harvest luncheon in the meeting hall, and of course, Rosemary had to come. She knew all this already, since Will had tried to be as clear as he could in what to expect, but still, she was glad she had someone to guide her out of the chapel and across the way to the large hall that the church used for receptions and other gatherings. Long tables had been set up with paper tablecloths, and colorful fall arrangements of silk autumn leaves and gourds were placed in the center of those tables.

Will had warned Rosemary that it would take him a little time to get out of his priestly vestments, so she took a seat at one of the tables, assuring Gloria that she was just fine and that Will would be along in a little bit. The other woman smiled and said she would be back, but there were some people she needed to talk to.

"Thank you for keeping me company," Rosemary added, and Gloria patted her on the shoulder.

"No worries," she said. "Honestly, I'm just glad that Will found himself such a lovely girl."

She hurried off then, while yet another flush rose in Rosemary's cheeks. Yes, it was nice to know that one of the people Will worked with closely seemed to approve of her, but she wasn't used to being praised quite so overtly.

And there he was, still in the long black robe

and priestly collar he'd worn under the formal over-garments he'd donned for the service, but not quite as forbidding. No, actually, she thought he looked positively yummy in the getup, which seemed to only emphasize the breadth of his shoulders and the narrowness of his waist. "Is it wrong that I want to do unspeakable things to you while you're wearing that outfit?" she murmured when Will came to sit down next to her, and a somewhat startled but pleased grin touched his mouth.

"Probably, but I don't mind." He leaned over and whispered, "Later," in her ear, and she chuckled, even as a warm thrill spread through her body.

Highly inappropriate for a church hall, and yet at the same time, she was glad to know he could still arouse her, that the terrible knowledge she'd been cursed with hadn't changed her that much. The night before, they hadn't made love, as if he'd sensed she wasn't quite ready to take such a step. Instead, they'd snuggled against one another, taking comfort in the other person's warmth, but had done nothing more. At the time, she'd been so tired and, frankly, depressed about the whole situation that she wasn't sure if she would ever feel desire for him again.

But a new day had apparently brought a new outlook. It also probably helped that the weather had turned sunny and bright, the clouds of the day before gone without dropping anything more than a little drizzle. Rosemary felt much more like herself, despite these unfamiliar surroundings.

"Don't think I'm not going to take you up on that offer," she replied in a low voice, then straightened a little and said much more loudly, "The hall looks great."

"Thank you," he said, gray eyes dancing with amusement at the abrupt about-face. "There was a whole team in here yesterday getting everything decorated. We do this every year the Sunday before Halloween."

"You don't have a Halloween party?"

"No. Some years ago, the powers-that-be decided a harvest luncheon was more 'wholesome.' That was before I was even added to the staff here." He paused and looked around, taking in the people laughing and talking while they stood in line at the buffet tables to heap their plates, the children at the "kiddie tables" off to one side. "Every once in a while, someone brings up the notion of trying a Halloween party instead, but this is sort of a tradition now, so we've stuck with it. There are usually plenty of other options for Halloween, so no one seems to mind too much."

"Like the 'trunk-or-treat' we have in the

Village in Glendora," Rosemary said, and Will tilted his head at her.

"In all the shops downtown, you mean?"

She nodded. "It's always the day before Halloween, though, so it doesn't interfere with the 'real' trick-or-treating—or the big Halloween festival the city hosts at Finkbiner Park. That's a few blocks over from Glendora Avenue. They have games and a costume contest and a haunted house."

"Sounds like Glendora is pretty into Halloween," he commented.

"I suppose you could say that." A sudden thought struck her, and she added, "Why don't you come over to the store and help hand out candy on Wednesday? It's fun to see all the kids in their costumes—and you'll get to see my nephew Tyler's costume, too."

"That does sound like fun," Will agreed. "I don't have to dress up, do I?"

"Well, it's kind of traditional," she said. "You could just wear what you have on, though."

At once, his hand smoothed the front of the black robe he wore. "This isn't a costume, Rosemary," he said, his tone more severe than usual.

"Sorry," she said at once, chiding herself for the gaffe. "It was just a thought. You could get a black satchel and a hat...do the whole *Exorcist* thing."

He shot her a pained look, and she couldn't help grinning.

"Sorry," she said again. "I'm just teasing. No, you can wear regular clothes, but it would be better if you dressed up. The kids like that much better."

"I'll see what I can do." He reached over and touched her hand, then got up from the folding chair where he'd been sitting. "I have to go talk to a few people—why don't you get yourself a plate, and I'll come back here and join you in a few minutes?"

This didn't sound like a very enticing plan, but she knew he was working and that he couldn't spend all his time babysitting her. "Sure," she replied. "But make sure you get yourself something to eat, too. A growing boy like you needs his lunch."

That comment made him grin, and he squeezed her fingers before saying, "Be back soon."

He began to move through the crowd, pausing here and there to speak to a member of the congregation. Not schmoozing, though; Rosemary could tell he was carefully listening to all the people he stopped to talk to, that his expression was calm and sincere throughout. One pale, thin woman who looked like she could be in her late fifties, and who also looked quite ill, shadows under her eyes and a pinched look to her mouth, took him by the arm and held it while they spoke, her gaze fastened on him as though she was drowning and he'd somehow thrown her a lifeline. Will took more time with her than anyone else, Rosemary noticed, and as their conversation was ending, he pulled her to him and gave her a brief hug.

Watching all this, Rosemary realized how much he cared about all these people, that if she was going to be with him, she would have to understand that the members of this congregation would have their own claims on his time. Yes, he'd taken a day away here and there as this crazy *Project Demon Hunters* mess demanded, but his duty to All Saints and the people who worshipped there had always remained in the background.

And that was all right. Expecting anything less would be expecting Will to be someone he wasn't, and she'd fallen in love with him partly because of his warm, generous nature, the way he was unlike any other man she'd ever known.

As that thought passed through her mind, she smiled. She'd been reluctant to come here, but now she knew why Will had made the request. He'd needed her to see this, to watch and understand.

She understood. And she loved him now more than ever.

Because they'd finally had a chance to go grocery shopping after church that afternoon, Will and Rosemary were able to sit down to a real dinner for the first time since she'd come to stay at his house. Nothing terribly fancy, just a roasted pork tenderloin they got at Trader Joe's and some wild rice and vegetables, but still, as he gazed at her next to him at the dining room table, he thought this was exactly what he'd been hoping for—Rosemary at his side, in this house, eating a meal the two of them had prepared together. They'd actually asked Audrey and Michael to come over, but their friends had demurred, saying they were going to the Bahooka to get their crab puff and piña colada fix while they were still here in Southern California.

"What about Fred?" Will had asked then, and gotten a huff of a laugh from his friend.

"Apparently, Fred has a hot date with Isabel McGuire," Michael replied.

That news startled him, but Will had to admit he wasn't exactly best friends with Rosemary's sister and therefore probably couldn't be expected to know every intimate detail of her private life. And when he passed on the information to Rosemary, she'd looked surprised as well.

"Seriously?" she asked as she reached for her glass of pinot noir.

"That's what Michael said," Will replied. "I didn't ask for details.'

"Oh, I wouldn't expect you to." She sipped her wine, expression thoughtful. "It's just that I know Isabel hasn't even *tried* to date since her divorce was final. We've all encouraged her to get back out there, but she's never seemed interested."

"I guess she was just waiting for the right computer hacker to come along," he remarked, and Rosemary grinned.

"Well, we girls do tend to like rebel types with long hair."

Will resisted the urge to lift a hand to his own short-cropped hair. "So, the exact opposite of me, is what you're saying."

Her dimple flashed into life for a few seconds before she said, "No, that's not what I said. I said we 'tend' to like. That suggests it's not all of us. I've always been a sucker for the 'still waters run deep' kind of guy."

"Good to know," he replied, then drank some of his own wine. "I'd hate to have to worry about you running off with some biker type."

"Fred's a biker?" Rosemary asked, eyebrows lifting slightly.

Will paged through his brain for the few tidbits

Michael had let drop about Fred Peñasco and realized none of them had ever hinted that he owned a motorcycle. Which didn't mean much. "I have no idea. I guess it was the tattoos and the ponytail that made me think it might be a possibility."

"I hope he is one," Rosemary said emphatically. "A few rides on the back of a Harley might loosen Izzie up a bit."

That mental image made Will want to chuckle, but instead he settled for a small shake of his head as he lifted a piece of pork tenderloin to his lips and chewed thoughtfully. Again, he thought of how much he appreciated this—just the two of them sharing a meal, having a conversation that didn't involve demons or psychic powers or long-lost fathers, whether angelic or demonic. Sometimes, the absolutely normal could be the most appealing thing of all.

After dinner, they took the remaining wine out to the living room with them and drank it slowly as they snuggled on the couch. Before long, they'd set down their wine glasses and begun to kiss, the show they were watching on Netflix long forgotten.

Her body felt so alive beneath him, so warm and wonderful. Will brushed a lock of hair away from her face and whispered, "Should we go to the bedroom?"

"No," she said at once. "I like it here. Do you mind?"

He shook his head. "I don't mind."

And then he was tasting her again, savoring the sweetness of wine on her lips, the richer sensation of her own flavor beneath the wine. Her fingers fumbled with the buttons on his shirt, and then it was on the floor, followed by her sweater, her jeans. Within a moment or two, they were both naked, and he took her nipple into his mouth, running his tongue over her pebbled flesh, listening to her moan at his touch. He shifted and could feel her moist womanhood rubbing against him, making him that much harder. But did she want it like this, so quick, hardly any foreplay at all?

Apparently, she did, because she murmured, "Do it, Will. Fuck me."

He didn't mind the rough language. In a way, he understood why she'd said it. She needed to reconnect—they both did, in the most basic and elemental way possible.

Without stopping to think, he sank into her, felt her surround him and pull him in farther, her legs wrapping around his waist so she could drive him that much deeper. A groan escaped his lips at the delicious sensation, at a joining that had been put off for too long.

They stayed locked together for some time,

until he could feel the orgasm rising in him—and in her as well, judging by the way her breaths came more quickly and her moans grew louder and louder. And then she cried out in earnest, and the climax surged in him, exploding through his body as he clung to her hands and rode it out. At last, he settled on top of her, feeling her heart pound against his.

"Thank you," she whispered, and he laid a gentle kiss against her temple.

"I love you," he said.

"I love you, too."

She stared up at him with wide blue eyes. Was that a glint of tears he saw? He couldn't tell for sure—and he knew he shouldn't ask. Rosemary had needed this to come back to herself, to come back to him, and he understood that she wanted simply to accept this gift and move on.

And that was what he would allow her to do. Both for herself…and for a future he hoped might now be within reach.

Chapter 14

BEING BACK AT THE STORE FELT STRANGE—
and yet good, too, a return to normality she'd
been desperately craving. Just as it had felt so real,
so ordinary, to get up and have breakfast with
Will and then kiss each other before they went
their separate ways for the day. Rosemary knew
she would miss him, but at the same time, she was
glad to have the store waiting for her. Celeste had
called the day before to confirm that Rosemary
had been coming in, and she'd assured her sister
everything was fine and there shouldn't be any
further disruptions to their schedule.

"Good," Celeste had said. "Because I'm just
buried trying to get this costume done on time."

"What is it?" Rosemary asked. "I'm dying to
know."

"State secret," her sister replied. "You'll see on

Wednesday when we come by for the trunk-or-treat."

Because obviously, Celeste wouldn't be working that night, since she and Kevin had to take Tyler around to all the shops. That was fine, since Rosemary loved working during the Village's Halloween festivities. Isabel would be there, too, since it got so busy that they really needed to have two people around to man the store and hand out candy.

"All right," Rosemary replied with an exaggerated sigh. "It had better be spectacular."

"It will."

They'd ended the call before Rosemary could ask whether Celeste had heard anything about Isabel's supposed date with Fred Peñasco, but that was probably fine. She didn't want to turn into a complete gossip...although on the other hand, she was kind of dying to know how Michael's hacker friend had convinced her sworn-off-men big sister to go out on an actual date.

And now it was just Rosemary in the store, since Mondays tended to be slow and there was no reason for them to have two people working. She could admit to herself that she felt a little nervous being there alone, although that was silly. No one was going to come in here and do anything, not with the busy nail salon next door and people coming and going from the law office on the other side of the shop. Despite these reassurances, she found herself looking over her shoulder more than once, as if she somehow expected Caleb Lockwood to come through the front door just as he had a few weeks ago, intent on turning her world upside down.

There was no Caleb, however. Just a steadier stream of customers than she'd thought there would be, although she supposed she should have remembered that Halloween week was often a little busier than other off-season shopping periods, mostly because people tended to be more interested in anything that seemed occult or supernatural in the days leading up to the holiday. At any rate, she had enough people shopping for books and Tarot cards and incense and smudge sticks that the day passed more quickly than she'd thought it would. In fact, she was so busy that she didn't feel the slightest bit guilty about calling the deli down the street to have someone deliver her lunch, the way she'd promised Will she would. Back before she'd had the specter of the Greencastle demons hanging over her, she'd wait for a big enough break in the steady stream of customers for her to hang up the "back at one" sign on the front door and slip out, but that wasn't happening this week.

Six o'clock came quickly, and she locked up and headed out, grateful that Will would be home already and waiting for her. In fact, he'd promised to make dinner because she had to work later than he did, for which she was grateful. She didn't mind cooking, but as someone who'd lived on her own for the past five years, it was kind of nice to know that she'd get home and not have to worry about figuring what to eat.

As she headed out of the parking lot, she realized she was already thinking of Will's house as "home." Maybe that was a little premature, but she couldn't deny the feeling. Which meant… what, exactly? Her own house was sitting empty, but she hadn't lived there for several months anyway, thanks to having to escape the construction next door. It was way too early to be thinking about getting rid of the place and making her arrangement with Will more formal, but the situation would have to be addressed at some point.

Don't think about selling it, then, she told herself. *Instead, you could get a management company and rent the place out.*

That would be a good interim solution, assuming she could find renters who would overlook the noise and dust from the massive remodel going on next door. However, house rentals in Glendora were in short supply, so she had a feeling that wasn't as big a problem as she first thought.

She filed the idea away for future reference. It

was something she and Will could discuss after Halloween. Maybe it was silly, but she'd started looking at the day as the dividing line between "now" and "then," as though anything that was going to happen would have happened by then, and afterward she could get on with the rest of her life.

Or maybe not so silly. Audrey Barrett might have come to her psychic powers later in life than most, but they were strong. Rosemary had been around enough clairvoyants to be able to tell when someone was faking, and Audrey hadn't been faking that strange spell she'd experienced the day before last. For just a few seconds, the veil had parted and allowed her to see into the future. Not with any detail, but just enough to let her know something was going to happen on Halloween.

In a way, it made sense. In the United States, Halloween was a fun holiday, a chance to get dressed up and go trick-or-treating—or, if you were too old for that sort of thing, to put on a costume and go to a party or out to club or whatever. But Rosemary and all those who followed the older religions knew it was far more than that. It was Samhain, the night when the veil between this world and the next was at its thinnest, when strange powers awakened and many possibilities presented themselves...not all of them benign. If something was going to happen, that would be the night for it.

All right, they would just stay on their guard and keep an eye out for any possible demonic manifestations—or part-demon meddling. She'd already told Audrey and Michael about the trunk-or-treat in downtown Glendora the night before Halloween, but Rosemary thought it would probably be a good idea to get together on the holiday itself. They could go to the festivities in Finkbiner Park and then out for a late dinner afterward. Maybe she could convince Michael to do the whole *Exorcist* thing for his costume, since Will didn't seem terribly down with that idea.

When she got to the house, a warm, savory aroma met her nose as soon as she opened the front door. Whatever Will had been up to in the kitchen, it smelled amazing.

"I'm home," she called out as she came inside and locked the door behind her, then made a detour to drop her purse off in the bedroom.

"In the kitchen," he called back.

Sure enough, he was standing in front of the stove, wearing a crazy apron printed to look like Boba Fett's Mandalorian armor, stirring a pot.

Despite the troubled thoughts that had passed through her mind on the drive home, she couldn't help but grin at the getup. "Nice apron," she remarked as she went over and planted a kiss on his cheek. He'd gotten a little stubbly during the day, so she could feel the roughness of his beard beneath her lips, but she didn't mind too much.

"You have a problem with Boba Fett?" he asked, raising an eyebrow.

"None at all," Rosemary replied. "He's pretty badass. I guess I just didn't expect to see you channeling your inner Mandalorian while stirring a pot of…." She had to let the comment trail off there, since although whatever Will was cooking definitely smelled great, she couldn't quite figure out what it was.

"Bouillabaisse," he supplied. "I suppose I should have asked you if you had any shellfish allergies before I started throwing this together."

"No food allergies at all," she told him. "I hardly ever eat red meat, and I try not to do much dairy, but those are just diet choices, not because I have an allergy."

"Good to know. This is almost ready—I'm just waiting for the rice to finish." He lifted his chin in the direction of a small rice cooker that sat on the counter opposite where he stood.

"Perfect. Should we have a salad with this?"

"If you want. Do you mind throwing one together?"

"No, or I wouldn't have asked."

She went over to the fridge and got out the bag of mixed salad greens they'd bought at TJ's the day before, dumped some in a bowl, and then threw in a bunch of grape tomatoes and sprinkled vinaigrette over everything. Since they didn't have any croutons, there wasn't much else to do except take the bowl out to the dining room table, which had already been set.

When she came back into the kitchen, Will was scooping the rice out of the cooker and into a bright blue bowl. "Want me to get that?" she inquired.

"Thanks. I just have to transfer the bouillabaisse to a bowl, and then we're set."

She took the bowl of rice into the dining room and set it down by the salad, then took a seat in the chair to Will's right. He'd already opened a bottle of wine—some kind of red blend they'd also gotten at TJ's—so after he came in with the main course, there really wasn't much left to do except pour the wine into their waiting glasses and then dish up a little bit of everything.

One mouthful told Rosemary the bouillabaisse tasted as good as it smelled. "This is incredible," she said. "I had no idea you could cook like this."

He gave a modest shrug. "It's not Cordon Bleu or anything. But I've taught myself to cook a few things over the years, and I wanted to have something nice for your first day back to work."

"I wasn't away from work for that long," she pointed out.

"I know. Still…." The word lingered on the air for a moment, and he reached for his glass of wine. "It was kind of a big step after everything you've been through."

Now it was her turn to lift her shoulders. "Maybe. I guess I really hadn't thought about it that way. But I have to admit that it's nice to come home to something like this."

Will's eyes met hers, intent, piercing. Clearly, he hadn't missed the way she'd said "home." However, he seemed to decide it was better not to comment on the remark, because he said, "How was work?"

"Fine," she replied, letting the moment slip past. "Busy. Which was good, because I didn't have much time to stop and worry about anything. But also quiet—nothing out of the ordinary."

"That's good to hear." He sipped some wine, then added, "It seems as if they really have backed off."

"I hope so," Rosemary said, although she knew she wasn't quite so sanguine about the situation. "Maybe they're trying to figure out what to do next."

"Or deciding that it's just not worth the effort."

Once again, she guessed that was more wishful thinking than anything else. On the other hand, maybe she was being too much of a pessimist about all this. The demons had already proven that their decisions and thought processes could be downright whimsical at times, certainly not anything that followed normal human logic. It could be that they'd decided to cut their losses and focus on something else. If that turned out to be the case, she'd certainly be grateful.

"Since everything's quiet," she said, "we need to figure out your Halloween costume. It can do double duty both on the night of the trunk-or-treat and on Halloween itself. And we need to get Audrey and Michael working on something for themselves."

His left eyebrow assumed an amused tilt. "I don't think they came all the way to California to spend time working on Halloween costumes."

"No, but we just agreed that the demons seem to be lying low, so Audrey and Michael have the time to come up with something. I mean, some people do dress in civvies for these things, but you'll see way more costumes than not."

"All right," Will replied, throwing up his hands in mock surrender. "I'll give Michael a call after dinner."

"And figure out what you're going to wear," Rosemary said, since she didn't want him to think that just because he'd promised to call Michael, Will was off the hook.

"Something simple, please. I'm not much of a costume kind of guy."

What about that getup you were wearing in church? That's not a costume? she thought, although she didn't think asking those questions out loud would score her any points. Will didn't consider his vestments a costume, but rather an outward symbol of his holy office in the church. "What, you don't want me to order you a full set of Mandalorian armor off Amazon?" she teased instead, and was rewarded with a flash of a smile.

"Too hard to go to the bathroom."

"True." A complication she hadn't really stopped to think about, but which seemed obvious after Will had pointed it out. "Cowboy?"

"Maybe," he allowed, expression guarded.

A thought popped into her head. "Ooh, even better—a cowboy like Wyatt Earp in *Tombstone*. You know, one of those long black frock coats and a black hat. That would be sexy."

"That sounds kind of complicated," he replied. "Also, Halloween is only three days away. How are you going to put something like that together on such short notice?"

"Don't you know you can get pretty much anything online with rush shipping?" she returned, and he smiled in a sort of deprecating way, as if admitting defeat.

"I'm not much of a shopper."

"Well, I'll figure it out," Rosemary said. "I usually dress as a gypsy, but if I really can get a costume like that together for you, then maybe I'll be a saloon girl this year."

An interested light danced in his eyes. "That sounds interesting."

"Ah'll see what I can rustle up, Will Gordon," she told him, adopting a fake drawl, and the twitch she'd spotted at the corner of his mouth turned into a full-blown grin.

"Sounds like a plan."

They chatted some more about the festivities in Glendora—including Will giving her the rundown on the sizes she'd need if she wanted to order any costume pieces for him—and came up with a few options for dinner on Halloween, depending on what Michael and Audrey were in the mood for. After their meal, Rosemary helped Will clear the table, but he told her he'd do the rest of the cleanup so she could get on with her shopping. Just as she'd thought, there were several websites that offered the kind of Wild West outfits she was thinking of, sites that catered to re-enactors and people who did cowboy shooting.

It was a good thing her expenses tended to be

low, because she went a little crazy and did some serious damage to her credit card between all the items she was ordering and the rush shipping she had to pay for on top of everything else. Rosemary wasn't quite sure why she'd decided to go all out this year. Maybe it was relief over escaping the Greencastle demons—coupled with a desire to focus on anything other than the horrible secret about her parentage they'd revealed—or maybe it was simply that this would be the first time she'd really been part of a couple at Halloween, the first chance she'd had to choose matching costumes so she and Will would truly look like they belonged together.

Whatever the reason, she was sort of glad he didn't come to check on her while she shopped. In fact, he was just drying his hands on a dishtowel when she came into the kitchen, all signs of meal prep cleared from the counters.

"Done shopping?" he asked.

"Yes, and it'll all be here on Wednesday morning. I had everything delivered to the store, since we'll both be at work and there wouldn't be anyone here to sign for the packages."

"'Packages'?" he repeated, looking slightly alarmed.

She shrugged. "Well, I had to shop around a little and get stuff from a few different places. Luckily, they're all located either here in California or in Arizona, so it's not like anything had to be sent from the other side of the country."

"Makes sense."

Relieved that he hadn't asked any probing questions about the amount of money she'd spent on their costumes, she asked, "Any chance you can get away early on Wednesday? That way, you can meet me at the shop and get changed there. The trunk-or-treat doesn't start until five-thirty."

"I can arrange that." He bent and kissed her, a gentle brush of his lips against her cheek. Even so, that light touch was enough to get her blood racing. She remembered how they'd had sex on the couch the night before like a couple of horny teenagers, and how amazing it had been, even though the sex had been hard and fast, with no real foreplay. Yes, Will was unbelievably tender with her—but he also knew how to rock her world.

"Good," she said, then went on her tiptoes and kissed him for real, a deep kiss, their tongues touching, her breasts rubbing against his chest as she wrapped her arms around him. "Now, let me thank you properly for that amazing dinner."

Tuesday morning, Will had a meeting with All Saints' senior priest and several of the deacons so they could start planning for the busy upcoming holiday season. Because he knew he'd be occupied for most of the hours leading up until noon, he'd put his phone in airplane mode so he wouldn't be interrupted. Once the meeting was over and he'd returned to his office, he got the phone out of his pocket and winced a little when he unlocked it. Two missed calls and five missed texts…all of them from Michael. But being Michael, he never said why he was trying to get in touch with Will. All the texts and messages simply said, "Call me when you get this."

Will glanced at the clock. A little past noon. There really wasn't time for him to drive out to Glendora to have lunch with Rosemary—or for her to come here to Pasadena to be with him—but he'd planned to at least call her and check in. However, whatever was going on with Michael seemed more urgent, so he uttered an inner apology to Rosemary before he touched the screen to return Michael's last call.

The phone picked up on the first ring. No greeting, only Michael saying, "Have you seen it?"

"Seen what?" Will returned, somewhat mystified.

Michael made an exasperated sound. "Jesus, Will, it's all over the internet!"

"Sorry—I've been in a meeting all morning. What's all over the internet?"

"The goddamn footage! They released it!"

For a second, Will could only sit there at his desk, phone pressed to his ear, as he tried to process Michael's reply. "But…you still have the hard drive, don't you?"

"Yes, but obviously, they must have made a copy of everything on it. No wonder they didn't seem all that concerned about trying to get it back after you and Rosemary took it from Daniel Lockwood's house. He'd already copied the files, so what difference did it make if you had the original drive?"

"But why would they release the videos? Caleb made it sound as though that was the last thing they wanted."

A derisive chuckle came through the phone's speaker. "Yeah, because Caleb Lockwood is such a paragon of truth and plain dealing. What's even worse is that they did a pretty slick job of hack-and-slash on the footage—none of the sequences are shown in their entirety…they've been edited to show Audrey getting attacked by demons, some of the sequence in the basement, but not the conclusion, not the part that showed the two of us driving those bastards straight back to Hell."

Will absorbed this latest wrinkle, then said, "Sounds like they want to frighten people."

"Exactly—and make it seem as if there's no

real way to fight a demon, which we both know is plain wrong."

And probably the timing of the videos being dropped on YouTube two days before Halloween had some significance. Was this yet another example of the demons wanting to cause whatever chaos they could, or was there something else going on here that neither he nor Michael had yet been able to figure out?

A chill worked its way down his spine as he asked, "Who uploaded the videos?"

"They were sent to a well-known YouTuber who does a lot of supernatural and occult stuff with a little conspiracy theory shit thrown in," Michael replied. "I reached out to the guy—we've had some interactions in the past—to say that it was all copyrighted material and that whoever had given the videos to him was violating the copyright, which now belongs to Colin Turner's sister Emma. But Troy just told me it was fair use and that if Emma wanted to have her lawyer talk to him, that was just fine. I very much doubt Emma will want to get involved in any of this, so it's not as if any of my threats have much weight behind them."

Will could tell that Michael was angry and worried and annoyed all at once…not a very good combination. And he couldn't really blame him. They'd been sort of waiting for the other shoe to drop—Rosemary's elaborate Halloween plans notwithstanding—but he didn't think any of them had been expecting something like this.

"So…what do we do now?"

"I'm not sure," Michael said. "My email's going crazy, and I'm sure I'll get a call from the cable network any time now, demanding to know what the hell's going on, but this is one situation where I can plead complete innocence. I didn't upload the files, and there's no way they can prove I did. On the other hand, we all need to keep quiet about the hard drive I do have in my possession. The network doesn't know about that, and we have to keep it that way."

"I won't say anything," Will told his friend, although he doubted the network would ever reach out to him. His connection to Michael Covenant was tenuous enough that most people didn't even know it existed.

"I know you won't. But let Rosemary know, too."

"I will." He hesitated for a moment, then went ahead and asked, just because he knew Rosemary would expect him to. "Is this going to change any of our Halloween plans? Because I need to tell Rosemary if that's the case."

Michael's reply was immediate, and emphatic. "No. Actually, I'm kind of relieved that we all had plans to get together—it's probably better if we're all together as much as possible. We already had decided to go out with Fred and Isabel tonight, so I don't think I'll cancel those plans, but Audrey and I will definitely be in Glendora tomorrow for this trick-or-treat thing."

"Trunk-or-treat," Will corrected him, although he allowed himself an inner sigh of relief. Rosemary wouldn't have been happy to have Audrey and Michael cancel, although anyone would have understood their reason for doing so.

In this case, though, there was strength in numbers, and Michael seemed determined for them to be together. As to what the demons intended with the unexpected dumping of the *Project Demon Hunters* videos on YouTube, Will honestly didn't know, but better for them all to be as prepared as possible.

Because the Lord only knew what might happen next.

Chapter 15

ROSEMARY KEPT ASKING HERSELF IF THERE was something she'd overlooked when she was in Greencastle, some hint Caleb had given her about the footage that she'd simply missed because she'd been so bound up in the sheer awfulness of learning her father might actually be a cambion, a half-demon. However, as often as she mentally replayed the scenes of the two days she'd spent there, she couldn't come up with anything that felt like a missing clue. In fact, the subject of the footage had barely even come up. It was as if Caleb and his father—and the rest of the Greencastle demons—had decided *Project Demon Hunters* was no longer an issue.

Except it had turned out that wasn't the situation at all. Actually, it was the exact opposite. Because the store was busy—she was covering

Celeste's hours as her sister worked feverishly to finish Tyler's costume so it would be ready for the trunk-or-treat—Rosemary didn't have any time to watch the YouTube videos Will had called her to tell her about. To tell the truth, even if business had been slow, she wasn't sure she would have wanted to watch the footage while she was by herself. It had been much better to wait until she got home from work, and she could sit on the couch and hold Will's hand as he played it for her.

She'd seen some of the footage before, and so she could tell how it had been edited, how key elements had been cut to make it seem as if the demons had had the upper hand in all those encounters. A decent job, too; she guessed it must have been Caleb who'd made the edits. He was the film school guy, after all.

And it was obvious that the videos had gone viral, because even though they'd been posted around 10 a.m. Central time and therefore hadn't even been up a full twelve hours yet, they all had more than two million views each. Word was spreading fast.

After they'd watched the last video—there were ten in all, some of them only a few minutes each—Will set down the remote. For a long moment, neither of them spoke.

Then Rosemary said, "It's bad, isn't it?"

"Well, it doesn't look good," Will replied. His

eyes were shadowed with worry, and she couldn't blame him. What kind of effect would those videos have on the general population? Would people dismiss the whole thing as a hoax of some sort, or would they look at those terrifying pieces of footage and realize there was no way any of that could have been faked, that—impossible as it might seem—it was all real? Will went on, "I talked to Michael again this afternoon. By that point, the network had gotten in touch with him to demand an explanation. He told them the truth—that he hadn't uploaded the videos and didn't know who was responsible."

"Oh, come on, Will," Rosemary protested. "We all know who's responsible."

"All right, we know it had to be one of the Greencastle crew," he said. "But we don't know which one for sure, which is probably good enough when it comes to denying all knowledge...at least, for now. Even so, they were making noises about a lawsuit, so I think Michael is probably going to be forced to lawyer up even though he had nothing to do with it."

Ouch. While she knew Michael could afford a damn good lawyer, legal troubles were still probably the last thing he needed to deal with, especially since any litigation would be handled here in California, and presumably he and Audrey planned to head back to Tucson after Friday.

Although maybe it wouldn't come to that—maybe the network's lawyers would figure out soon enough that Michael had nothing to do with the leak and that they needed to look elsewhere for their culprit. Most likely, they'd attempt an internal audit, since of course they knew nothing about the backup footage Colin had hidden on an external hard drive and therefore would suspect that it had to have been one of their own people leaking the files stored on the network's servers.

"I'm sorry about that," she said. "Michael doesn't deserve to get that sort of mess dumped on him."

"He'll handle it. He sounded a lot more pissed off than worried, so it's probably going to be more of a nuisance than anything else." Will ran a hand through his hair and then reached for the glass of water he had sitting on the coffee table. After taking a sip, he said, "You can't see the comments because we were watching the videos on my Apple TV interface instead of watching them online, but there's a lot of chatter about this—and not just in the YouTube comments. It's gotten picked up in all sorts of forums dedicated to the supernatural and the occult."

"People trying to debunk the videos?" Rosemary asked, knowing she sounded a little too hopeful. Because the best possible outcome would be to have everyone decide the footage had been faked somehow and move on with their lives.

"Unfortunately, no." He paused, then amended his statement, saying, "Well, of course, there are a lot of skeptics. But there are also a number of people using all kinds of technical arguments to show how the footage couldn't have been faked, that it truly is real. And those voices seem to be getting louder."

She shrugged, although she knew trying to act dismissive probably wasn't going to work here. "It's blowing up right now because it's fresh. I'm sure in a day or two, people will have moved on to some other sensation. After all, there's no real way to prove those videos are real…or fake. People can argue the subject *ad nauseam* because that's what people do, but it's not going to change anything."

Will gazed at her for a long moment, expression troubled. At last, he said, "I hope you're right, Rosemary. I really do."

"But you don't think I am." She didn't bother to phrase the words as a question, not when she could see the truth of his feelings on the matter in his eyes.

"No," he said heavily. "I really don't."

Maybe he should have been expecting this. Word

of the footage had continued to spread; when he checked YouTube that morning before heading off to All Saints, he saw that most of the videos now had more than three million hits each. That was a lot of impressionable minds getting bombarded with images the human brain wasn't quite equipped to handle.

The voicemail on his office phone at the church was filled with messages from people asking questions about the videos, needing some kind of reassurance that Hell wasn't real and they'd only been the victims of an elaborate YouTube prank. Will knew he needed to return every single one of those calls and offer what comfort he could…but at the same time, he also knew he'd be lying if he told those people that yes, it was all a fake, that Hell and the demons who were supposed to dwell there were nothing more than products of the human imagination.

Whatever he would have liked to believe on the subject, Hell was very real…as were the demons who made it their home.

So he picked up his phone and returned the calls one by one, doing his best to sound calm and soothing, to tell people they had nothing to fear. Even as he spoke, though, he knew he was offering half-truths at best. No, he hadn't faced down those demons with Michael and Audrey, and yet he knew they were all too real. In some cases, belief in the power of the Holy Spirit was enough to hold those demons at bay...but not always. And especially not with the Greencastle demons, whose human blood paradoxically made them much more difficult to fight.

He knew he'd promised Rosemary he would try to leave early, but he had to spend so much time on the phone that it was doubtful he'd be able to get away much before five. The traffic heading eastbound would be horrendous, too.

"Troubling day," came Stan's voice from the doorway, and Will looked up from his satchel, where he'd been stuffing a few bits of paperwork to take home.

Damn it. While at any other time, he would have been glad to stop and talk with Stan, to get his take on the situation with the *Project Demon Hunters* footage, Will knew he didn't have the luxury of a leisurely chat, not if he wanted to get to Glendora any time close to five-thirty.

"Yes," Will said. "I've been trying to reassure people that we don't know for sure that any of those videos are even real, but it's been an uphill battle."

Stan crossed his arms and frowned slightly, deepening the lines around his dark eyes. "The footage does look fairly convincing."

"Wasn't it all from a failed TV show? They can do pretty amazing stuff with computer animation these days, even on projects that don't have typical big Hollywood budgets." There, that sounded reasonably skeptical, but not so vociferously so that it might make Stan suspicious.

"That's what I read. But even so—I've watched the videos for myself, and if those were truly effects and not real-life action, then they were some of the best computer animation I've ever seen. I also tried to offer what comfort I could to those who called asking questions, but it's difficult when even I'm not certain what I'm looking at."

"I'm sure a lot of experts are dissecting every frame," Will said, doing his best to sound unconcerned by the whole thing. "And I think I'm going to wait to hear what they have to say on the subject before I try to pass judgment."

"Probably a wise course of action," Stan replied. "I'll try to do the same."

"Anyway," Will went on, "I have an event in Glendora I need to get to. Something I promised I would do with Rosemary and her family."

"Well, then, don't let me keep you." Stan paused there for a few seconds, then added, "She seems like a lovely young woman. I'm glad you brought her to the service on Sunday so she could get acquainted with the congregation."

"Yes, she told me she had a very good time," Will responded. That was mostly the truth— Rosemary hadn't been effusive about the experience, and she hadn't promised that she would return any time soon, but neither had she said she'd felt uncomfortable or unwelcome. Which was probably the most he could hope for, considering how out of her element she had been.

"Good to hear. And have a good evening, Will."

He returned the pleasantry, then closed up his satchel as Stan left the doorway and returned to his own office down the hall. Probably about time for him to be packing it in for the day as well, although Stan didn't have far to go, since his house was only about a mile away, in the lovely historic neighborhood that bordered CalTech.

As expected, the traffic on the eastbound 210 was miserable, but at least it was just usual rush-hour sluggishness, no accidents or road construction or anything that might have made the situation any worse than it already was. Will pulled into the parking lot behind Sisters We at exactly 5:25. Cutting it close, but technically, he wasn't late.

There were already families with young children heading out from the parking lot to the street, so he knew he didn't have a moment to spare. Rosemary had told him to come and knock at the back door, since that was where the shop's bathroom was located and where she planned to leave his costume hanging up for him.

A minute after he rapped on the door, she opened it, looking harried—but also pretty spectacular. She hadn't allowed him to see the costume she'd ordered for herself, and so he didn't know quite what to expect, but what he hadn't expected was to see her in a purple brocade corset with a lacy black camisole underneath, black flounced skirts revealing fishnet hose underneath, and lace-up Victorian boots. Her mass of curly hair had been pulled up away from her face and adorned with a purple feather held in place with a jeweled clip, and her makeup was much more dramatic than anything she normally wore.

"Wow," he said, duly impressed.

"You're late," she replied, her severe tones at odds with her flamboyantly seductive appearance.

"Sorry—it was crazy today. I had to do a lot of hand-holding."

At once, the slight frown that had creased her brows disappeared. "Oh, wow—I hadn't even thought what you might have to deal with at the church today. It's okay—Isabel is holding down the fort, but I need to get back out there and help her. All your stuff is hanging in the bathroom, steamed and ready to go."

She went on her tiptoes and gave him a quick kiss on the cheek, then hurried off toward the front of the shop. Will saw the bathroom door standing open, the light on, and so he went in there and inspected his costume. It looked just as impressive as her saloon girl outfit, although far more sober—a long black frock coat and matching black wool trousers, a vest in subtle shades of slate blue and black, a white shirt with a high winged collar.

He got dressed as quickly as he could, marveling a little at how well everything fit. When he was done, he placed the wide-brimmed black felt hat on his head and grinned into the mirror.

"Eat your heart out, Wyatt Earp," he said, and turned off the bathroom light.

Up front, Rosemary and Isabel were busy handing out candy to the first wave of trunk-or-treaters who'd arrived on the scene. Isabel was costumed as Professor McGonagall from Harry Potter, her curly hair pulled back from her face into a severe knot and her elegant, slender form made even more striking by the dark green velvet robes and tall pointed witch hat she wore. The entire ensemble was so professional-looking, he wondered where she'd gotten it.

When he greeted her and then asked about the costume, she gave him a pleased smile. "Oh, I made it—well, everything except the hat. I bought that on Etsy."

Rosemary had mentioned that both her sisters sewed, but for some reason, he hadn't thought they were skilled enough to be professional costumers. He wondered why Rosemary didn't sew as well, although he supposed it was possible she just wasn't interested. "It's an amazing costume," he told her. "You look like you walked right off the set of one of the Harry Potter movies."

A faint flush spread along her cheekbones, emphasizing her resemblance to her younger sister. Still, she seemed to brush off the compliment, saying, "Wait until you see what Celeste made for Tyler."

Will glanced over at Rosemary, who was busy handing out snack-size Snickers and Kit Kats to a group of kids who looked to be around seven or eight, and included a ballerina, a little girl in a long black dress and carrying a test tube who he thought was supposed be Marie Curie, and a pretty convincing werewolf. She grinned and said, "I'm in the dark, too. Since I wasn't involved in making it, I get to be surprised along with everyone else."

"You all take Halloween pretty seriously, don't you?" he asked as he went over to Rosemary so he could grab another bowl of candy and be ready for the next group of children who came along.

The two sisters exchanged a glance. "Well, for anyone who follows the old religion, Samhain is a very important holiday," Isabel said. "But yes, we're all big fans of Halloween. Our mother really got into it when we were kids—sewed us some amazing costumes, decorated the house like crazy back before it was as popular as it is now."

"It was lots of fun," Rosemary chimed in. "Mom used to dress up as a witch and sit on the porch in a rocking chair, and she'd hold a big bowl of candy in her lap as she sat there and rocked. You had to reach in the bowl and try to get a piece of candy without her grabbing you. She had dry ice fog swirling around and everything."

Will tried to visualize pretty, cheerful Glynis McGuire dressed up as a scary witch and didn't succeed very well, but he supposed you had to be there. For a moment, he recalled the Halloweens back in his Massachusetts neighborhood when he was young—the crunch of dead leaves under his feet, the scent of wood smoke that seemed to hang in the air...the sweaters his mother tried to force him to wear with his costumes because it was really too cold to go around without one. Luckily, he always won those battles, but he had a feeling she made the effort every year because otherwise she wouldn't have felt as though she was doing her motherly duty.

Just good, simple fun from a time when the world didn't seem quite so frightening and demons were something you used in ghost stories to scare the crap out of your friends. Too bad they'd turned out to be all too real.

Luckily, those dark thoughts were chased away by the arrival of another group of trunk-or-treaters, and for the next twenty minutes or so, Will and Rosemary and Isabel didn't have much time to chat, since the kids were coming in steady waves now, the volume growing greater and greater as more parents got home from work and started to make the rounds with their children.

And then, just a little after six, Celeste and Kevin showed up with Tyler.

No wonder they'd tried their best to keep the project a secret. Because their son was so young—Will remembered that Rosemary had said Tyler was two—they'd concocted a costume that allowed him to ride around in his wagon while they pulled it. Of course, you had to strain to see the wagon at all, because it was covered in a sort of crazy quilt of metallic gold and silver and copper fabric, stitched to look like a pile of treasure. Sitting in the middle of the quilt was Tyler himself, wearing a dragon costume in shades of dark copper and brown and umber. His little face was just barely visible through the dragon's mouth, but he looked mightily pleased with himself.

"Holy crap," Rosemary said as she stared down at her nephew. "That's amazing."

"Thanks," Celeste said, looking justifiably proud of herself. Her hair was braided back in an intricate style, and Will noticed that she wore fake prosthetic points on her ears. Judging by the ears and the elaborate green costume she wore, he guessed she was supposed to be an elf of some sort.

"Smaug, right?" Rosemary asked then, and Tyler grinned from inside the dragon head he wore.

"SMOG!" he shouted.

Right, from *The Hobbit*. Will hadn't seen the films, so he didn't know who Celeste was supposed to be. But Rosemary's brother-in-law, buried under a long white wig and fake beard and gray robes, was undoubtedly dressed up as Gandalf.

"Well, Smog," Rosemary said, obviously mispronouncing the name on purpose, "do you want some candy to add to your treasure?"

"Snickers!" Tyler shouted.

Rosemary grinned. "Okay, kiddo, Snickers coming right up." She dug around in the bowl she held and extracted two of the miniature candy bars, and dropped them into the large plastic pumpkin Kevin was holding.

"What do you say, Tyler?" Celeste prompted.

"Thank oo, Auntie Rosemy," Tyler responded.

Will couldn't help smiling a little at the boy's mispronunciation of his aunt's name. Then again,

"Rosemary" was kind of a mouthful for a two-year-old.

The two-year-old in question was staring up at him now, blue eyes wide even shadowed as they were by the head of the dragon costume he wore. "You're scary," he announced, and Rosemary and Isabel both chuckled, even as Celeste looked reprovingly at her son.

"He's not scary, Tyler," she said. "He's a cowboy."

Apparently, Tyler was having none of it, because he replied, "He doesn't have a cowboy hat."

"It's kind of cowboy hat," Rosemary put in, obviously seeing the need to defend her companion. "He's Wyatt Earp, a famous gunslinger."

But it seemed Tyler had decided to be contrary. "He doesn't have any guns."

"No guns on Halloween," Will said, doing his best to mimic a western drawl. "That's the law."

Tyler's eyes grew even more owlish. "Really?"

"Really."

At that moment, a large group of trunk-or-treaters began to enter the shop, which was already starting to feel a bit crowded. "We need to keep going and make the rounds," Celeste said. "But you all are coming to the carnival at Finkbiner tomorrow night, right?"

"Wouldn't miss it," Isabel replied. "Go on—load up on candy."

"That's the plan," Kevin said, voice a little muffled by the heavy beard he was wearing. "We'll try to stop by again after we've done the circuit."

"Have fun!" Rosemary called out, and her sister smiled and gave her a thumbs-up as Kevin squeezed Tyler and his wagon out through the door.

After that, they were busy for quite a while and didn't have a chance to talk much, because the waves of children just kept coming. Will knew that Glendora was bigger than it seemed, but he honestly hadn't expected there to be quite so many kids, enough that he started to wonder if Isabel and Rosemary had enough candy on hand to feed them all. Yes, he'd seen the bags of fun-size candy bars stashed under the counter, but it still didn't quite seem enough.

However, he pushed his worries away, figuring that the McGuire sisters had been working this event for years and most likely knew exactly what to expect. And he was actually glad of the crush, just because the constant influx of new faces and new costumes meant he didn't have much time to think about anything else, including the *Project Demon Hunters* footage that was now making the rounds on the internet. It was a problem they couldn't ignore forever, but for now it was enough to hand out candy and to praise the kids' costumes, and in the few moments where they had a bit of breathing space, to allow himself a glance at Rosemary and admire how beautiful she looked. Of course, she was lovely with no makeup and her hair mussed from sleep, but it was also fun to see how she could change her appearance so drastically when she wanted to.

And fun was something they all needed right then. Halloween was nearly upon them, and he had no idea what to expect, but for now it felt good to live in this moment and enjoy it, to pretend that no shadow hung over them and that they had nothing bigger to worry about than where they planned to go out to eat after the trunk-or-treat officially ended at eight o'clock.

He was also starting to wonder what had happened to Michael and Audrey, since they'd promised to attend the event and it was now almost seven o'clock. But even as worry started to sink its claws into him, the two of them walked through the shop's entrance, and Rosemary let out a delighted peal of laughter.

"Yay—you did it after all!" she exclaimed.

Because although Will would never have worn his vestments as a costume, Michael obviously had no such scruples. He'd slicked his over-long hair back as best he could, and wore a black suit with the priest's collar prominent at his throat and a black fedora covering his head. In one hand, he held a black satchel. Next to him, Audrey was wearing a sparkly red devil costume which, although not as skimpy as some he'd seen, still showed a good deal of leg and cleavage.

"Well, it was kind of a moral imperative," Michael said.

"I wanted to be a nun," Audrey put in, sounding a bit aggrieved. "But they were out of my size, so Michael suggested this."

"I can see why," Rosemary replied with a grin. "Going to take her home for a bit of exorcising after this, Michael?"

He tried to look stern, but there was a glint in his gold-gray eyes that told Will his friend probably planned to do that very thing. "Hey, she picked it out."

"Because it was the least offensive devil costume in my size," Audrey said. "But whatever. We're here. Have we missed much?"

"Well, you didn't get to see my nephew," Rosemary said. "But Celeste and Kevin said they'd swing by before they left, so all is not lost."

Although Audrey had looked a little worried to hear she might have missed the star of the show, she relaxed slightly when she heard they'd have a second chance to see Tyler. "Oh, good. I know we'll get to see his costume tomorrow, too, but I was looking forward to that."

"Fred didn't come with you?" Isabel asked, trying to sound casual but not doing a very good job of it.

Michael and Audrey exchanged a glance. Then Michael said, "He told me to send his apologies— he's trying to get a costume together and he sort of ran out of time for tonight. But he said he'd definitely come tomorrow night for the carnival and dinner afterward."

She relaxed visibly. "Oh, that's fine. I told him he didn't need to worry about a costume, but he seemed to think it was important since the rest of us were dressing up."

"And I wasn't going to try to dissuade him," Michael replied. "I know what Fred's like when he gets the bit between his teeth."

They all smiled at that remark, but soon after, it was back to handing out candy, since another group of trunk-or-treaters showed up then. Seeing that they were busy, Audrey and Michael excused themselves, saying they were going to roam a bit but would be back in a little while.

"Don't want to miss Tyler a second time!" Audrey said, and Rosemary gave her a thumbs-up.

Shepherding this latest group of children was a woman who looked to be around Isabel's age, maybe a little older. After the kids had gotten their candy and were about to move on to the next shop, the woman with them said, "You all look amazing! I know it's kind of late notice, but we're having a Halloween party at the Castle tomorrow night, and I'd love it if you could drop by."

"'The Castle'?" Will repeated, wondering if he'd heard her correctly.

"Rubel Castle," Rosemary said. "It's kind of a landmark."

The woman smiled. "Yes, we actually got our historic designation a while back, but I know a lot of people have never heard of it."

"And you're with the historical society, right?" Rosemary asked. "I think I remember seeing you at the booth at the street fair last spring."

"Yes, that's me," the woman replied. "Lena Margolies. Anyway, come by if you can. Just tell them Lena sent you. But I have to run—I need to keep an eye on the kids. Have a good one!"

She went out, and Will sent a questioning look at Rosemary.

"It should be a lot of fun," she said. "I did a tour of Rubel Castle a few years ago—it's this crazy place that this guy named Michael Rubel and a bunch of his friends built over the course of several decades. People still live there, although Michael Rubel himself died some time ago."

Isabel spoke then. "It does sound like fun. I'd heard that they had Halloween parties there, but it's sort of an invitation-only kind of thing."

"Well, it sounds like we have an invitation," Michael said. "The question is…should we really accept it?"

"Why not?" Rosemary demanded, hands on her hips. A big amethyst glinted from her hand, a ring Will didn't think he'd seen before.

"Are you forgetting Audrey's vision? The one that indicated this would all be over by All Saints Day? That seems to imply that something is going down tomorrow night on Halloween."

"We don't know what it is, though," Audrey pointed out. "Honestly, wouldn't we be safer at a party surrounded by people?"

"Strangers," he returned, and Rosemary shook her head.

"Not complete strangers. I mean, all right, I didn't know Lena by name, but I've seen her before. I'm sure there will be other familiar faces at the party, because it's a locals-only sort of thing. And it does sound like fun. You'll love Rubel Castle—it's built of stone with all sorts of found objects embedded in the concrete. There's a caboose and underground rooms and all sorts of crazy stuff. I can't think of a better place to spend Halloween night."

For a moment, Michael was silent, obviously pondering what Rosemary had just told him. Then he looked around at the eager faces that surrounded him and appeared to relent. "All right," he said at last. "But I'm stocking up on holy water, just the same."

"Well, it goes with the costume," she said with a grin, and he sent her a pained look.

The discussion was effectively tabled then, since Celeste and Kevin returned with Tyler, and there was much oohing and aahing over his Smaug costume. He'd gotten quite the haul at the trunk-or-treat, and clearly was ready to go home so he could devour his spoils.

"Only two," Celeste warned him, but he didn't seem too worried by the restriction.

"Four," he said, holding up five fingers, and Kevin smiled.

"We'll see, buddy."

They made some quick plans for their meet-up at the Halloween carnival the following afternoon, then rolled Tyler away.

There was still almost an hour left until the trunk-or-treat officially ended, but Will could tell it was starting to wind down. They handed out candy—and still had several unopened bags left, which sort of shocked him—and then closed everything down a little after eight. Rosemary suggested heading over to a place called Luca Bella, which was just down the block and around the corner. Everyone agreed this sounded like a good idea, rather than driving somewhere else in all their various cars. Isabel bowed out, saying it had been a long day…although Will got the impression that she simply didn't want to be the fifth wheel and so excused herself.

But even without her, dinner was a lively affair —the food was good, the wine list decent, and everyone seemed to be doing their best to pretend all was well in the world. Even Michael, who usually tended to be the one to bring people back to reality, apparently had decided to let it go. Maybe he'd decided, much as Will had, that since they had no idea what the Greencastle demons were even up to, they might as well relax and enjoy themselves now while they had the chance.

The next day could be decidedly different.

Chapter 16

Although the internet buzz about the *Project Demon Hunters* footage didn't seem to have died down—if anything, it had only intensified—Rosemary still found herself looking forward to Halloween night. She hadn't experienced any strange premonitions or feelings, and neither, apparently, had Audrey.

"You may all be putting more meaning into that 'flash' of mine than you should," Audrey had said when Rosemary called during her lunch break. "It's not as if I have some kind of world-class reputation as a clairvoyant or something."

"No, but your intuition has been pretty good in the past," Rosemary replied. "Still, I know what you mean. The footage is out there, and the world hasn't ended."

Audrey had made a disgusted sound at that

comment. "Well, your world hasn't. Michael's been on the phone with his lawyer all morning."

Uh-oh. "That bad?"

"I don't know yet. But when you get right down to it, Michael really didn't have anything to do with what happened to the footage. I know he and Colin had discussed doing something similar, but it's not a crime to talk about something. So this may end up being a bunch of sound and fury, but we won't know for a while yet."

"And here I am, dragging him out to a Halloween party."

"It'll do all of us some good," Audrey said, obviously doing her best to make sure Rosemary wouldn't feel guilty about playing social director. "And actually, we looked up that Rubel Castle place online after we got home last night, and it seems like an amazing place. Michael's actually really interested in checking it out, says he wants to see if it's at all psychically active."

That sounded like something Michael would want to do. It was too bad Colin Turner was gone; he probably could have shot some interesting footage at the castle. Assuming, of course, that the historical society would have even allowed a camera crew in the place.

"You'll love it," Rosemary told her friend. "It's the kind of crazy spot that you'd never expect to find in sleepy old Glendora. How could I turn down a chance for us to spend Halloween in a place like that?"

"You couldn't. We're really looking forward to it—even if Michael is being all doom and gloom about my supposed 'prediction.'"

"He shouldn't be. For all any of us knows, it was simply telling us that we were past the worst and there was nothing else to worry about."

Even as she spoke those words, though, Rosemary couldn't help feeling that she was being overly sanguine about the situation. It still felt as though she'd missed something vitally important, although she couldn't say what. And things had been quiet ever since she'd returned from Indiana. Surely if something was going to go down, she should have caught a hint of it. Even her dreams had been calm, placid. Although she couldn't exactly explain how or why, it was almost as if the stream of impressions she tapped into to get a reading on a place or an object had simply been turned off.

It seemed Audrey wasn't quite convinced, either, because she only said, "Maybe," and left it there. They didn't have the time to get into it any more than that, because one o'clock was almost upon them, and Rosemary needed to unlock the door and take the "be back in" sign down.

After saying that she and Michael would be at the shop a little before five, Audrey hung up.

Rosemary threw the wrapper from her sandwich in the trash and reopened the store, although she didn't expect to get too many customers. The lead-up to Halloween was busy, but once the day itself arrived, things tended to quiet down. Fine by her; she already had a sign in the window that said, "closing at 4:30 on Halloween," so would-be customers would know what to expect. She hadn't dressed up that day since there weren't any events in the downtown area itself, and she needed that extra time to change. Will planned to get into his costume at the house; it wasn't that far out of the way, and dressing up in advance would simplify things for everyone.

Four-thirty rolled around, and Rosemary turned the "closed" sign around and locked the door, then headed back to the bathroom so she could get changed into her costume. Because Halloween itself was quiet, Isabel hadn't worked that day, and instead planned to come by a little before five.

It felt kind of strange to climb out of her clothes and into her costume, knowing she was all alone in the place, and so Rosemary got dressed as quickly as she could, fingers flying up the metal clasps on the front of her corset. Once she was fully dressed—or as dressed as she could be, in that kind of getup—she worked on dark-ening her makeup, pulling her hair up and fastening the feather to one side with its jeweled clip.

All that done, she folded her street clothes and put them in the little overnight bag she'd used to carry some of her costume bits and pieces, then stowed it on a spare stretch of shelf in the storage room.

When she turned around, she saw Madeline Nash standing in front of her.

A gasp escaped her lips. "M-madeline," she stammered. "What are you doing here? I thought you'd moved on."

The ghost stared at her with blank, dark eyes. "You didn't keep it safe."

"What?" Rosemary asked. "Keep what safe?"

"The footage," Madeline whispered. "They took it, and it's everywhere."

Guilt assailed her, even though Rosemary knew she and Will and everyone else had done their best to keep Colin's files out of the demons' hands. "I know," she said sadly. "We tried, Madeline. We didn't know that they'd made a copy. But it will be okay—people forget about this stuff when the next shiny thing comes along. We just have to be patient."

"You don't understand," the ghost said. "It's out, and so is its power. You can't stop that."

"What power?" Rosemary tried to sound calm, but that comment about the footage's "power" had made an uneasy chill shudder its way down her neck. "What are you talking about?"

But the ghost was already growing dim. "Can't...stop...it...."

And then she was gone.

Rosemary stared at the spot where Madeline's ghost had been standing—floating, really—but there was no trace of her.

Three knocks sounded on the back door, and she nearly jumped out of her skin. Then she realized it had to be Will, showing up right when he'd said he would. With shaking fingers, she unlocked the door and opened it. He stood outside, almost impossibly gorgeous in his Wild West getup, but she found she wasn't quite as thrilled by the sight as she knew she should be.

"Hi, Rosemary," he began, then stopped as he appeared to get a better look at her. "What's the matter? You look like you've seen a ghost."

She gave him a humorless grin. "I have."

"What?"

Rosemary closed the door and locked it, saying, "Madeline Nash was here just a minute ago."

Will glanced around, as if expecting to see some trace of the ghostly visitor. "I thought she'd moved on," he said, his voice troubled.

"So did I. But apparently, she had different ideas." Now that Will was here, Rosemary realized that her hands were shaking. She clenched them as she went on, "It seems she isn't too happy with us for letting the demons release the footage."

"We didn't exactly 'let' them," he said.

"I know. I tried to tell her that. Anyway, she said something about the power in them being 'out' and how we couldn't stop it now."

His brows drew together as he appeared to puzzle through that remark. Then his expression grew even grimmer. "I wonder if she was talking about what I've been seeing—people's faith being challenged by all this."

"It's not that bad, is it?" Rosemary put a hand on Will's arm, trying to reassure herself with the sense of strength she got from that touch. "I mean —it's just some viral videos. This sort of stuff always peaks and then gives way to the next big thing."

"Except most viral videos don't make people question their beliefs about God and the universe," he replied, crystalline eyes cloudy with worry.

No, she supposed not. But since there wasn't much any of them could do about it, she tried to reassure herself that Madeline appearing now wasn't the dark portent it appeared to be. "I still think you're overestimating people's attention spans," she said lightly, and he seemed to relax a little.

"I hope you're right."

Another knock on the back door. This time, it was Isabel outside, back in her Professor McGonagall costume. She looked at her sister and said at once, "What's the matter?"

Rosemary glanced at Will, and he gave a barely imperceptible lift of his shoulders.

But because it was Izzie—who would be able to tell right away if her sister was trying to keep something from her—Rosemary explained what had happened.

Isabel shook her head. "This isn't good."

"I know that, but, as I was just telling Will, I don't know if there's much we can do about it."

"Maybe not, but…we should all be careful tonight."

"Already planning on it," Will said, hands resting on his hips. No, he wasn't wearing even fake guns as part of his costume, but something about the way he stood seemed to indicate he was mentally preparing for a different kind of battle than the one that had gone down at the OK Corral.

Isabel gave a nod, although her expression was still troubled, as if she wasn't sure whether any of them were prepared for what might be looming on this particular Halloween. Before she could speak, though, there was yet another knock at the back door.

Michael and Audrey this time…and with Fred Peñasco accompanying them, although it took Rosemary a second or two to recognize him. She had absolutely no idea where he'd managed to dig up the costume, but he was dressed as Professor Snape from the Harry Potter movies, right down to the shaggy black hair.

"I thought Isabel and I should be a matched set, since the rest of you are," he explained as the group entered the receiving area at the back of the store. "So, I found myself a Snape costume."

"How do you just 'find' a Snape costume?" Rosemary inquired, surprised enough by his appearance to momentarily forget about her encounter with Madeline's ghost.

"Well, if you're Fred, you dig around on the internet," Audrey said. "And then you pull in a few favors."

Fred gave a modest shrug, a gesture that looked vaguely ludicrous under all those heavy, sweeping robes. "I knew somebody who knew somebody. They tracked the costume down for me. And here we are."

"You look wonderful," Isabel said.

He raised a skeptical eyebrow. "Even with this hair?"

The question elicited a smile. "Even with that hair." She looked away from Fred, over at her sister, and Rosemary gave the faintest shake of her head. Maybe it was foolish not to tell Michael and Audrey and Fred what had just happened with Madeline's ghost, but Rosemary didn't see the point in upsetting everyone. They were going to have a good time tonight, even if it killed her.

"Well," she said briskly, "we might as well head over to Finkbiner Park. I was going to suggest we walk, but if we're going to go up to Rubel Castle immediately afterward, then it doesn't make much sense to do that. Maybe we should carpool?"

"Two cars, though," Michael replied. "None of our cars are big enough to cram all six of us in."

Which was true, especially with several of them wearing bulky costumes.

"Well, the four of you can go in Audrey's car," Will suggested. "And Rosemary and I can take mine. We'll collect her car from the parking lot here at the end of the night. It'll be safe, won't it?"

"Oh, sure," she said. "I've left it overnight here once or twice."

"And I walked, so I don't have a car," Isabel put in. "So that makes it that much easier. My mother went with Celeste and Kevin because she wanted to see Tyler in the costume contest."

"Sounds like it's all handled, then," Will said. "What time is the contest?"

"Oh, not until six," Isabel replied. "We have time."

Even so, they all trooped out of the store then, Rosemary pausing to lock up and turn on the alarm as she went. She waved at the other two couples as they got into Audrey's CR-V, then gingerly climbed into Will's Dodge Challenger—a feat that wasn't as easy as it looked, what with her floofy skirts and feather in her hair, not to mention the corset. It was a real one with metal bones, made for reenactors, and bending over in the thing was kind of a challenge.

"I don't know how women managed back in the day," she remarked as Will helped her with the seatbelt, since she wasn't very bendable.

"I kind of doubt they were getting in and out of muscle cars," he replied, smiling a little. "And also, they were used to wearing those things."

She supposed so. Well, at least after this evening, she wouldn't have to wear the corset again until next Halloween…unless Will asked nicely, of course.

The thought made her smile to herself, an expression he obviously caught, even though she'd thought his attention was on the road, since they'd just pulled out of the parking lot and onto Meda Avenue.

"Looking forward to partying at Rubel Castle?" he asked.

"Oh, yes," Rosemary replied. It was probably better not to mention what she'd really been thinking about. "I can't wait for everyone to see the place. It's really amazing. But also...I suppose I was thinking about how nice it was to have all of us together in one place, being able to go out and do something social. I doubt that Michael and Audrey were visualizing this sort of outing when they came back to California."

"No, probably not," Will agreed. A small hesitation before he went on, "It seems like Fred is pretty taken with your sister. I doubt he would have put that much effort into hunting down that Snape costume if he wasn't interested in her."

Rosemary had been thinking much the same thing, so she nodded. "That was really sweet of him. And it looks to me like Isabel is actually receptive, too, which is surprising. Not that Fred isn't worthy of her or anything, but just that she's been so down on the whole dating thing for the past few years that we all sort of decided she'd given up on men."

Will's brows lifted slightly. "It doesn't look that way to me."

"No, me neither. And Fred isn't so far away that the two of them dating is totally out of the question. Michael said he lives in Redlands, right?"

"I think so," Will replied, although his attention was obviously fixed on the road ahead of them, since they'd already made the short hop to the street where Finkbiner Park was located. It was still a block south of them, but there didn't seem to be many parking spaces available.

"Drive another block," Rosemary instructed him. "We'll have to walk across the park, but it's probably not so crowded on Minnesota Avenue."

"Got it."

He followed her instructions, and just as she'd hoped, there were still spots available on the street that bordered the northwest side of the park. They slid in behind a Ford Explorer and parked the car, then got out. Since it was still early in the evening, daylight lingered, although the shadows grew long and Rosemary knew it would be dark soon enough.

"That way," she said, pointing, and headed out across the field toward the area that had been set up for the Halloween carnival. The scent of kettle corn drifted on the air, and she could hear kids laughing and shouting in excitement.

The event wasn't actually a full-blown carnival, since there weren't any actual rides. But there was a haunted house and a hay bale maze, and booths where you could try your hand at winning a stuffed animal, or pause and get your face painted. In the bandstand, a group that looked as if it was made up of local high school kids was playing a revved-up version of "The Monster Mash."

And there were Michael and Audrey and Fred

and Isabel, walking in from the other direction. It seemed they'd had better luck getting parking than Will and Rosemary had. Isabel waved, and the two of them sped up their pace a little to meet up with the rest of their group.

"Any sign of Mom and Kevin and Celeste?" Rosemary asked as they approached, and Isabel shook her head.

"No, but I'm sure we'll bump into them soon enough. What's the plan?"

"Mill about aimlessly until the costume contest starts?" Rosemary suggested, and everyone chuckled.

"Mill about, it is," Michael said. "I think I'll start with the kettle corn."

They all ended up getting some, since they wouldn't be eating any "real" food for another couple of hours. Afterward, they walked around and looked at the various costumes and ate kettle corn, until at last they bumped into Glynis, who was with Kevin.

"They're already getting the kids lined up for the costume contest," she said, explaining why Celeste and Tyler were absent. "But it should be starting in a few more minutes."

Rosemary extended her bag of kettle corn toward her mother, offering some, and Glynis shook her head. With a shrug, Rosemary asked,

"Are you coming to Rubel Castle with the rest of the gang?"

"I thought I would, since it sounded like an open invitation. I've lived in the San Gabriel Valley my entire life, and yet I somehow never managed to visit the Castle."

"Perfect timing, then."

A woman wearing a black long-sleeved T-shirt and a headband with cat ears walked onto the stage that had been set up at one end of the carnival, leaned into the microphone at the side of the stage, and welcomed everyone to the carnival, then announced that the costume contest would be starting in five more minutes.

Good. While it had been fun to walk around and chat, Rosemary knew she was anxious for the costume contest to start so they could head up to Rubel Castle once the contest was over. And since Celeste and Kevin planned to bring Tyler along, at least for a little bit, it wasn't as though she'd be abandoning them to go party elsewhere.

Will leaned in close and murmured, "Do you think Tyler's going to win?"

"I don't see how he couldn't," she replied. "I mean, I've gotten to see a lot of kids' costumes between yesterday and today, and I haven't seen anything that was better than what Celeste made for Tyler. But I guess we'll just have to see. He's so young, I don't think he even really understands what the contest is about, but I know Celeste would like to win—both for bragging rights, and because the grand prize is a hundred-dollar gift card to JoAnn Fabrics. She could do a lot of damage with that."

"Like starting on next year's costume?"

"Exactly," Rosemary said with a grin.

The cat-eared emcee came back and said they were getting started, then announced the first entry, a little girl in a blue dress and a long white wig—Elsa from *Frozen.* An assortment of monsters, fairy princesses, and other characters marched across the stage after her…and then Tyler came on somewhere in the middle, accompanied by Kevin, who was pulling the wagon.

The crowd started cheering loudly, telling Rosemary that they'd just seen their favorite. Some of the other costumes were very well done, including the kid in Mandalorian armor made out of cardboard and papier maché, but none of them could really compare to Tyler's gleaming, golden Smaug costume.

So, it wasn't all that much of a surprise when Tyler won first place. Celeste came out with him to accept the gift card—and the surprise basket of Halloween candy that went along with it. From the resigned expression on her face, Rosemary guessed her sister could have done without another load of candy in her house, but she supposed Celeste would figure out something to do with it that wouldn't involve getting her son high on more sugar than he was allowed to eat in a year.

Afterward, Kevin and Celeste and Tyler met up with the rest of their group and were congratulated all around. Looking triumphant but a little tired—Rosemary had to wonder how much sleep her sister had lost getting that costume done on time—Celeste said, "Are we heading out now? I can tell Tyler is starting to get a little pooped, so I don't want to keep him up too late."

"That was the plan," Rosemary said. "We'll carpool and meet there. I know Lena is expecting all of us, so it shouldn't be a problem if we don't all arrive at the same time."

Celeste nodded. "Good. Okay—see you there."

They went their separate ways then, Rosemary and Will headed back to his car, while the rest of the group went in the opposite direction to retrieve their own vehicles. Rosemary explained how to get to the castle, along with alternates for parking if there wasn't anything available on Live Oak Avenue, the street where Rubel Castle was actually located. The spot in question wasn't that far from Finkbiner Park, so in less than five minutes, they'd arrived at their destination, getting a spot around the corner on Palm Avenue.

"Ready?" Rosemary asked, and Will nodded.

"Yes. You know, this will be my first castle."

She grinned. "You're going to love it."

Honestly, Will hadn't quite known what to expect of the place. In the middle of a quiet, upscale neighborhood on the east end of town, gray stone walls loomed out of the darkness, topped with honest-to-God turrets and crenellations. He paused on the steeply sloping street in front of Rubel Castle and stared up in awe. "It really is a castle."

"Well, yeah. Why else would they call it that?" Rosemary tugged on his hand, pulling him along, and he followed, doing his best not to gape at his surroundings.

Through a tall iron gate, and then into a courtyard crowded with people in all sorts of wild costumes—court jesters and gypsies and fairies and devils. Will recognized the woman who'd come into Sisters We the night before and extended the invitation to Rosemary, mostly because she was wearing a long black dress and a choker made of lace but otherwise hadn't done much to alter her appearance for the occasion. She sat at a table in the center of the courtyard, a cash box on the table in front of her.

"Hi!" she said brightly as Rosemary and Will approached. "We're not charging to get in or anything, but the historical society would appreciate a donation."

"No problem," he said at once, digging in his pants pocket for his wallet so he could pull out a twenty-dollar bill. While he certainly didn't mind making a donation to a worthy cause, he thought it was a little shifty that Lena hadn't mentioned the donation angle when she invited Rosemary and her friends and family.

Apparently, Rosemary was thinking about the same thing, because she frowned slightly as Will handed over the money, although she didn't comment. "Anything we need to know about the party?" she asked, tone carefully neutral.

"Not really," Lena replied. "There are refreshments over in the next courtyard and a cash bar. Water and sodas are free. We have access to the upper levels chained off to avoid any mishaps, and also to keep people from wandering into the private spaces where we still have tenants."

"So, people really do live here?" Will glanced up at the high walls of the castle, at the windows he spied in some of them, where dim lights showed in the darkness.

Lena gave him an indulgent smile. "Yes, there are a few apartments that are still occupied. So, just try to respect their privacy, you know?"

"No worries," Rosemary said. "I doubt I'm going to do much climbing in these heels."

"Good idea," Lena said with a chuckle. "Enjoy yourselves."

Will took Rosemary's hand in his, and they left the courtyard where they'd been standing and moved on to the next one. As Lena had said, there were long tables set out with a dizzying assortment of goodies arranged on them. To one side, there was a tiki-style bar with a guy in a pretty decent Beetlejuice costume playing bartender.

"Do you want something to drink?" Will asked. "It's probably a good idea to hang out here until the rest of our party arrives."

"Sure," Rosemary replied at once. "I think I ate enough kettle corn to create a nice cushion."

Probably, that sugary snack wasn't the best base to lay down in terms of consuming alcohol, but there was also plenty of food here to ensure they wouldn't exactly be drinking on an empty stomach. Will asked the bartender for a couple of glasses of red wine—he guessed they only had one kind, so he didn't bother to specify the varietal—then handed over a ten-dollar bill and got a couple of plastic cups of wine in exchange. He took them over to one side, where Rosemary was looking at her surroundings with a faint abstracted frown pulling at her brows.

"Everything all right?" he asked her as he handed over one of the cups.

She accepted it, took a cautious sip, and nodded approvingly. "That's actually not bad."

Will allowed himself a swallow. Yes, for something they were selling for five bucks a glass, it was more than decent. It seemed as though whoever had organized the Halloween party here wasn't trying to make a profit on the concessions.

"Anyway," Rosemary went on, "there's something about this place. It gives me a weird feeling."

Her comment set off alarm bells in his mind, but he told himself there wasn't necessarily any reason for worry. "Weird" could mean all sorts of different things. "Weird how?"

She frowned briefly, as if she was having trouble quantifying something that was difficult to pin down. "I don't know, exactly. The energy here is different from any other place I've ever been. It's strong."

"Evil?" he asked, hoping he didn't sound too concerned.

"No. It's more…neutral. But zingy at the same time."

"Do you remember feeling it when you first visited here back in high school?"

At once, she shook her head. "I don't think so. Or at least, if I felt something, it wasn't like what

I'm feeling now. But that was ten years ago…a lot has changed since then."

And a lot had changed for Rosemary just in the past couple of weeks. Will wasn't terribly surprised that she was having a different experience now than she'd had as her younger self.

"I'll ask Izzie and Celeste when they show up —and Audrey," Rosemary added. "It might be nothing."

Or it might be everything, considering the prediction Audrey had made about All Saints Day. Except Rosemary had just said that what she was feeling now wasn't good or evil, which seemed to indicate it couldn't involve the Greencastle demons.

"There they are," Will said, glancing away from her to see the entire contingent enter the courtyard, with Kevin towing Tyler in his wagon at the head of the group. Tyler was looking around in awe, mouth open.

Once they were close enough for conversation, Isabel said, "This place…."

Rosemary's expression shifted to almost one of eagerness. "You feel it, too?"

"How can you not?"

"I don't feel anything," Fred said, in skeptical tones that would have been worthy of Professor Snape himself.

"You're not psychic, Fred," Michael remarked.

He tilted his head back to look up at the crenelated towers above them. "But to the rest of us, this place is positively buzzing."

"Why, though?" Audrey said. "I mean, I can sense it—it's like the static I feel when I forget to put a dryer sheet in with the laundry—but what does it mean?"

Michael paused in his inspection of their surroundings to glance back at her. "I'm not sure yet. But I think we should all probably stay on our toes."

"It's a party, Michael," Rosemary said. "Do you honestly think anything is going to happen with all these people here?"

It was a good question, mostly because the forces of darkness tended to attack when victims were alone and isolated. Although the party was ebbing and flowing around them, and the grounds of the Castle so complicated that Will couldn't get a very good sense of the general layout of the place, he guessed there had to be several hundred people here. Not exactly an optimal setup for an attack—at least, not if the attackers wanted to escape notice.

Obviously, those same thoughts had been passing through Michael's mind, because he hesitated before answering. "I don't know," he said at last. "But this energy we're feeling here—it has to mean something."

"Maybe all you're feeling is the energy of the hundreds of people who worked on the Castle through the years, who poured their life force into creating this place," she told him.

He was silent again, looking around. "I suppose that's possible."

"Cookie!" Tyler shouted then, breaking the tension in the group. Obviously, he'd gotten tired of the talking and had spotted the goodies on a nearby table.

"Let's try one of those little sandwiches first, buddy," Kevin said, unzipping part of the gold lamé "hoard" that covered the wagon so he could extricate his son. He added to Celeste, who was looking a little concerned, "I think they're just ham and cheese. It'll be fine."

"Okay," she said. "No peanut butter."

He only shook his head, as if amused that she thought he'd forget such an important detail. Carrying Tyler, he went over to the table and put together a little plate, then turned back to Celeste. "Why don't you all take a look around? I'll stay here with Tyler and make sure he gets some dinner."

"I don't know...." Celeste began, clearly not thrilled at the prospect of leaving her son and husband behind.

"I'll stay with them," Glynis offered. "I'm sure

there'll be plenty of time for me to poke around later. Go on—have some fun."

"It would be easier to do some exploring without having to haul that wagon everywhere," Rosemary said.

That argument seemed to clinch things, because Celeste gave a lift of her shoulders, as if deciding it wasn't worth arguing about. "Okay. But only for ten minutes or so."

"Sure," Rosemary responded. "We can still see a lot in that amount of time."

Apparently, she'd decided to act as tour guide, since she'd been to the place before, and no one else had, not even Isabel. Half-drunk cup of wine in one hand, Rosemary led the group around the ground level of the place—there was actually a huge underground apartment that had once been a water storage tank—and showed them the blacksmith's shop, the cement walls embedded with glass bottles, the various other odds and ends that had been incorporated in the construction of the place. Looking at everything, Will got the impression that there had probably been a lot of weed involved in the building process, which made sense, since the majority of it had taken place during the 1960s and '70s.

When they returned to the courtyard a little more than ten minutes later, Kevin was sitting there, looking up at the moon as it began to rise over the eastern walls of the Castle. However, neither Glynis nor Tyler were in sight.

"Kevin, where's Tyler?" Celeste asked, moving past Rosemary and Will so she could approach her husband.

Before he could answer, Glynis appeared, coming in from the other direction. Celeste whirled to face her, looking worried.

"Mom, do you know where Tyler is?"

At once, Glynis looked over at Kevin, who hadn't moved from the folding chair where he sat. "He was with Kevin just a minute ago. I had to go to the ladies' room, but I was only gone for a couple of minutes at the most."

Kevin blinked, then said, "Tyler's fine. He went with Lena."

"What?" Celeste demanded. "Why would you let him do that? We don't even know the woman!"

"Rosemary knows her," he said.

Next to Will, Rosemary shook her head. "We're acquainted, but not that well. Where did they go?"

He heard the tension in her voice, but it seemed she was doing her best to remain calm. While he guessed this was all a misunderstanding, he couldn't ignore the strange, blank expression on Kevin's face, which seemed very unlike him. Will didn't pretend to know the other man very well, but even his brief acquaintance with Rosemary's brother-in-law had been enough to show he tended to be a cheerful sort of person, the kind of guy who smiled more often than not.

"Something's wrong," Isabel said. She stepped forward, away from the group, and went to stand next to Celeste. "Kevin, where did Lena take Tyler?"

"He's right here," came a woman's voice.

There was Lena, striding into the courtyard, Tyler's hand gripped firmly in hers as his little legs tried to keep up with her brisk pace.

"He's fine," she continued. "Or at least...he will be...if you do what I ask."

And as Will stared at the woman, her face rippled and shifted, just as her form altered, growing taller and broader. In a few seconds, it wasn't the friendly member of the local historical society staring back at them.

It was Daniel Lockwood.

Chapter 17

THE PLASTIC CUP OF WINE FELL FROM
Rosemary's hand and clattered against the flag-
stone-paved ground. There had been very little
wine left in it, so it didn't splash much. However,
she wasn't thinking about the wine.

How could Daniel Lockwood be here?

But even as she stared in horror, she realized
he wasn't alone. Costumed figures moved to stand
next to him, their faces shifting as well, no longer
half-familiar neighbors from her hometown, but
the rest of the Greencastle contingent, including
Gerald, who stood behind Daniel, his expression
stony, unreadable.

As well as the Beetlejuice who'd been serving
drinks. He came out from behind the bar, and
suddenly the crazy makeup and striped suit and
wild hair were gone, and it was Caleb standing

next to his father, arms crossed, that hateful smirk back on his face.

"Let him go!" Celeste burst out, then ran toward her son.

At once, Daniel Lockwood raised a hand, and she fell to the ground, apparently stunned.

Rosemary cried, "No!" and began to move forward, but Caleb spoke then.

"I wouldn't do that if I were you, Rosemary. She's fine—just knocked out. Whether she—or the rest of you—remains fine is entirely up to you."

Out of the corner of her eye, she could see Michael step out from the rest of the group. Off to the side, Glynis made an abortive movement, as if she intended to go to her unconscious daughter. Michael gave the slightest shake of his head, apparently telling her to remain where she was, and so she stopped in place, hands clenched at her side.

"What do you want?" Michael asked, his voice clear and cold.

"Oh, we want lots of things," Daniel replied. He glanced down at Tyler before returning his attention to the man who stood a few yards away. "And we intend to have them. We've been denied long enough."

If Tyler had looked at all afraid—if he'd been struggling or crying the way a little boy gripped by a strange man should have been—then Rosemary would have taken the chance and run forward, relying on her strange powers to shield herself from Daniel's attack. But her nephew only stood there calmly, gazing off into the middle distance as if he didn't have a care in the world. Clearly, whatever spell or magic or whatever you wanted to call it that Lockwood had employed to keep Kevin quiescent had also been used on Tyler.

Because her nephew wasn't in obvious distress, Rosemary forced herself to hold her ground. "'Denied'?" she repeated, hoping she sounded incredulous enough. "I've been to Greencastle, remember? You all seem to be living pretty comfortably for a bunch of people who claim to have been 'denied' anything."

Daniel lifted a scornful eyebrow. "You don't know what you're talking about. Do you think a few creature comforts can compare to what we should have had, considering our birthright as the sons of demons? No, it's time to bring our master back, to give him the dominion that is his right. And this is the night when it can come to pass."

Master? Rosemary thought frantically. *Does he mean Satan? But Michael and Audrey never even mentioned the Devil being involved in any of this....*

Her thoughts were whirling around in her head, flying this way and that like falling leaves in an autumn gale. If she could just concentrate, figure out how to get Tyler away from that monster—

Michael surprised her by uttering a derisive laugh. "Your 'master'?" he said. "Audrey and I sent him to Hell six months ago, and we'd be more than happy to do it all over again if you even try to summon him here."

"And this time, they'll have help," Will added, hand hovering by the pocket of his frock coat, where Rosemary guessed he had stashed some of those plastic vials of holy water.

Unfortunately, Daniel didn't seem too worried by the not-so-subtle threat. His lips lifted in a thin smile, and he said, "I'm afraid you don't have the upper hand here." His glacier-pale eyes shifted back to Rosemary, seeming to bore into her. "It's very simple, my dear. You have the power of our blood. Help us now, and I'll return your sister's son to you."

"'Help you'?" she repeated. "Help you do what?"

Caleb sent her a pitying glance, as if he couldn't believe her stupidity. "If you really need it spelled out, Rosemary, we need you to help us open the gate to let Belial out. He wants to come back to this world, wants to reward all his faithful servants."

"And that will include you," Daniel said in

coaxing tones. "Anything you want—it will be yours. Just join your strength to ours on this holy night, in this holy place."

"What's so holy about it?" Audrey asked, speaking for the first time.

Daniel's glance raked down her, from the glittery devil's horns half-hidden by her lustrous brown hair to the red knee-high boots she was wearing. If Rosemary had been on the receiving end of that gaze, she knew she would have wanted to take a bath, since it was all too clear what the half-demon thought of her friend's skimpy costume…and the woman wearing it.

A few feet away, Michael bristled, but he didn't take the bait. Voice cold, he said, "Yes, tell us what a demon-blood like you would know about 'holy.'"

Rosemary wanted to flinch at the insult, although she knew it hadn't been directed at her personally. Yes, that same blood flowed through her veins, but that didn't mean she intended to act like it did.

"At the center of this property, two ley lines intersect," Daniel said, gaze still fixed on Audrey, as if he hadn't even heard what Michael had said. "You know what a ley line is, don't you, my dear?"

Her lips thinned under their coating of red lipstick, but she said calmly enough, ignoring the condescension, "They're invisible lines of electromagnetic energy that supposedly connect places of cultural or mystical significance."

Another of those thin smiles, and Daniel said, "Oh, there's nothing 'supposed' about what they do. As you said, they carry the Earth's energy within them, and they're a source of unimaginable power...if you know how to tap into it. One passes below DePauw University in Greencastle, which is part of the reason why we settled there. In fact, that same line travels all the way here and passes under this structure, and continues to a spot a little less than a mile to the west of us."

"To Whitcomb's mansion," Michael said, nodding faintly as if Lockwood's revelation had just confirmed a theory.

"Very good. Yes, all these places are connected. But what makes this spot even more significant is that the ley line which runs under Greencastle and the Whitcomb mansion intersects with another line here, making the energy of those lines that much greater. Add to that the negative energy we've unleashed on the world by the release of the *Project Demon Hunters* videos, and we have a potent combination." Daniel looked back at Rosemary, expression softening. "You are very powerful, my dear. More powerful than you can imagine. It's time for you to join those who share your blood and bring Belial back to us."

She glared at him, hands planted on her hips even as her body thrummed with fear for her nephew. Yes, so far, Tyler seemed unharmed, and yet she guessed that Daniel wouldn't hesitate to hurt him if she refused to do as he asked. But there was no way in the world that she could possibly assist the Greencastle demons in bringing Belial back from his exile in Hell. That meddlesome demon had already done enough damage; she shuddered to think what kind of foul acts he'd try to perpetrate if he were set free on this plane of existence, unhindered by any need to conceal who or what he was.

Although she had no intention of helping Daniel Lockwood—or the rest of them—Rosemary knew she needed to stall for time until she could come up with a way to get Tyler safely away from the cambion leader. "And what is Belial going to do once he gets here? Take up residence in the Whitcomb mansion? Last I heard, someone else was already living there."

It wasn't Daniel who answered her, but Caleb. Taking a step forward, he said, "No, he has no need to masquerade as Matthew Whitcomb any longer, and so there's not much point in him living in that house, is there? He'll find a suitable body to inhabit, just as he always does. But it's nothing that needs to affect you, or anyone in your family. In fact, you won't even notice that he's returned to this plane—well, except for the riches that will be your reward."

"You don't know much about me, do you, Caleb?" she returned, her tone acid. "If I gave a shit about being rich, do you think I'd be part-owner of a small indie bookstore in the San Gabriel Valley?"

He didn't look offended by her response. "Well, I would have *liked* to have gotten to know you better…if you'd only allowed me to."

Next to her, Will bristled, but Rosemary could tell he wasn't going to rise to the bait. No, like everyone else, he was holding back, knowing that one false step could lead to pain or worse for little Tyler. They were waiting for her to salvage the situation…and she had no idea what to do.

However, since the demons appeared willing to continue the conversation, it seemed clear enough that they couldn't continue without her assistance. If she kept stalling them, maybe they'd run out of time.

Right, when the clock strikes midnight? she scoffed at herself. *That's almost four hours from now, and I kind of doubt they're going to be willing to stand here and chat for that long.*

Probably not. They were going along with her for now because they felt they had the luxury of time, but sooner or later, their patience would run out. Then they'd all be in a heap of trouble.

And as much as she might wish for some of the other partygoers to come along and interrupt this terrible little tableau, Rosemary knew she couldn't hope for such a rescue, either. The party had gone eerily quiet ever since Daniel and the rest of his demons came on the scene, and she had a feeling that any humans left in the place were under the same kind of spell that had made her brother-in-law so passive, so useless. Why the rest of them hadn't been affected, she wasn't sure, although she suspected that the psychic powers her mother and Isabel and Celeste all shared had protected them, and the same for Michael and Audrey. That didn't explain why Will and Fred were also unaffected, but maybe having so many psychics around them had created something of a shield.

At any rate, the important thing was that she knew she couldn't expect anyone to help her. Had she ever been in such a tight spot before? She didn't think so, simply because as the youngest child, she'd always had someone there to bail her out.

Not this time.

"Is that what you want, Caleb?" she asked. "To get to know me a little better?"

His eyes held hers. "Among other things. You belong with us, Rosemary. You belong with me.

Not with that so-called man of God standing next to you."

She opened her mouth to protest, but there was no time, because Will had stepped forward and thundered, "Begone, foul spirit! I banish you in the name of Christ!" And he pulled a vial of holy water out of his pocket and splashed it across Caleb's face.

To her shock, he actually recoiled in pain, angry red welts marring his model-handsome features. The other part-demons stared at him in consternation, clearly not expecting this sort of attack to have had any kind of effect.

That appeared to be the only signal the rest of Rosemary's companions needed, because Michael charged forward as well, holy water flying as he invoked the Father, the Son, and the Holy Spirit. The demons cried out in pain, and Fred, apparently seeing that he wasn't of much use in that sort of confrontation, moved quickly to grasp Celeste by the arms and haul her out of harm's way.

But Daniel grabbed Tyler and held him up, long fingers digging into the little boy's midsection. Tyler let out a screech, although Rosemary couldn't tell for sure whether it was in pain or because he was so shocked by the older man's sudden movement.

"Stop!" he called out. "Unless you want this child's brains splashed all over the pavement."

At once, Will and Michael paused, and Audrey and Isabel froze in place, their faces white with fear. The part-demons who flanked Daniel also went still, although their labored breathing was loud on the air, and Rosemary could clearly see the livid marks on their faces where the holy water had splashed them.

Why had it worked here? She'd seen for herself how Will's holy water hadn't done a damn thing to Caleb when Will had doused the part-demon with it at Colin Turner's house in Glendale, so why now?

However, she knew she didn't have time to pick apart the mystery. She needed to make sure nothing happened to her nephew. Not on her watch.

"Put him down, Daniel," she pleaded. "Please."

He didn't move, only stood there with Tyler's legs dangling in the air. Cold eyes met hers and held. "Of course, I will—if you promise to help us."

Come on, come on, she begged her brain. But that useless organ seemed incapable of coming up with a plan to simultaneously rescue her nephew and incapacitate Daniel Lockwood. Next to his father, Caleb was grinning in triumph. As she watched, the red marks on his face slowly began to fade.

So, while the holy water could hurt them temporarily, it wasn't enough to incapacitate them in any meaningful way.

Great.

For what felt like forever, Rosemary stood there, fists knotted in impotent fury at her sides. But it didn't seem as if there was anything she could do. Bringing Belial back to this world might cause horrible suffering, and yet, in that moment, she could only see little Tyler's terrified face, the hitching sobs that tore their way out of his chest. For some reason, he seemed to have broken free of the demon's spell. Was that because he'd been shocked from it when Daniel grabbed him, or had the half-demon decided it was better to have him awake and aware on purpose in order to torture him further?

The thought made her lips thin. No matter what, this had to end…even if it meant acknowledging that she'd lost, that the demons had beaten her.

She pulled in a breath and lifted her chin. "Okay," she said. "You've won. I'll help you. Just please—put him down."

"Rosemary, no—" Will began, but Michael clamped a hand on his arm, as if understanding that she had no cards left to play.

"Very good," Daniel said. "Come over here, please."

Dully, she crossed the several yards that separated them and then paused next to the demons' leader, Caleb flanking her on the other side. Inwardly, she was screaming at herself to do something, but there was nothing left to do. She tried to hearten herself with the inner reminder that Michael and Audrey had once beaten Belial, and so she had to hope they could do it again...but she didn't know for sure. From the way they'd described it, that had been one hell of a fight.

As soon as she stopped moving, Daniel lowered Tyler to the ground...but he didn't let go of the boy's arm. No, it seemed clear enough he wasn't going to release her nephew until he knew for sure that she was going to assist them in their diabolical plan.

"What do I need to do?" she asked.

"Join with us," Daniel replied. "Take Caleb's hand."

Inwardly, she shuddered at the thought of having to touch the man she'd dated so briefly, but this wasn't the time to be squeamish, not with Daniel still clutching Tyler by his tiny bicep. She swallowed some more air and reached out, felt Caleb wrap his fingers around hers. His grasp was tight enough that she couldn't quite prevent herself from flinching, but she made herself remain where she stood.

Will looked as though the only thing

preventing him from launching himself forward to rescue her was Michael's iron grip on his arm. Audrey and Isabel and Glynis were white-faced, while Fred stood grimly next to Celeste; he'd set her down on a folding chair at the same table where a glassy-eyed Kevin still sat, and kept watch on both of them.

"Now what?" Rosemary asked.

"Reach out for the power of the ley lines," Daniel instructed her. "It should be easy for you to sense. We're going to take that power and use it to form a gateway, and then bring Belial through that gate."

She shut her eyes. In a way, that was much better, because then she couldn't see the dismay in Will's face, the mixed anger and frustration in Michael's expression, the very real fear that clung to her mother and Audrey and Isabel like an extra garment. In the darkness behind her closed lids, Rosemary thought she saw two shimmering pathways snaking through the dark, intersecting somewhere beneath her feet.

"Belial," Daniel intoned, and the rest of the demons took up the chant, murmuring it in deep voices that seemed to shake the ground itself.

Too much to hope that it was an actual earthquake, a temblor that would interrupt their horrible ceremony and prevent the gateway from forming. No, it was only the power of their demon blood, reaching out for the energy of the ley lines and changing it somehow, making it shift and shudder into another shape, now a great arch looming up in the black night.

She could feel Daniel's will pressing against hers, and she knew she couldn't stand there and do nothing for any longer. No, she had to use her own power to touch the energy flows and bend them to her will so the gateway became more and more solid. Shadows appeared to flow and take their own shape inside that gateway, shapes that seemed to grow corporeal as she watched, turning into a great horned man with eyes of fire.

A whimper escaped her throat as cold enveloped her body, turning her limbs to ice. Rosemary knew she should do something to stop this, and yet she also knew if she rebelled, tried to sabotage the summoning in any way, Daniel would take his revenge on the helpless boy he held. She couldn't allow that to happen, couldn't let any harm befall her nephew.

The dark shape drew closer to the gate, malevolent red eyes sweeping over her. In just a few more seconds, he would be through it, and this would be all over.

Or worse, it would only be beginning.

Out of nowhere, brilliant white light flared up in the darkness, illuminating the black gate and all the strange runes and sigils etched into its surface, even though Rosemary couldn't remember consciously putting any of them there. She threw up her hands, breaking her contact with Caleb.

And her eyes met those of her father.

At least, the man she'd thought was her father until Daniel Lockwood had convinced her that her true father was the half-demon Gerald Gates. She stared at John McGuire in utter shock.

Because if Daniel had been telling the truth, then John McGuire had been dead for ten years, and the man she'd thought she and Will had met in Indianapolis only a demon wearing a dead man's face. But if Daniel had been lying—

"Quick, Rosemary," her father said. "Join your power with mine."

"But—"

The protest barely made it to her lips before Daniel grabbed hold of her, letting go of Tyler. Her nephew had the presence of mind to run to his Aunt Isabel, who scooped him up and took him out of the line of fire, running over to stand next to Fred.

That was all Rosemary could see, because Daniel's other hand settled at her throat, squeezing ever so slightly. John McGuire remained where he was, watching calmly.

"You can't interfere…*angel*," Daniel said, all but spitting the last word. "It's not allowed."

"Well," Rosemary's father said, his tone mild,

"I've always found it easier to ask for forgiveness than for permission."

His hands lifted, and a shimmering white light surrounded them—the same shimmering light Rosemary herself had summoned when she'd fought to protect Will and herself from Caleb's attack in a confrontation that now felt as if it had taken place a hundred years ago. Somewhere inside, the ache that had settled there ever since Daniel Lockwood convinced her she was part-demon began to slip away.

"Yes," her father said. "They lied. That is all they can do. It's time to send them where they belong, don't you think?"

She couldn't nod because of Daniel's grip on her throat. However, she knew it didn't matter. All she needed was her mind...and the power that had come to her from her father.

Brilliant white light flared out around her, and immediately Daniel Lockwood let go of her, staggering back a pace. She took advantage of his distraction to run forward to her father, felt his hand grasp hers.

"All of us," he said clearly. "I need all my daughters...and my wife."

Just out of the corner of her eye, Rosemary could see Isabel and Glynis take Celeste by the hand, could see Celeste blink and appear to come back to herself. Seeming to understand that he needed to stay out of the fray, Fred picked up Tyler so the two sisters and their mother could hurry forward and join their strength with the angel who was their father...and Glynis's husband.

The light surrounded all of them, blinding as the arc from a blown transformer. Rosemary felt it surge through her, bright and brilliant and yet warm and welcoming at the same time, like feeling the sun on her face after the long night of an Arctic winter. They held hands, Rosemary and Glynis on one side and Isabel and Celeste on the other, and the energy blazed out from them, wrapping around the demons, who screamed and howled in pain, Gerald's handsome features contorted in agony, Caleb looking almost resigned, as if deep down he'd known it might turn out like this...Daniel's pale eyes blazing in fury. Smoke rose from their bodies as they writhed in the grip of the light...

...and then they were nothing but smoke, seeping down into the flagstones beneath their feet, disappearing from view as their bodies melted to nothing. In her mind's eye, Rosemary saw the dark gate they'd constructed collapse upon itself, burying the demonic man-shape that had risen within it. And to her ears came a howl of rage, of impotent fury, until it died away entirely.

She blinked, and saw that they were alone

now in the courtyard, her sisters and her father and mother, Will and Michael and Audrey standing off to one side, Fred over by the table where Kevin had been slumped in his folding chair the whole time. Now, though, he was stirring, and sat up and blinked at everyone. He put a hand to his head, as if it hurt, then glanced up at Fred, who bent and set Tyler down on the ground.

"Did I miss something?" Kevin asked.

And everyone burst into laughter.

Epilogue

THE SUN BLAZED DOWN, SO WARM AND
bright, it was hard to believe that the date was
November first. They'd all congregated at Glynis's
house because that had felt like the right place to
gather, but the lovely weather had drawn them
outside to the backyard, where the scent of roses
drifted on the air, thick as incense.

Rosemary held Will's hand as they sat on one
of the outdoor love seats on the back porch.
Michael and Audrey sat on the love seat opposite
theirs, while Fred and Isabel occupied two of the
chairs. They weren't holding hands, but Rosemary
had spied Fred whispering something to her sister
earlier—and had also noted the uncharacteristic
flush that had touched Isabel's cheeks. From the
look of it, getting dragged into a demonic

conspiracy had only helped bring them together, rather than sending Fred running for the hills.

And a few feet away, Glynis stood next to her husband, his fingers twined with hers as they stood and watched Celeste and Kevin play catch with Tyler out on the lawn. It didn't seem that Tyler had suffered any ill effects from their confrontation with the Greencastle demons—in fact, he kept asking if they were going to go back to the "haunted castle" soon, because he'd had so much fun.

"I'm going to have a hard time explaining you," Glynis said as she gazed up into John McGuire's face. "The whole world thinks you're dead, you know."

He grinned, then lifted the glass of sangria he held and took a sip. "I'm sure we'll figure out something. Maybe tell everyone I've been working secretly for the government all this time."

"So…you're really back?" Rosemary asked, and Will's fingers tightened on hers. They'd shared their own speculation on her father's sudden reappearance, but the night before, John had only told everyone that he'd explain everything the next day, saying it was better for them all to slip away quietly before any of the other partygoers came back to themselves enough to realize that something pretty strange had just gone down in one of Rubel Castle's courtyards.

Her father nodded. "Daniel Lockwood was right about one thing—interference isn't allowed. Coming back to help you—even to stop a demon and save my grandson—that cost me my wings. But it was worth it. Belial couldn't be allowed back into the world."

"You'd think your—well, you'd think the people in charge might see it that way," Michael remarked, and John shrugged.

"Yes, but rules are rules. It's fine. I'm condemned to live a mortal life…but that doesn't mean I won't get back to Heaven eventually." His gaze strayed to his wife's face, glowing with happiness and looking ten years younger at the prospect of having the man she'd lost forever suddenly returned to her side. "Only next time, I won't be there alone."

She leaned her head against his shoulder, even as Audrey spoke. "And Belial is really gone?"

"Well, he's stuck in Hell, where he should be," Rosemary's father said. "I'm not saying that someone might not try to summon him again, but the chances of their being successful aren't very good. He took a direct hit from the gate collapsing on him, and he's probably going to be licking his wounds for a while and in no shape to go anywhere."

"And the Greencastle demons?" Michael put in.

"In Hell as well. Stuck there forever, because they were just human enough that they have no chance of ever being summoned."

"Good," Will murmured, but Rosemary remained silent.

It wasn't that she mourned Caleb—God, no—but at the same time, she couldn't help thinking about all the people the Greencastle demons had left behind…Caleb's mother, the other wives… that girl Tiffany, who planned to get engaged to Sean. Except Sean was now gone, along with all the rest of the part-demons. Losing fourteen people like that at the same time would leave a gaping hole in the fabric of a town as small as Greencastle. How in the world could anyone come up with an explanation for what had happened?

They probably wouldn't. Those men would just be gone, and it would be a crazy mystery that would get picked apart for the next ten years. But in the end, the world would be a better place with them gone. No worries about generation after generation of demon-kind populating the town and hatching their own dark plans.

It was better this way.

Her father gazed down at her. "You did well, Rosemary."

"Me?" she said, then shook her head. "I don't

know how you can say that. I couldn't come up with a single way to defeat them."

"But you didn't lose your cool," he told her. "You stood up to them until you realized you couldn't any longer, not without bringing harm to your own flesh and blood. Don't be too hard on yourself—fourteen to one are pretty big odds."

She supposed he was right. A little flicker of warmth grew inside her, a warmth she realized came from hearing her father's praise. When she was a child, she hadn't heard it all that often, and she'd done her best to excuse him because she knew he was busy with his work and often preoccupied. Now, though, as she looked at him and finally saw the tension gone from his face, she realized his detachment had only been a defense mechanism, a way of keeping himself from getting too close to the family he knew he would have to leave one day.

"He's right," Will said gently, and she at last allowed herself to smile.

"I suppose so." She looked around at everyone. "We kicked some demon ass, didn't we?"

"Definitely," Audrey said. "You McGuires are a force to be reckoned with."

Yes, they were. And now it wouldn't just be her and her two sisters and her mother, but her father as well. And Will, and Kevin and Tyler, and Michael and Audrey…and probably Fred as well, even if he didn't know it yet. All of them coming together in a circle of friends and family, doing what they could to drive back the darkness with their light.

She saw Will smiling down at her, saw the sunlight catch in his clear gray eyes, and knew the love that had always eluded her had come into her life, steadfast and true, better than anything she ever could have imagined. He would be there beside her, no matter what happened, no matter what challenges they faced. His actions had already more than proven that.

And it was enough. His love, here in the light, was enough.

The End

This concludes the *Project Demon Hunters* series. Thank you so much for taking this journey with me, and with Michael and Audrey and Rosemary and Will. Turn the page to see all of my books, including my brand-new series, the Witches of Wheeler Park!

Also by Christine Pope

THE WITCHES OF WHEELER PARK

(Paranormal romance)

Storm Born

Thunder Road

Winds of Change (July 2020)

PROJECT DEMON HUNTERS

(Paranormal Romance)

Unquiet Souls

Unbound Spirits

Unholy Ground

Unseen Voices

Unmarked Graves

Unbroken Vows

THE DEVIL YOU KNOW

(Paranormal Romance)

Sympathy for the Devil

Charmed, I'm Sure

A Wing and a Prayer

THE WITCHES OF CANYON ROAD*

(Paranormal Romance)

Hidden Gifts

Darker Paths

Mysterious Ways

A Canyon Road Christmas

Demon Born

An Ill Wind

Higher Ground

Haunted Hearts

THE WITCHES OF CLEOPATRA HILL*

(Paranormal Romance)

Darkangel

Darknight

Darkmoon

Sympathetic Magic

Protector

Spellbound

A Cleopatra Hill Christmas

Impractical Magic

Strange Magic

The Arrangement

Defender

Bad Blood

Deep Magic

Darktide

THE DJINN WARS*

(Paranormal Romance)

Chosen

Taken

Fallen

Broken

Forsaken

Forbidden

Awoken

Illuminated

Stolen

Forgotten

Driven

Unspoken

THE WATCHERS TRILOGY*

(Paranormal Romance)

Falling Dark

Dead of Night

Rising Dawn

THE SEDONA FILES*

(Paranormal Romance)

Bad Vibrations

Desert Hearts

Angel Fire

Star Crossed

Falling Angels

Enemy Mine

TALES OF THE LATTER KINGDOMS*

(Fantasy Romance)

All Fall Down

Dragon Rose

Binding Spell

Ashes of Roses

One Thousand Nights

Threads of Gold

The Wolf of Harrow Hall

Moon Dance

The Song of the Thrush

THE GAIAN CONSORTIUM SERIES*

(Science Fiction Romance)

Beast (free prequel novella)

Blood Will Tell

Breath of Life

The Gaia Gambit

The Mandala Maneuver

The Titan Trap

The Zhore Deception

The Refugee Ruse

STANDALONE TITLES

Hearts on Fire

Taking Dictation

Night Music

Golden Heart

* Indicates a completed series

About the Author

USA Today bestselling author Christine Pope has been writing stories ever since she commandeered her family's Smith-Corona typewriter back in grade school. Her work includes paranormal romance, fantasy romance, and science fiction/space opera romance. She makes her home in Arizona's beautiful Verde Valley.

Christine Pope on the Web:
www.christinepope.com

f facebook.com/ChristinePopeAuthor

twitter.com/ChristineJPope

pinterest.com/ChristineJPope

www.ingramcontent.com/pod-product-compliance
Lightning Source LLC
Chambersburg PA
CBHW021131260626
47169CB00005B/1557